Sean could see the anguish in her wide brown eyes, still damp with tears.

"It's okay. I've got you," he murmured, moving his hands around to her back in the beginning of an embrace.

Surprisingly, she didn't pull away, but leaned against him with a sigh.

"What I meant to say was that I was so cold to you, so withdrawn those last few months. I was just so self-involved, so focused on trying to have a baby that it must have seemed that nothing else mattered to me. I *am* truly sorry, Sean."

"I just wanted you to be happy, Charlotte. I still want you to be happy."

The longing in his wife's eyes sparked anew the heat that had never stopped smoldering in Sean. Before he could take the time to consider the possible consequences, Sean bent his head and claimed her luscious mouth in a kiss.

Dear Reader,

Several years ago, a close friend's daughter decided to adopt a child. She soon discovered that although she was a stable, healthy young woman and a dedicated teacher, her options were limited because she was also single.

Laura chose to pursue the foreign adoption alternative. Her journey to Kazakhstan to adopt the elder of her two daughters was the inspiration for *The Baby Bind*. She has since rounded out her very special family with the recent adoption of her younger daughter, a little girl who was born in China.

Raising children seems to become more of a challenge every day. Yet it's heartening to see how many people choose to become loving, caring, devoted parents despite all the uncertainties they face.

This story is for all you parents out there and for all who hope to be parents one day. May all the dreams you have for yourselves and for your children come true!

Sincerely,

Nikki Benjamin

THE BABY BIND

NIKKI BENJAMIN

SPECIAL EDITION®

Published by Silhouette Books

America's Publisher of Contemporary Romance

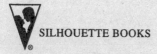

SILHOUETTE BOOKS

ISBN-13: 978-0-373-24842-1
ISBN-10:   0-373-24842-3

THE BABY BIND

NIKKI BENJAMIN

was born and raised in the Midwest, but after years in the Houston area, she considers herself a true Texan. Nikki says she's always been an avid reader. (Her earliest literary heroines were Nancy Drew, Trixie Belden and Beany Malone.) Her writing experience had been limited, however, until a friend started penning a novel and encouraged Nikki to do the same. One scene led to another, and soon she was hooked.

Chapter One

For a long time Charlotte Fagan sat alone in the close confines of her small, elegant sports car, huddled in the darkness, hands clasped in her lap. An icy January rain pounded hard against the canvas roof just above her head and ran in rivulets down the windshield, blurring her view through the glass. But the storm that raged outside her car was nothing compared to the storm that raged in her heart.

Charlotte hadn't been sure that she was making the right choice when she left the small town of Mayfair, Louisiana, almost three hours earlier and had begun the long drive to New Orleans. Her gaze fixed upon the tall old town house tucked deep in the heart of the French Quarter, she still wasn't sure.

There had been a time when she could have, *would* have, asked anything of her husband without the slightest hesitation—a time when she had been able to trust him with her deepest, most intimate needs and desires. He had willingly, lovingly, tenderly given her everything that had been within his power to give.

Now, however, she knew that convincing Sean to help her was going to be a challenge. Separated by a physical distance of two hundred miles and the emotional distance of living apart for half a year, with only the tenuous-at-best connection of a telephone line between them, she was certain that the odds of winning him over were zero to none.

Unbeknownst to him, Sean held the possibility of a dream come true, an opportunity for her happiness—in fact, the very key to her happiness—firmly in his hands. She needed his cooperation—she needed it desperately. But for the first time since that summer day ten years ago when he'd promised to love and cherish her always, Charlotte wasn't sure that he would offer it.

She had spotted his signature red SUV at the curb on her first pass down the street. She had also detected the faint glow of light sliding through the wide wooden slats of the shutters covering the long, narrow front windows on either side of the equally long, narrow front door. No doubt about it, at least in her mind. Her husband was most certainly at home on this stormy night.

But was he home alone?

Never in the past had Sean given Charlotte reason to believe that he would be anything but faithful to her and the vows of their marriage. But the distance between them had grown so great lately that she could no longer be absolutely sure of him in any way.

Unclasping her hands, Charlotte reached across the car's console, picked up the bulky brown envelope she'd tossed on the passenger seat less than five minutes after retrieving it from her mailbox in Mayfair, and rubbed a finger over the neatly printed return address on the shiny white label.

After ripping the envelope open and scanning the contents, she hadn't even thought about continuing up the long gravel drive to the old plantation house she and Sean had so lovingly restored early in their marriage. She had wanted only to show the paperwork enclosed to her husband and know that he felt the same excitement and the same joy that had blossomed in her soul, as she'd quickly read through the various documents.

Though it had already been early evening and a steady rain had been sluicing down relentlessly, Charlotte had wheeled her car into a narrow U-turn and headed back to the two-lane highway that would take her to the interstate leading straight to the city.

More than once along the way, she had considered turning around and returning home again. The storm had made driving slow and tedious. And though flooding wasn't likely in the French Quarter, Charlotte was nervous about traveling through the rest of the city, post-Hurricane Katrina.

Her initial impulse to share with her husband what had been good news to her had also faded, taking with it the flurry of hope in her heart, and the sense of urgency that hope had engendered.

Pragmatic once again, Charlotte had acknowledged that the sheaf of papers and the small glossy photograph in the plain brown envelope she now held in her hands contained no magic elixir that could remedy all that had gone wrong with her marriage. But there was also the promise of a dream about to finally come true and with it the opportunity for another kind of happiness—*her* happiness, at least.

A gust of wind rattled up the narrow street, rocking

Charlotte's car. The gaslight half a block away flickered ominously, sending shadows scuttling along the deserted sidewalk. Instead of letting up as she had been hoping, the rain drummed even more insistently outside her meager, not to mention increasingly cold and damp, little shelter.

Though her hasty drive to New Orleans now seemed rather foolish, she had no desire to drive all the way back to Mayfair without talking to Sean. She not only had important news to share with him—news that affected him as well as her—but also a duty to do so without delay. She wouldn't intrude for long. She would simply state the facts of the matter. Then she would express her need for his assistance, and hope for at least some consideration from him in return.

As she tucked the envelope inside a zippered pocket of her tote, then fished for the compact collapsible umbrella she'd stashed under her car seat, Charlotte knew that approaching Sean wouldn't be such a big deal if she could anticipate how he would respond. But after half a year apart there was very little she knew for sure about how her husband felt about anything or anyone, including her.

The umbrella was all but useless in the face of the stormy onslaught she battled from car to curb, then along the slick sidewalk and up the three narrow stone steps to the front door of the town house. Though her calf-length black wool coat worn over gray wool pants and a turtleneck sweater kept her mostly dry, her feet, shod in black leather pumps, were soaked after only a few steps.

Finally standing on the small stone porch, her hands numbed by the cold and damp, she almost lost her grip on the handle of her umbrella as another blast of wind swirled around her.

Too bad she hadn't thought to take her gloves from her tote when she'd tucked the envelope safely inside it. Bundling her chin-length chocolate-brown curls into a headscarf wouldn't have been a bad idea, either—if only she'd had one with her. She would have preferred not to look like a mad woman tonight, but there was little she could do about that now.

Pressing one trembling finger against the brass button that rang the doorbell, Charlotte reminded herself that her appearance mattered not at all. Sean had seen her in a worse state on more than one occasion in the past, and hadn't shunned her. Of course, he had still been in love with her those other times that she hadn't been at her best—

Without any warning—not even the sound of the bolt sliding in the lock—the front door of the town house swung open. Huddled close to the facade, as she was, not to mention totally unprepared for her husband's sudden looming presence in the doorway, Charlotte took a startled step back.

At the same instant that the heel of her right shoe slid over the rain-slick stone, another gust of wind caught the umbrella. Thrown completely off balance, Charlotte let go of the umbrella, and as it sailed into the night, she stumbled again and started to fall.

Sure that she was about to land in a heap halfway down the porch steps, she uttered a small, frightened cry. Then, as suddenly as she'd begun to go down, she found herself caught up in the grip of her husband's arms. With a smooth, steady swoop, he lifted her neatly off her feet, then cradled her securely against his chest.

Blinking up at Sean in dismay, the full force of the rain soaking her hair, her face and her coat, as well as *his* hair and face and rumpled white dress shirt, Charlotte was overcome by the most disconcerting urge to…giggle. The situation into which she'd gotten herself was so utterly unexpected and so utterly ridiculous that despite the stern and disapproving look on her husband's face, she really couldn't help but laugh.

Not a little burble, either, but an irreverent, unrestrained ripple of hilarity that first brought tears to her eyes, and then with a startling shift, drew darker, more painful tears from her soul.

Sean swung around with her still in his arms, a muttered curse rattling deep in his throat, walked back into the town house and unceremoniously kicked the door shut with one well-placed foot. Caught up so protectively in his firm yet gentle grip, Charlotte leaned her head on his shoulder and sobbed like an exhausted, overwrought child.

Though she knew she was making a spectacle of herself, she couldn't seem to stop the tears pouring from her eyes. She had dammed them up deep inside of her for so long that getting a grip on her runaway emotions now seemed all but impossible.

As if oblivious to the fact that they were both sopping wet, Sean strode through the entryway, heels rapping on the hardwood floor, crossed the very old, very exquisite Oriental carpet in the living room, then settled on the equally old, equally exquisite burnished brown leather sofa.

His hold on her remained determined, perhaps even a little tender. But as her sobs finally began to subside, he spoke to her in a tone that blended exasperation, anger and reproach in an all too familiar way.

"I'd really appreciate it if you'd tell me what, exactly, is going on here, Charlotte." His slow, deep, delectably Southern voice drawled over her, around her, inside of her, soothing her, although likely not by design. "Are you all right?"

She hadn't been *all right* for longer than she could remember. Living through six months of long, lonely days and even longer, lonelier nights had left her feeling bruised and battered.

But she knew that wasn't what Sean had meant, and even if it had been, making such a reply wouldn't have garnered her the least bit of sympathy. Not when she had been glad to see him go that sunny Sunday afternoon just days before they would have celebrated their tenth wedding anniversary, and, much to her regret, had made no effort to hide her feelings from him.

"I'm okay, really—okay…"

Not quite able to look at her husband eye to eye yet, Charlotte breathed in his familiar scent as she rubbed her cheek against the rough wet texture of his cotton shirt.

"You didn't sound okay a few minutes ago," Sean pointed out, not unkindly.

"I'm perfectly fine. I just need to…to talk to you about something," she said, finally shifting in his embrace so that she could look up at him and meet his questioning gaze.

She'd had no more than a glimpse of him before she'd slipped on the step and he'd so gallantly saved her from a nasty fall. With the light at his back, he'd been only a silhouette then, mostly shadowed by the darkness of the night. In the soft glow of the living-room lamps, Charlotte now had a chance to study his features for the first time in half a year.

His appearance hadn't changed much in the time they'd lived apart. His face—defined by high cheekbones, square jaw and hawk-like nose—was still as ruggedly handsome as ever. But his short, thick, very wet, raven-black hair was more liberally salted with silver than she remembered.

There was also more than a hint of weariness evident in his expression and wariness in his pale gray eyes that held, as well, a definite chill.

"Must be something serious or you wouldn't have driven two hundred miles in the middle of a rainstorm on a weeknight," he said. "I seem to remember that you don't like being on the road in bad weather and that your workload at the high school rarely allows you an evening off."

Sean was right. Whenever possible, she avoided driving any distance at all during stormy weather. She was also extremely conscientious about her job at Mayfair High School. One of three guidance counselors, she was quite busy during the spring semester when the eleventh graders were busy sending out college applications and the twelfth graders were engaged in a scramble to find student loans and/or jobs at local businesses around town.

"Yes, it's serious, at least to me," Charlotte replied. "Very serious…"

"I'm assuming it's not a simple matter, though—something we could have discussed over the telephone." Sean hesitated, eyeing her with the first indication of alarm, the frown already furrowing his forehead deepening incrementally. "Are you ill, Charlotte? All those fertility drugs— have they caused a problem with your health?"

He paused again, the brush of his fingertips against her cheek as soft, and fleeting, as a butterfly's wings, reminding her of the warmth and tenderness he had once shown her so freely.

Then he added with very real concern, "You have to know I would certainly take something like an illness seriously."

The hope that all was not lost between them after so many months spent apart sparked anew in Charlotte's heart. Obviously, Sean hadn't stopped caring about her completely, though she had given him good reason to do just that during those last few weeks before he'd finally walked out on her.

Of course, *he* had been the one to call a permanent halt to what he'd so inelegantly termed their *baby chase*. And *he* had been the one to say with undeniable certainty that perhaps it was just as well that they weren't able to have a child—the child she'd wanted so desperately for so long. He couldn't have said anything more hurtful to her if he'd tried.

Charlotte had always believed that she was meant to be a mother. Her mother and grandmother—now deceased—had told her so many times. Yet she had failed to live up to the legacy left to her by the two strong women who had devoted their lives to raising her after her father's death. She had accomplished everything else she had ever set out to do; everything except conceiving a child. Now she might have one last chance at motherhood, but she had to play her cards just right.

"I know you would take it seriously if I were ill, but I'm not." Charlotte offered her husband a slight smile meant to be reassuring. Then, in an attempt at levity, she added, "But I'm likely to end up with a raging head cold before the week is over if I don't get out of these wet clothes soon." She pushed a lock of dripping hair away from her face, shivering as a few drops of icy water trickled down the side of her neck. "You wouldn't by any chance have a spare pair of sweatpants, a sweatshirt and some heavy socks I could borrow, would you?"

At five foot eight, Charlotte was only a few inches

shorter than Sean, and with her slim, boyish figure she could also wear some of the same clothes he did, and in the past, often had.

"Of course, I would." Though he didn't actually return her smile, the grim lines on either side of his mouth softened just a bit. "I'd also like to suggest that we each take a shower then meet in the kitchen for sandwiches and coffee. I don't know about you, but I haven't eaten since lunch."

"That's an excellent idea," Charlotte agreed. "I haven't eaten yet, either."

Looking away from him, she scooted off his lap as gracefully as possible, encumbered as she was by the wet wool of her coat, pants and turtleneck sweater. She also tried to ignore, as best she could, the painful stab to her heart as she recalled all those nights in the past when they had showered together.

Sean stood, too, shoved his hands in the side pockets of his suit pants, and shifted a little uncomfortably. Charlotte risked another glance at him, but he kept his gaze averted, obviously as ill at ease with their situation as she admittedly was.

"There are fresh towels, soap and shampoo in the bathroom on the second floor. I'll get some sweats and socks for you and put them in the guest room," he said, then finally turned to lead the way to the narrow staircase off the entryway.

"Thanks, Sean—thanks a lot," Charlotte murmured as she followed him up the stairs.

Once upon a time, she would have gone with him to the master suite—complete with its own tiny fireplace—that took up the entire third floor of the town house that had been Sean's boyhood home. She would have stood with him under a rain-shower spray of hot water in the separate glass-enclosed stall in the master bathroom, or soaked with him in the huge, old-fashioned, claw-footed tub.

But tonight she walked alone down the dimly lit second-floor hallway to the bland, yet tidy, guest room and the small, serviceable bathroom as her husband continued up the staircase without so much as a backward glance.

Had he gotten so used to living on his own since they'd been apart that he no longer missed her? Or had he been so glad to get away from the turmoil rocking their marriage during those awful weeks before he'd left that he had never really missed her at all?

Stepping into the bathroom and closing the door, Charlotte caught sight of herself in the oval mirror above the freestanding white porcelain sink. Thankfully she didn't look as bad as she'd thought she did, but she didn't look especially good, either.

With all trace of her makeup washed off by the rain, her face was paler than she would have liked. The dark shadows that seemed to have taken up permanent residence under her wide, golden-brown eyes also stood out prominently. Her normally curly brown hair hung flat and wet against her head, as well, making her appear downright woebegone.

Which she wasn't really, and refused to pretend to be with Sean.

In fact, she wasn't a pathetic person by any stretch of the imagination. She was a strong, independent, intelligent woman who'd just happened to get soaked during a rainstorm. The last thing she wanted to stir in her husband was pity, and the best way to avoid doing that, she decided, was to pull herself together and put on a happy face just as quickly as she could.

Shivering despite the blast of hot air coming from the

vent in the ceiling, Charlotte turned on the taps in the shower, then undressed quickly, piling her wet clothes in a neat-as-possible heap atop the wicker hamper. Once she was warm and dry again, she'd hang everything up, but for now, her major goal was to chase the damp chill from the marrow of her bones.

She stood for a long time under the pounding, steamy spray, content just to let the soothing flow ripple over her. Her physical discomfort began to retreat and so, too, did the threads of tension stiffening her shoulders and knotting the small of her back until she could finally luxuriate in a froth of cleansing bubbles. The familiar scent of the lavender soap and shampoo she'd chosen in another lifetime soothed her, as well, not only revitalizing her, but also putting her in touch with her femininity once again.

Feeling infinitely better, Charlotte stepped out of the shower stall at last, swaddled her hair in one big, fluffy white towel, and used another to blot the moisture from her skin. Gathering her wet clothes, she returned to the guest room, hung everything on the padded hangers she found in the closet, then dressed in the dark gray sweats and wool socks Sean had left for her on the bed as promised.

She took a few moments more to towel-dry her hair, finger-combing her damp curls into some semblance of order. Then, with more than a modicum of her confidence restored, she unzipped her tote and took from it the brown envelope. Drawing a deep, steadying breath, she opened the clasp, pulled out the sheaf of papers and scanned them one last time before putting them away again.

Smiling to herself, Charlotte headed out of the bedroom, moving silently across the deep pile of the carpet, then grinned outright as she inhaled the mouthwatering aroma of a muffuletta sandwich warming in the oven. She hadn't had one of those since the last time she and Sean had been together in New Orleans almost nine months ago.

That night they had sat together in the kitchen and shared the round loaf of Italian bread stuffed with ham, salami, provolone cheese and savory olive salad. That night, she had assumed that they'd also shared the hope that she would soon be pregnant with their child. But sadly, she had discovered how wrong she'd been on that account just three months later.

Apparently her beloved husband had simply been humoring her. Tired of the pretense he'd upheld for almost two years, he'd expressed his wishes in no uncertain terms, and when she'd failed to go along with what *he* wanted, he'd packed up his belongings and moved into the New Orleans town house without even the slightest hint of regret.

Charlotte had been so devastated by his betrayal that she'd been almost glad to see him go. For a long time afterward, she hadn't really missed him much, either.

With her hopes and dreams of having a child dashed completely, it had also been all she could do to get through each day. The only way she'd thought she could be a mother was with Sean's cooperation, and he'd refused to continue giving it.

That was still true, of course. But now all it would have to cost him was a little of his time.

As she started down the staircase, Charlotte wanted to believe that her husband hadn't hardened his heart to her so much that he would withhold from her that one small gift. Unfortunately, she didn't have a lot to offer him in return. But maybe, just maybe, the promise that she would never ask anything else of him again in her life would be enough to convince him that they would both be winners in the end.

Chapter Two

Sean had intentionally made short work of his shower, then quickly pulled on faded jeans and a black cashmere sweater before heading downstairs again. He had needed some time alone in the small, modern kitchen of the town house while the muffuletta sandwich he'd bought on his way home from the office warmed in the oven.

Time to brace himself with a stiff drink and gather his scattered wits so that he'd be ready to face Charlotte with a measure of calm.

She had been just about the last person that he'd expected to find standing on his doorstep on this stormy January night. Not only for the reasons he'd given her—her dislike of driving in bad weather and her stressful, time-consuming job at Mayfair High School—but also because of the emotional distance that had grown so impossibly great between them in the half year they had lived apart.

Charlotte had been so obviously glad to see him move out of the house in Mayfair six months ago, and since then, she hadn't seemed the least bit interested in having him move back home again. Even over the holidays she had seemed more than content to be alone—although technically she hadn't exactly been *alone*.

She had spent Thanksgiving with her friend Ellen Herrington, and Ellen's family, then she'd gone on a ski trip to Colorado with another friend, Quinn Sutton, during the week between Christmas and New Year's.

Not that Sean had begrudged his wife having the companionship of her friends during what was a typically lonely time of year for adults on their own. He certainly hadn't wanted her to spend the season feeling as miserable as he had.

But Charlotte had always talked about how important it was to her to share special occasions like Thanksgiving and Christmas and New Year's with family. And he was her only family now, just as she was *his* only family, or had been until anger, fatigue and frustration had forced him to call a time-out in their ten-year marriage.

Granted he could have gone about it with more consideration. But at the time, tensions had been running so high between them that he hadn't exactly been thinking straight. All he'd really known for sure during those last few days they'd been together was that he was very close to losing his wife completely. Leaving on his own had seemed a wiser choice than being asked, or even *told*, to go.

Sean had only meant for the separation to be temporary, though. He'd been sure that a short period of time apart would be good for both of them—a time during which they could each adjust to and accept the prospect of a different kind of future together. Especially since the alternate future he'd had in mind could be as fulfilling as the one they'd once anticipated having.

But somehow he'd screwed up big time, simply by expressing what he had honestly and truthfully come to believe. A lot of couples didn't have children, often by choice, and they remained happily married.

How awful had it been to acknowledge that as far as he was concerned, he and Charlotte didn't have to have a child in order to be content with the life they'd made together?

Neither one of them had been uplifted in any way by their consistent failure to conceive a child. How much more agony had Charlotte expected them to suffer in search of the one goal they had seemed destined never to attain? Why hadn't she been able to see, as he had, that maybe they just weren't meant to be parents?

Sean certainly hadn't had the first clue about how to be a father. His own had been away on business so much that he hadn't been much of a role model. His father's cool, distant and demanding demeanor had been extremely off-putting, as well. Though Sean had done his best to please him as a child, he hadn't ever really wanted to pattern his own behavior after his father's.

There was also the fact that Sean's doting mother had often treated his father like the odd man out on those rare occasions when he had been at home with them.

During those last few months when he and Charlotte had been together, she had become so completely focused on baby making that Sean had experienced a similar sense of exclusion. And he had begun to suspect that he might be in for an even worse fate once a child was added to the increasingly dissatisfying mix of *his* marriage.

Charlotte, too, had grown up without a father. But unlike

Sean, she never seemed to have experienced any sense of loss or to have missed the presence of a man about the house. He could see where maybe one day she would be so devoted to loving and caring for a child, as her mother and grandmother had been devoted to her, that she wouldn't miss the presence of a husband, either.

Calling a halt to the fertility treatments and the in vitro procedures so that they could reassess their situation had seemed like a better idea than continuing to attempt to conceive a baby with so much uncertainty eating away at his heart. But had he realized six months ago that his abrupt decision to move out of the house in Mayfair, albeit temporarily, would cause such a rift between him and Charlotte, he never would have done it.

He would have tried instead to convince his wife that they could be as happy together as a childless couple as they'd been during the eight years they'd shared before she'd insisted that it was time for them to have a baby. Of course, such an attempt would have been frustrating at best, if not downright futile, Sean reminded himself as he added a little more whiskey to the ice cubes in his glass.

His determination not to pursue the possibility of parenthood any further had created an impasse unlike any other he and Charlotte had faced during their marriage. And Charlotte's refusal to at least *try* to understand, much less accept, his reasoning had only made bad matters worse.

All of which brought Sean back to the same conclusion he'd come to over and over again during the time he and Charlotte had lived apart.

Despite his own diffidence about becoming a father, he had gone along with Charlotte's desire to have a baby because he had loved her enough to respect her wants and needs. But every attempt to conceive a child had ended in failure.

As he had told her before he'd moved to New Orleans in June, and as far as he was still concerned, unless and until she could show the same respect for *his* wants and needs, they really were better off apart.

So, Sean wondered, yet again, what had brought his wife to their town house in the French Quarter on such a dark and stormy night?

Apparently not the threat of a serious illness, much to his relief, he acknowledged. But the possibility that she'd come here to personally present him with a formal request for a divorce was almost as painful for him to contemplate.

Maybe he was dwelling too much on negatives, though. Maybe what Charlotte wanted from him was reconciliation, and maybe, just maybe she'd finally come to terms with the agreement she'd have to make in order to have that happen.

The alcohol buzzing through Sean's system had eased somewhat the initial tumble of emotions he'd experienced upon first seeing his wife outside his door. But the sudden thought that Charlotte might want to give their marriage another chance made his heart pound and his gut clench all over again.

Such an offer from her would go a long way toward dispelling the anger and disappointment that still lingered, haunting him—

"Either my senses are deceiving me, or you have a muffuletta sandwich warming in the oven."

The sound of Charlotte's voice, just a little too cheerful, startled Sean from his reverie. He had been standing at the counter, head bent, contemplating the whiskey and ice in the glass he held, and so hadn't seen her approach through the doorway that connected the long living/dining room and the kitchen.

Now eyeing her as she hesitated uncertainly a few steps away from him, he wished that he'd focused more fully on the moment at hand. Remembering the past had been all good and well, but his introspection had left him far more vulnerable than he wanted to be to his wife's considerable charms.

Gazing at Charlotte for a long, steady moment, Sean experienced the same stirring of physical desire that had caught him unawares when he'd first swept her into his arms on the front doorstep. Even dressed in baggy sweats and floppy socks, with her dark hair curling damply against her much-too-pale face, she looked sexy as hell to him.

He'd like to blame the six months of celibacy he'd endured for his response to her allure, but Sean knew there was much more to it than raging testosterone. No other woman he had ever met—no matter how poised, polished, glamorous or willing—had ever appealed to him in quite the same way that his wife did, even when she was barely pulled together.

This wasn't the time to let her know it, though. Until he found out what she wanted from him, Sean deemed it better to mask his intimate thoughts and desires behind a cool and businesslike facade than risk being hurt by her yet again.

"Yes, there's a muffuletta sandwich warming in the oven," he confirmed in a polite tone of voice. "I bought it at Central Market on my way home from work."

Having gathered his wits about him, he resisted the urge to return her slight smile. There was no sense encouraging the kind of camaraderie they would have once shared. Not if she was about to ask him for a divorce, he thought, eyeing the brown envelope she held so tightly, clutched to her chest.

"I haven't had one of those since...since the last time we were here together," Charlotte said, her smile turning wistful.

"Lately I've been buying only a half sandwich," Sean admitted. "Otherwise I'm too tempted to eat the whole thing myself, usually in one sitting. I asked for a whole one tonight, although I'm not sure why."

"Lucky for me you did, or you'd probably be serving me peanut butter and jelly."

"Oh, I would have been able to produce a fairly good grilled-cheese sandwich for you," Sean advised her, finally allowing himself the barest hint of a smile.

"Well, that's good to know."

Charlotte walked to the island that took the place of a kitchen table, slid onto one of the tall black enamel stools and carefully set the envelope facedown in front of her.

"The sandwich should be ready in a few minutes." Sean turned to the counter, set aside his glass and took the carafe off the stand of the coffeemaker. "I'll make some coffee for you, too."

"Actually what I'd really like right now, Sean, is a little whiskey on ice," she said, surprising him not only with her brusque tone, but also with her unapologetic air.

While Charlotte had never been a teetotaler, she had always preferred a modest glass of wine to hard liquor. Since she'd given up even wine during the two years she'd been trying to conceive, Sean hadn't seen her drink anything stronger than club soda in quite a while.

"I have some wine—" he began, glancing back at her.

"Thanks, but I'd prefer the whiskey tonight. It will take away the chill in my bones a little faster."

"I can turn up the thermostat if you're cold."

"Just give me the whiskey, Sean," she said, suddenly

sounding exasperated. "I promise I won't get all goofy on you. One bout of hysterical laughing and crying is enough for one night, even for me."

Sean was about to state that he hadn't been concerned about a repeat of her earlier behavior, but he knew that he'd be lying. The more relaxed Charlotte became, the more likely she'd be ruled by her emotions.

As he'd discovered more than once already, that would then make it almost impossible for him to deal with her in a rational manner.

Trying not to appear too obvious, he took a glass from the cabinet, filled it with ice, wordlessly poured the smallest measure of whiskey possible into it, then set it in front of her.

She met his gaze with a slight arch of her eyebrows, just enough to let him know she wasn't stupid. Then she lifted the glass to her lips and took a healthy sip without the least hint of a grimace.

For just an instant, Sean wanted to reach across the island counter, put his hands on her shoulders and—what? Shake her senseless or pull her into his arms and kiss the smirk off her lips?

He'd be damned if he knew for sure.

"Do you think our sandwich is ready yet?" she asked as he turned to fill the coffeemaker with water, a spark of humor evident in her softly teasing tone.

Our sandwich? It was *his* sandwich, and he damn well didn't appreciate her proprietary air. But to say so would only reveal to her the emotional turmoil roiling in his belly.

"Why don't you set out some plates and napkins for us while I put the coffee on?"

"Okay…."

Charlotte slipped off her stool and next thing Sean knew she was standing mere inches away from him, her arm brushing against his as she reached up to open a cabinet door. Had he realized ahead of time that asking her for a little help would put her in such close proximity to him, he would have never done it.

His intention had been to keep relative peace between them, and he'd succeeded...to a point. Busy with dishes and napkins, Charlotte was neither guzzling whiskey nor ragging his butt. Moving around the narrow confines of the kitchen, though, she arrested his senses completely, making him just as crazy, only in another kind of way.

The scent of her favorite soap and shampoo drifted all around him, a pleasant counterpart to the spicy aroma of the sandwich coming from the oven. The subtle waft of flowery fragrance had an equal ability to stir up memories of better days...and nights, as well.

And the nudge of her hip—surely accidental—reminded him of how lithe and firm her body was beneath the sweats she wore. Fragile, too, he added to himself as he gave in to temptation and watched her arrange the plates and napkins on the island counter—not across from each other as he would have preferred, but more intimately side by side.

He had been almost sure earlier, carrying her to the living-room sofa, that she had lost weight during the months of their separation. Not a lot, but enough so that it had been evident in the sharper angles of her bones as well as in the slightly narrower shape of her face.

"All ready if you are," Charlotte said, glancing up at him as she sat on her stool again.

Her expression shifted from open, almost eager, to wary

and uncertain in an instant, warning Sean that his concern for her had likely shown on his face as something more akin to anger. No big surprise, since he didn't like the idea that she might not have been taking adequate care of herself the past six months. But neither stirring her apprehension nor putting her on guard would do either of them any good.

"Would you like me to freshen your drink?" he asked, the echo of false cheer in his voice signaling that he was in danger of overcorrecting.

"I'm fine for now," she answered quietly, obviously even more leery of him.

"I'll just get the sandwich out of the oven, then."

Relieved to have something to do, Sean slid the muffuletta off the cookie sheet onto the cutting board, deftly sliced it into quarters, then transferred it onto a serving plate that he deposited on the island counter with the merest hint of a flourish.

"Mmm, it looks as good as it smells," Charlotte murmured, helping herself to a piece of the sandwich, careful to capture all of the melted cheese that oozed out of the bread. One bite later, she smiled at him blissfully. "Tastes as good as it smells, too."

Trying to ignore the arrow-to-heart effect of the dreamy look in her dark eyes, Sean slid onto one of the stools across from her. He moved his plate and napkin in front of him, then took a quarter of the sandwich for himself.

"I'm glad you like it," he said, his tone once again cool.

The look she shot at him in return held the smallest measure of disappointment.

"What's not to like? It's hot and fresh and full of good stuff, and I'm really hungry."

Sliding her gaze away, Charlotte reached for her

drink, took a fortifying swallow, then silently tucked into her sandwich.

Sean gladly followed her lead, though his eyes lit more than once on the brown envelope she had yet to mention. Much as he wanted to know what it held, there was a part of him that dreaded the moment when he'd find out.

Without the give and take of conversation to slow them down, they polished off their meal in a matter of minutes. Still quietly introspective, Sean rinsed their empty plates and put them in the dishwasher. He then added ice and another small measure of whiskey to each of their glasses, and finally sat across from Charlotte once again.

She had her hands clasped tightly atop the island counter. At the base of her throat, her pulse fluttered, and she seemed determined to look anywhere but at him. Her sudden anxiety fed Sean's, making him fear again for the true state of her health.

Other than having to deal with a serious illness, what else could tie her in such knots?

Not the decision to file for divorce—she had to know he wouldn't argue with her about it if that was what she really wanted. Not the decision to ask him to come home again, either—again, she had to know he would move back to Mayfair in a minute, as long as she agreed to his terms regarding any further pursuit of parenthood.

Finally unable to wait any longer for Charlotte to begin on her own, Sean put a hand over hers. With the other he tapped the brown envelope once, his heart hammering inside his chest.

"Now that we've finished eating, do you want to tell me what this is all about?" he asked as gently as he could.

"That would probably be a good idea, wouldn't it?"

Charlotte opened her clasped hands, holding on to him for a long moment as she sent an inquiring yet apprehensive smile his way.

"Yes, that would be a very good idea."

Sean gave her hands an encouraging squeeze. Then he let go of her and sat back on his stool, crossing his arms over his chest.

Lowering her gaze, Charlotte picked up the envelope and fumbled with the clasp, her fingers trembling enough for him to notice. He was half tempted to take the damn thing away from her and rip it open himself, but she was jittery enough already.

He expected her to pull out all of the paperwork the envelope obviously held. Instead she removed only a single sheet to which something was attached with a paper clip. She gazed at the paper for several moments, her expression softening perceptively. Finally she looked up at him again, and Sean saw the faint shimmer of tears in her eyes. Yet again, he couldn't help but fear the worst.

"Just tell me, Charlotte," he said, his voice a ragged, insistent growl filled with more menace than he'd intended. "Whatever it is you've come here to tell me, please…just do it now."

Charlotte sat back on her stool and blinked at him, momentarily looking as if she'd been struck a blow. Then she tilted her chin defensively and eyed him with sudden, steely resolve. All trace of her earlier fragility, as well as her uncertainty, disappeared in an instant.

"Do you remember that we talked about adoption last year?" she asked, her tone surprisingly matter-of-fact.

"Yes, of course, I remember. We even filled out some forms and agreed to have a home study done by an agency here in New Orleans that arranges adoptions of foreign children."

Sean hesitated, confused by the tack Charlotte had taken. The home study had been done long before he'd moved out of the Mayfair house. But they had been so focused on their last, ultimately unsuccessful in vitro procedure that they really hadn't pursued the adoption alternative any further.

Or rather *he* hadn't pursued the adoption alternative any further, Sean amended.

Realization suddenly dawning as to where Charlotte must be headed, he pushed away from the island counter, stood and raised his hands in an emphatic gesture meant to fend her off.

"No, Charlotte," he continued with a mix of anger and frustration. "No way am I going to agree to adopt a baby. I made my feelings about parenthood very clear six months ago. We gave it our best shot and we failed and enough is enough. I haven't changed my mind about that since then, and I'm not going to change my mind about it now."

There was no denying the flash of hurt in his wife's eyes as she stared at him reproachfully, but he braced himself against the pain he knew his words had caused her. Unwilling to hear any defense she might choose to offer, he allowed her no chance to speak.

"I went along with the testing, not to mention the fertility treatments, the scheduled sex and the in vitro procedures even though none of the doctors we consulted could give us any concrete reason why we were having trouble conceiving on our own. I did it all for *you* because you wanted a baby so much. But as I tried to tell you six months ago, in the process I realized that I'm just not cut out to be a father. I also asked you to try to accept and understand *my* feelings, but you refused to do it."

"Believe me, Sean, I *have* accepted how you feel about being a father," Charlotte insisted, her voice a firm, quiet counterpoint to the echo of his own rising tone.

Sean had always prided himself on his ability to handle problems in his personal life in the same businesslike manner in which he dealt with professional problems. He counted his quiet competence as one of the main reasons why he'd had such success with the corporate security company he'd started after he'd completed his service in the military.

He knew from long experience that flying off the handle rarely earned anyone anything they really wanted. In fact, he only had to look back half a year to be reminded of where the last volatile confrontation he'd had with his wife had gotten him.

Marshaling his resources, he picked up his glass, looked away from Charlotte and took a long swallow of whiskey as he quickly counted to ten. Then he set aside his glass, took a steadying breath and spoke again.

"So why are you bringing up the subject of adoption now?" he asked, pleased that he managed to sound reasonable once again.

"Because I still want to be a mother—I still *need* to be a mother—and now I have the chance. But only if you'll help me," Charlotte answered in a rush, the look in her eyes one of pleading. "We've been approved to adopt a baby girl—as a couple."

She set the paper and attached photograph on the island countertop and pushed it toward him with a fingertip. But Sean was too stunned by what she'd just said to acknowledge it even with a glance.

Adopt a baby girl? Was Charlotte nuts?

"All I'm asking is that you go with me to Kazakhstan to complete the adoption process," she added, so amazingly calm and collected that all he could do was stare at her in disbelief. "Of course, we'll have to pretend that we're still happily married and living together in Mayfair, but only for a few months. Then you can move back here again and file for divorce if that's what you want to do. I promise that I'll agree to whatever terms you choose, and I won't ask you for anything more ever again—not even child support."

"Surely you can't be serious—" Sean began, still unable to believe that she was not only asking something so preposterous of him, but also doing it in such an amazingly blithe manner.

He had prepared himself for the revelation of a serious illness, a request for a divorce, or in the best of all possible worlds, an offer of reconciliation on his terms. But to even *suggest* that he travel halfway around the world with her—to Kazakhstan, of all places—to adopt a foreign child he neither wanted nor needed in his life... She couldn't possibly be thinking straight, could she?

"I've never been more serious about anything in my life," Charlotte assured him, her voice wavering, but not her gaze. "Please, Sean...please, *please* help me bring our little girl home."

"She's *not* our little girl, Charlotte—"

"Yes...yes, she *is*. Just look at her—she's beautiful...."

Sean didn't want to do it—didn't want to look at the small color photograph attached to the sheet of paper lying on the countertop. But neither could he ignore completely the desperate urgency he heard in his wife's voice.

Obviously she was well on the way to irrationality regarding this business of adoption. Maybe by cooperating with her just a little he'd eventually be able to calm her down enough to make her see reason.

His mouth set in a grim line, Sean stared at Charlotte for a long, unhappy moment. She continued to meet his gaze without flinching, and at the same time, pushed the photograph a tad closer to him across the countertop.

With a reluctance much greater than he should have been experiencing under the circumstances, Sean finally shifted his gaze to the small photograph. His eyes focused on the child's face captured on it and his breath caught in his throat.

Not a tiny baby, but a toddler of more than a year in age, the little girl in the photo was beautiful, indeed. But she was also so much more than that. With her wispy brown hair and wide brown eyes, her pale porcelain skin and bow-shaped lips, she was the very image of his wife. There was something about the tilt of her little chin and the calm, direct expression on her face that also reminded him of…himself.

She could have been Charlotte's child—and his, Sean thought, his heart softening unexpectedly. Anyone who saw the three of them together would easily assume Charlotte and he were the child's biological parents.

For a long moment, he wondered why she looked so serious, then imagined how much fun it would be to make her giggle, just like Charlotte often did when he said something amusing. Surely that was a familiar spark of mischief he saw in the little girl's big brown eyes.

Only he hadn't the first clue how to make a child giggle, Sean realized. More than likely, with his background and upbringing, he'd actually be more apt to make her cry.

Then Charlotte would sweep her off to cuddle and coddle, leaving him on the outside looking in.

Reminded all over again of the perils inherent in his vision of fatherhood, Sean gave himself a firm mental shake. He simply couldn't afford to waver any further from the position he'd already taken. Bad as it was to be alone, being *hurt* and alone would be even worse.

"You're not going to help with the adoption, are you?" Charlotte asked, the threat of tears evident in her quiet voice.

Having judged his mood all too accurately, she stood now, too, and reached for the photograph with a trembling hand.

Sean wanted to give Charlotte all the reasons why he couldn't help her. He wanted to ask her, yet again, to understand and accept how he felt about being a father. But what he found himself actually saying surprised him as much as it must surely have surprised his wife.

Catching her hand in his, he stopped her from picking up the photograph. Then, in a gruff voice he barely recognized as his own, he made the only offer he could in good conscience.

"If adopting this child is that important to you, then I will help you in any way I can," he said.

"Oh, Sean—" Charlotte began, the smile lighting up her face a glorious thing to behold.

"But," he interrupted her, his voice flat and his gaze steady as he held up a warning hand to her.

He refused to be diverted from the course he'd chosen by either acknowledging or encouraging her initial joy.

"What?" she asked with confusion, her smile quickly fading.

Sean hesitated for the space of a heartbeat. Then he laid out his terms in a steely tone.

"I'll help you only with the understanding that once we're home again and you're settled with the child, our marriage will be over, and I'll be filing for divorce."

Chapter Three

Charlotte stared at Sean, the echo of his last words resounding between them in the brightly lit kitchen, punctuated only by the still steady drumbeat of rain against the window above the sink.

She felt as if she'd just been treated to a wild, unwanted roller-coaster ride. The emotional ups and downs she'd experienced in the space of just a few minutes had taken her from hope to disappointment, joy to confusion, then to the final rattling halt of sad realization.

Charlotte had seen the way Sean's expression had warmed and softened when he'd first allowed himself to look at the photograph of the little girl they'd been chosen to adopt. She had sensed, as well, the melting of his heart as he'd wordlessly acknowledged how eerily the child's physical features resembled their own.

She had been so sure that he must have thought—as

she had—that the toddler in the photo had been born halfway around the world, in answer to all her prayers, especially for them.

In all honesty, his reaction to the photograph had seemed to mirror hers so completely that Charlotte had been certain that Sean would be able to set aside his concerns about his ability to be a good father at last and gladly agree to pursue the adoption with her. He had to have seen, as she had, that here was the child she had been meant to mother. Here, indeed, was the child she had been meant to call her own.

But in the blink of an eye, he'd withdrawn into himself again, the lines and angles of his handsome face deepening. Having obviously reminded himself that by adopting a child he would also be taking on the burden of fatherhood—a burden he no longer wanted—he had visibly hardened his heart to her.

Charlotte had been ready to put away the photograph, to admit defeat and start the long drive back to Mayfair. Sean had always been a decisive man. Once his mind was made up, he rarely, if ever, changed it.

The six months he'd chosen to live in the New Orleans town house rather than with her in Mayfair were proof enough of how true that simple fact remained. Had she remembered how unwavering he could be several hours earlier as she stood beside her mailbox back home, she likely could have saved herself a lot of grief.

He had surprised her, though, with a one-two punch that had momentarily rendered her speechless. First he had offered to help her with the adoption in any way he could, sending a shaft of joyous hope straight to her heart. But then he had laid out his terms in such a cool, calm, businesslike manner that Charlotte had barely been able to swallow around the clog of anguish that lodged in her throat.

She knew that she shouldn't have been all that surprised by the bargain Sean expected her to make with him. Six months ago he had stated very clearly how he'd felt about continuing their seemingly futile quest to conceive a child. He had also warned her only a few minutes ago that his feeling on the subject hadn't changed.

But apparently Sean had made a decision regarding their marriage, as well. A firm decision, in fact, since he hadn't given her any choice in the matter, had he?

He hadn't said that she could either adopt the child or work with him to put their life together back on track again. He had simply offered to help her with the adoption, and then he'd said he would be filing for divorce.

Charlotte wasn't sure what she would have done if Sean had actually asked her to choose between him and the child. She still loved him, just as she had almost since the first day she'd met him, and surely would until the day she died.

They had been so happy together for such a long time. He hadn't been wrong back in June, either, when he'd insisted that they could be happy together again without the baby she'd been so desperate to have.

Only then she'd been in the midst of a hormone-induced emotional turmoil that hadn't allowed her to see reason in anything he'd had to say to her.

No, Charlotte didn't think she would have ended her marriage to Sean in exchange for the chance to have a child. But if their marriage was already over in *his* mind, as it certainly seemed to be, then she might as well do whatever she could to at least have the child she'd always wanted, and had always believed she was meant to have.

"I realize that my terms probably seem harsh to you," Sean added, finally breaking the silence that had stretched between them so uncomfortably for the past few minutes.

Letting go of her wrist, he took a step back from the island that separated them and crossed his arms over his chest again. Charlotte saw in his stance a reflection of the brook-no-argument mentality he'd adopted six months ago, and allowed herself a small inner sigh of resignation.

No sense making things more difficult than they had to be. He was willing to give her some of what she wanted from him, some of what she needed. Why risk having him withdraw the offer he'd willingly made by voicing an all-or-nothing demand that he obviously didn't have the heart to honor?

"No, not really, all things considered," she replied, sitting on her stood again.

She tried to smile so that he would know she understood and accepted the decision he'd made, and harbored no ill will as a result. But she couldn't be sure if she'd succeeded as he continued to eye her in a grim, uncompromising manner.

"I realize that I'm asking an awful lot of you," she continued. "I want you to know how grateful I am that you're going to help me. I also want you to know that I'll try to make it as easy as possible for you to get through the whole…process—"

"Before we go any further here just tell me one thing, will you?" Sean cut in. "Did you move forward with this business of adopting a foreign baby after I left Mayfair back in June?"

"No, of course not," she answered without hesitation, stung by the accusation of equivocation on her part underlying his question. "For the first few weeks after you left me, it was all I could do to get out of bed each morning.

Then I had to focus as much energy as I possibly could on getting ready for the start of the school year."

She paused and drew a quick, angry breath.

"I certainly wasn't plotting to thwart you in any way," she added. "I'm not that kind of person, and you, of all people, should know that by now. I wasn't expecting to find this in my mailbox." Charlotte tapped a hand on the envelope for emphasis, and tipped her chin up angrily. "But I *am* happy that I did, and I don't intend to pretend otherwise."

"I don't expect you to."

Typically, Sean didn't attempt to defend his questioning of her or to backpedal even the slightest bit. But for just an instant, Charlotte was sure that she saw the merest flicker of hurt in his pale gray eyes.

Her response must have touched a nerve with him, as well. Though how exactly, she couldn't really be sure. Unless he *had* meant to offer her an ultimatum earlier— either go forward with adopting the child or work together to save their marriage.

"I don't suppose you'd consider—" Charlotte began, then looked away when his expression hardened again.

He hadn't said that reconciliation was an option. In fact, he'd been quite firm about his intention to file for divorce once the adoption process had been completed.

"What?"

"Nothing," she said, pushing away from the counter, envelope in hand.

"Is there anything else you'd like to know right now? Otherwise, I'll just run upstairs, collect my clothes and head on back to Mayfair. We can discuss the adoption again in a few days—"

"You are *not* driving back to Mayfair tonight," Sean said. "The weather has only gotten worse since you've been here, and that's going to make it even more dangerous for you to be on the road than it was earlier, especially on the interstate."

"I'll be fine—" Charlotte assured him.

She didn't really want to drive home tonight. But neither did she want to spend the night in the town house with her husband, knowing as she now did that their marriage was over.

"There's also a lot more I want to know about this adoption business," Sean added, riding over her feeble protest. "Do you have any idea of exactly what we're going to have to do? Has the agency given you any information on where we're supposed to go to collect the child and a specific time frame for doing so?"

Charlotte didn't much care for the way he phrased his rapid-fire questions—adoption *business, process, collecting* of a child. He made it sound so cold, so…clinical—as if becoming the parents of the precious little girl in the photograph were just another transaction to be brokered as quickly and efficiently as possible.

But she also had to admit that he had a right to know up-front all that he would be required to do.

Unfortunately, Charlotte couldn't provide him with the information he wanted in the same concise manner he'd just requested it, though she was sure most, if not all, of it was contained in the envelope.

"I don't know," she admitted. "I haven't had a chance to look through all of the paperwork the agency sent us."

"All the more reason for you to spend the night here. That will give us a chance to sort through the packet together," Sean said amenably enough, then added, "unless you're ready to call it a night, in which case I don't mind reading over the information on my own."

Deftly outmaneuvered, Charlotte realized that Sean had given her two choices, neither of which would allow her to leave New Orleans that night.

Going through the adoption-agency information was going to take awhile, and according to the clock on the kitchen wall it was after ten o'clock already. She was barely alert enough to drive now, although with a little coffee she'd probably be good to go. But a couple of hours from now even coffee wouldn't help her to stay awake during what would be a long, tedious drive in stormy weather.

The only way she could possibly get away that night would be to leave the envelope with Sean so he could review the contents on his own, and she certainly wasn't prepared to do *that*.

"I suppose we might as well go over everything together," she said at last, though not nearly as graciously as she should have.

"Would you like some coffee before we get started?" Sean offered with the benevolence of one who had triumphed.

"Yes, please."

Charlotte sat on her stool again, making an effort to tamp down her irritation. How bad could spending one night in the guest room of the town house really be when it would also give her a chance to cement her new affiliation with her soon to be ex-husband?

Obviously, she was about to find out.

"Do you still take cream and sugar?"

"Do you still make coffee strong enough to hold a spoon upright?"

"Cream and sugar it is," Sean acknowledged with the first hint of humor in his voice that she'd heard all evening.

Reminded of how charming he could be when he put his mind to it—as he was apt to do whenever he'd gotten his way—Charlotte was tempted to lower her guard just a little.

She was stuck in the town house with him for the night, so why not relax and enjoy the companionship Sean now seemed willing to offer her? With the rain still thundering down outside, the small kitchen, light and bright, provided a warm and cozy haven for the two of them.

Only by Sean's choice they weren't really a couple anymore—at least not in the same sense that they'd once been. If she allowed herself to pretend otherwise even for an evening, she knew that she would find it even more painful to face the reality awaiting her in the not-too-distant future.

Better to think of her husband as a business partner from now on, Charlotte warned herself as she took the sheaf of paperwork from the envelope and laid it out on the island countertop. A *temporary* partner with whom she would have dealings for only a short time before he walked out of her life for good.

"You're looking just a mite grim all of a sudden," Sean observed as he set two steaming mugs of café au lait on the counter, then sat on the stool across from her again. "Have you come upon something disturbing among all those papers from the adoption agency?"

"The number of forms alone that we're supposed to complete is daunting," Charlotte replied, glad to have something to use as a blind for her disquieting emotions.

She took a swallow of the hot, sweet, creamy coffee laced with chicory. Then she spread the various forms out in front of her, reading headings aloud as she turned them toward Sean for his perusal.

"To start, we need a written referral from the adoption agency in New Orleans, criminal background checks from the local and state police, and clearance from Immigration and Naturalization to bring the child into the country. Then we have to apply for approval from the adoption agency's sister agency in Kazakhstan, as well as from the orphanage there. There's also a form requesting a formal invitation from the orphanage to adopt the child and another one requesting a visa from the Kazakhstan government allowing us to travel to the city of Almaty where the orphanage is located."

Charlotte risked a quick glance at her husband. She was afraid that the sheer volume of paperwork required to set the adoption process in motion would be enough to make him change his mind. Even with the agency's help in assembling the necessary dossier—a service they offered that had been included in the fees she and Sean had already paid—the work involved would be time consuming.

Then they would have to spend approximately four weeks in Kazakhstan, meeting with agency and orphanage personnel and bonding with the child. Only after significant bonding between the adoptive parents and the child had occurred would their request for adoption be presented to the court and approval finally be given.

"They're quite thorough, aren't they?" Sean glanced at her, then focused on the forms again, adding, "That's reassuring, at least to me."

"Me, too," Charlotte agreed, releasing with relief the breath she'd been holding.

Sean hadn't sounded as if he'd been thinking about

backing out of his end of the bargain they'd made…at least not yet.

"With so many checks and balances in place, once the adoption has been completed and we're home again, there shouldn't be any problem with anyone challenging our rights as the child's parents," he continued, surprising Charlotte with his use of *we* and *our*, and the plural *parents*.

Just a slip of the tongue, she told herself, trying hard not to get her hopes up again. But she had to admit that Sean wasn't distancing himself nearly as much as he'd led her to believe he would earlier. Especially considering the fact that he wasn't planning on sticking around to be a full-time, or even part-time, father once they'd finished with the *business* of adopting the child.

"That was one of the things that impressed me the most about the Robideaux Agency when we first began looking into the possibility of adopting a child," Charlotte said. "They have an excellent and well-established reputation for setting up successful legal adoptions of healthy foreign children. They also provided us with a lengthy list of references from other adoptive parents who had used their services."

Sean shot her a long, measuring look, his pale gray eyes seeming to assess her response in a calculating manner.

"You've certainly done your homework," he drawled, his tone not altogether approving.

Charlotte's initial response to his comment was to blink at him with a mixture of surprise and confusion. Then she realized he was once again inferring that she'd gone behind his back somehow by contacting the Robideaux Agency without his knowledge.

"Yes, I did," she admitted, eyeing him narrowly as she barely controlled her anger. "But that was over a year ago when we first talked about the adoption option and we realized that at our age we had a better chance of adopting a baby from a foreign country. You told me then to be very careful not to get involved with a fly-by-night organization, and I was. In fact, I told you quite a lot about the Robideaux Agency before we had our first meeting with our counselor there, and it was my understanding that you approved of the way they handled their adoptions. Although I'm thinking that you must not have paid much attention to what I told you or you would have remembered it now."

"There was a lot going on in our lives a year ago, Charlotte," Sean retorted defensively. "My business had almost doubled as companies around the city and state began to see the need to increase their on-site security following the hurricane. You were in the midst of another round of fertility treatments then, too, and miserable most of the time as a result. You'd end up in tears during just about every conversation I tried to have with you—"

"Probably because you so obviously resented taking any of your precious time to actually *listen* to me," Charlotte cut in, no longer able to hide her ire. "How was I supposed to respond when you were constantly rattling the change in your pockets, checking your watch or staring out the window like a condemned man hoping for a reprieve every time I turned to you for comfort?"

"All you talked about was how tired you were, how sick the drugs made you feel and how depressed you were. Then there were the twice-daily reports on how your temperature had either gone up or down, and how we had to schedule down to the exact *minute* when I'd next be expected to perform sexually. *That* was really something to anticipate, too," he snapped sarcastically. "You lying in bed about as relaxed and willing as a terrified virgin, hands gripping the sheets—"

Charlotte looked away from him, remembering how her confidence in herself as a woman had dwindled more and more as one barren month followed another. Then, smiling ruefully, she shook her head as she spoke her next thought aloud.

"Then I find out that the whole time I've been beating myself up for my inability to get pregnant you actually weren't all that thrilled about the prospect of fatherhood."

"Not the *whole* time," Sean insisted quietly.

"So I was only making a fool of myself for what—six to eight months before you finally spoke up? That's such a relief to know," Charlotte allowed, taking her own turn at sarcasm as she gathered the forms from the adoption agency and started to stuff them into the envelope.

"I never once thought you were making a fool of yourself, Charlotte," Sean said, his tone softening unexpectedly at the same moment she felt the touch of his hand on her wrist. "But I *was* worried about you—the way you kept *obsessing*—"

"So you left me and now I'm all better," Charlotte interrupted him bitterly as an unexpected rush of tears stung her eyes.

"Rehashing the past isn't really getting us anywhere now, is it?"

Again Sean's voice was surprisingly gentle.

"I have to agree, especially since we'll be divorced by this time next year." Forcing herself to get a grip on her roiling emotions, Charlotte met her husband's gaze again. "But you've insinuated twice already that I've been less than honest with you about what I might have done to further our chances of adopting a child. I'm not going to sit by quietly and let you get away with it. I've always been truthful with you, Sean—*always*—and I swear to you that I always will be. But if you can't, or *won't*, trust me—"

"I *do* trust you," he cut in, tightening his hold on her wrist just enough to help to make his point. "Obviously I jumped to some wrong conclusions earlier and I apologize."

Charlotte eyed her husband skeptically for several moments. She was still more than a little angry with him, and she was deeply hurt, too. He could say that he hadn't thought she'd made a fool of herself by trying so desperately to have a child that she'd been completely unaware of his true feelings. But that was how he'd made her feel six months ago and that was how she felt now.

Taking the time and energy necessary to nurse her grievances against him was a luxury, though—one she couldn't afford at the moment. Sean's offer to help her with the adoption had been tentatively made, at best. By continuing to behave toward him in a hostile manner, especially now that he'd eaten a small slice of humble pie, she might just cause him to withdraw that offer altogether.

"Just don't do it again, okay?" she asked, still refusing to allow her gaze to waver.

"I won't—I promise." He finally let go of her wrist after another small, seemingly meant-to-be-affirming squeeze. Then he stood again, looking very weary all of a sudden. "I'd really like to read through the information from the adoption agency more closely, but right now I'm beat. Is there any chance we could pick up where we left off again in the morning, more cordially? I'm not sure how anxious you are to get back to Mayfair, or how you feel about missing a day of work. But I was thinking that since you're already here, maybe we could try to set up an appointment to meet with our counselor at the agency sometime tomorrow, too."

Exhaustion had been creeping up on Charlotte, as well, making her much more sensitive than she should have been. A good night's sleep would better her mood quite a bit. Since she was going to have to spend the night in New Orleans, she didn't have any great desire to rush back to Mayfair the next day, either.

What could it hurt to stay in the city tomorrow so that she and Sean could go over the paperwork together and, if possible, talk to their counselor at the agency? She might as well take advantage of his willingness to cooperate with her while she could.

"That sounds like a good idea to me. I'll call the school district's automated line before I go to bed tonight and arrange for a substitute to take my place tomorrow."

"The more we can get down now, the better."

"Yes, I agree."

Sean smiled approvingly as Charlotte stood, too, the envelope in hand. She thought he would say something more or, at the very least, offer to go upstairs with her as he had earlier. But he stood with his hands in his pockets, apparently content to wait for her to make the next move.

"I guess I'll call it a night, then," she murmured after a few more moments of silence passed between them.

Feeling oddly out of place in the once familiar and much loved old town house, Charlotte turned to leave the kitchen, walking alone through the living/dining room to the staircase off the entryway.

She and Sean had shared so many happy times here together. They had visited the town house often, especially over weekends during the fall and winter months, so that they could enjoy the city's various cultural events. But her memories of those days and nights were now bittersweet.

There would be no going back to the life they'd once had together. Sean had made sure she understood that, and she did. She could mourn the past and the loss of his love all she wanted, but it would gain her nothing in the end.

So she would look to the future, instead, where another kind of life awaited her, and another kind of love would fill the painful emptiness that now made her heart ache.

On her own in the guest room with the door politely shut, Charlotte called to arrange for a substitute to take over for her at the high school the next day. She washed her face and brushed her teeth, then turned back the serviceable navy-blue-and-white striped comforter on the bed, slipped beneath the blankets and switched off the lamp on the nightstand.

She could still hear the rain tapping against the windowpanes, but more gently as the worst of the storm finally seemed to be over. The steady patter should have lulled her to sleep in short order. She was tired enough to want as well as to need the rest. But her mind still raced along too busily to shut down on her command.

Her own fault, she admitted, remembering how eagerly she had welcomed the mug of coffee Sean had set before her. Revved up by such a hearty dose of caffeine so late in the evening, she would likely toss and turn until dawn. That, in turn, would leave her at a distinct disadvantage when it was time for her to face her husband once again.

With a quiet sigh, Charlotte sat up in the bed and pushed aside the blankets. There was only one antidote she could think of for sleeplessness—a glass of warm milk dosed with a small shot of whiskey. She didn't want to go downstairs again, especially if Sean was still in the kitchen. But suffering through a restless night would be much worse.

Still debating her alternatives, she switched on the lamp, then cocked her head to one side and looked up at the ceiling. From above came the muted sound of measured footsteps punctuated by a squeak or two as Sean walked across the floor. A few moments later, the pipes gurgled with running water and Charlotte made her decision.

She could run down to the kitchen, heat up some milk in the microwave oven, dose it with whiskey and be back in the guest room in a matter of minutes, all without Sean being any the wiser.

Feeling like a thief in the night despite her equal right to make herself at home in the town house, Charlotte crept down the hallway to the staircase. Ten minutes, at the most, and she'd be back in her bed, door shut, laughing at herself for being so apprehensive.

What was the worst that could happen to her, anyway—getting caught by her husband of ten years with the milk jug in one hand and the whiskey bottle in the other?

She made it to the kitchen without a problem, prepared her nightcap and was halfway across the living room, mug in hand, when she realized that she'd much rather sip her spiked milk curled up on one of the upholstered wing chairs tucked between the front windows.

The house was peacefully quiet, the darkness of the room broken only by the pale glow of gaslight coming through the slats of the wooden shutters. The intimate ambience suited her mood so much better than that of the sterile, unfamiliar guest room.

Soothed by the hot drink, Charlotte thought back over her conversation with Sean and the angry words they'd exchanged. He had been right when he'd said rehashing the past was a waste of time, as she'd acknowledged then. Still, she couldn't help dwelling on some of the harsher accusations he'd made. Not only had they been very revealing; they had also held more validity than she liked to admit.

She hadn't realized at the time that she'd been so hard to live with all those months she'd been trying to get pregnant. With Sean's comments fresh in her mind, however, she could look back now and understand how problematic her self-involvement must have been for him.

She had always been successful at everything she'd ever attempted to do. But she had consistently failed at the one thing she'd always been meant to do. So caught up in her own misery had she been that she'd stopped being the fun-loving, affectionate, desirous and desirable wife, best friend and playmate Sean had loved. Instead she had become an intense, emotional, unhappy woman with a mission, not to be diverted in any way, shape or form.

But she had thought that Sean wanted a child as much as she did. She had been so driven, so demanding of herself and of him, because she'd assumed they had the same goal in mind.

If only Sean had said something sooner about how he really felt. If only he hadn't just packed up and left her…

The tears that had threatened earlier began to trickle down Charlotte's cheeks as she thought of all the mistakes she'd unknowingly made, and how fatal those mistakes had been to her marriage.

She had been so sure that all she needed was a child to

make her life complete. Now she realized, much too late, that her quest had cost her the one thing she would have never willingly given up in exchange—the man she loved with all her heart and soul.

Chapter Four

Never lay out the terms of a business deal unless you're absolutely sure that you can, and will, follow through with them yourself....

That simple piece of advice, given to him by his father over a dozen years ago, echoed in Sean's mind as he paced from one end of the master suite to the other. With only one lamp lit on the bedside table, the corners of the familiar room were bathed in dark, not altogether welcoming shadows that suited his mood much more than he would have liked.

Climbing the staircase to the third floor of the town house, he had thought that he would be asleep almost as soon as his head hit the pillow. By the time he'd changed into a pair of fleece pants and a waffle-knit, long-sleeved T-shirt, brushed his teeth and turned back the bedcovers, though, an odd, unforeseen sense of restlessness had settled over him.

First and foremost, Sean couldn't help but be distracted by the fact that after six long months, Charlotte was tucked into bed within incredibly easy reach, mere moments away.

If he so desired, he could go to her in the guest room, slip into the bed beside her, take her in his arms, kiss her and caress her. He could make love to her as he once had, and as he'd dreamed of doing more nights than he cared to count over the past half year.

And, oh, how he wanted to do *that,* as his turgid state now reminded him.

But along with his near desperate yearning to make love to his wife had come all the reasons why there could be no satisfying of his baser instincts that night, or any night for as long as he could imagine into the future. Reasons that began and ended with the terms he'd offered Charlotte in exchange for helping her go forward with the adoption of the child she wanted—apparently more than she wanted *him.*

She had taken no offense at all when he'd said that he would be filing for divorce after the adoption was final. Possibly she'd been a little surprised, perhaps even a little hurt, but only momentarily. With a measure of serenity and pragmatism that had left him surprised and hurt, she had offered agreement and understanding instead of the demurral that he'd fully anticipated.

Sean wasn't sure why he'd tossed out the fillip of divorce, but the moment he'd spoken the words aloud, he'd been sorry. He didn't want to end his marriage to Charlotte. He just wanted her to honor his wishes about having, or more precisely *not* having, a child.

He had thought that faced with the prospect of divorce, she would at least ask for a little time to consider the downside of going ahead with the adoption. But she hadn't been deterred in the slightest. Which had led him to believe that she'd been pursuing the option of adopting a foreign child even after he'd revealed his true feelings about fatherhood.

Charlotte had been so hurt and so angry with him when he'd accused her of going behind his back that she'd convinced him that he had made the wrong assumption. Yet she hadn't denied her happiness at the opportunity she'd been given to have the child she wanted, even knowing their marriage would be over as a result.

Her jibe about his lack of attention had stung him, as well, causing him to reciprocate in kind—not the wisest move he could have made under the circumstances, he now admitted to himself.

He had said a lot of things to her that he probably should have kept to himself. But continuing to hide the pain he had suffered those last few months before he'd moved out of the house in Mayfair, not to mention the sense of abandonment that had overwhelmed him at times, had no longer been possible for him to do.

Charlotte hadn't been the only injured party in their relationship—he had been hurt, too. His tears hadn't been shed, though. They had been swallowed along with his sense of loss, his damaged pride and his constant awareness of how powerless he was to give her the baby she wanted.

Charlotte hadn't been the only one faced with failure on a daily basis. How had she thought he'd felt each month when she'd come to him, sobbing, to announce the start of another menstrual period? Had she never once imagined that, looking in the mirror, he saw someone so deficient that he couldn't provide his wife with the happiness she deserved?

Sean had always hated knowing that he was at least

partially to blame for Charlotte's sadness and depression. To his way of thinking, ending their baby chase had seemed as good a way as any to go back to those days when they'd been able to laugh together, to play together, to be each others best friend and loving confidant.

But his wife hadn't wanted that. She'd only wanted a child—a child he hadn't been able to give her...until now.

That, Sean knew without a doubt, was why he hadn't been able to refuse outright to help Charlotte with the adoption.

He wanted to resent everything about the orphaned little girl waiting for them in Kazakhstan, but he couldn't be that hard-hearted. For one thing, the child would make his wife happy in a way he obviously no longer could. And for another, he liked the idea of being the one to provide the little girl with a safe and loving home where she would be nurtured with Charlotte's love, and care and kindness.

He had no doubt that Charlotte would be a wonderful mother, and though he wouldn't subject the child to his lack of parenting skills, he would see to it that she never lacked for anything, whether it was a secure home, clothes, toys, trips abroad, the best education available—

Not a minute too soon Sean caught himself in mid-fantasy and gave himself a firm mental shake. He'd allowed himself to get carried in a direction he'd already made clear to Charlotte that he wasn't going. He wasn't about to become the child's father—at least not in any way but name only. He would provide for her, though, and for Charlotte. After all, he wasn't selfish or cruel or mean-spirited.

Having settled that bit of business with himself, Sean sat on the edge of the bed and assessed his chances of finally being able to sleep. Still zero to none, he admitted after a minute or two, his brain buzzing in six different directions.

He thought of the contract that he had to review; a fairly simple agreement to provide a security guard for a small trucking company in Baton Rouge that had been having problems with not-so-petty theft at their warehouse. It was in the briefcase that he'd left on the dining-room table when he'd first come home, but it wouldn't be any trouble to go down and get it. If anything was likely to put him to sleep, it was thirty-odd pages of legalese.

Sean only hesitated a moment or two on the second-floor landing. From there, he couldn't tell whether the guest-room door was open or closed—the narrow hallway was much too dark. Not that it would have mattered to him, one way or the other.

Charlotte hadn't seemed upset about his decision to file for divorce and she hadn't asked him to reconsider. Their marriage must already be over as far as she was concerned, in which case, it was unlikely that she'd welcome any advances on his part. Better to keep his distance than risk the most hurtful kind of rejection he could get from her.

At the bottom of the staircase, Sean halted again, head tilted to one side. Something about the quality of the silence surrounding him gave him pause, but he wasn't sure why. While the rain had stopped, he could still hear water dripping from the branches of the trees lining the street just outside the front door. He was sure he'd heard something else, though—a shuffling, or perhaps a snuffling sound that he couldn't quite place.

When he heard nothing more after a minute or two, he finally moved into the living room, only to stop again, his heartbeat accelerating, not with fear but exhilaration. Charlotte was sitting in one of the wing chairs between the front windows.

Had he been a superstitious man, Sean would have been tempted to believe that he'd conjured her with his lustful thoughts. As it was, he sensed that something besides mutual longing had brought his wife to her favorite retreat within the walls of the old town house.

"Hey…" he said, pausing a few steps away from her. "Are you okay?"

"Couldn't sleep," she replied, her voice sounding a little rough around the edges. She held up what appeared to be a coffee mug. "I thought a little warm milk might help. What about you?"

Though he couldn't see Charlotte's face, Sean was fairly sure that she'd been crying as recently as a few moments ago. Obviously she was trying to hide that fact from him in her own dignified way, and he thought it best to go along with her.

"Couldn't sleep, either. I thought reading the contract in my briefcase might be just the antidote."

Charlotte shifted in the chair, moving to stand up. She swayed a bit, though, and instantly he reached out to steady her.

"Oh, sorry…" She gazed up at him for a long moment, then added, "I didn't mean to…to…."

Sean looked back at her as her voice trailed away. He was now close enough to see the anguish in her eyes, still damp with the tears she'd shed.

"It's okay. I've got you," he murmured, moving his hands up her arms to her shoulders, then around to her back in the beginning of an embrace that drew her closer still.

Surprisingly, she didn't pull away as he'd fully expected, but leaned against him instead with a soft and weary-sounding sigh.

"No...I wasn't really talking about being so clumsy, although I'm sorry about that, too. What I meant to say was that I didn't mean to be so cold to you, so withdrawn those last few months we were together. I didn't even realize that was how I'd been behaving until you brought it up tonight. I know that's no excuse for hurting you, especially since your feelings were always important to me. I was just so self-involved, so focused on what I wanted that it must have seemed that nothing else mattered to me. I also realize that it's a little late for an apology, but I *am* truly sorry."

"We were both very self-involved back then," he acknowledged, smoothing a hand over the soft tangle of her hair.

He wished that she had used the present tense when she'd spoken of his feelings being important to her, but at least she had taken responsibility for the pain she'd caused him and apologized for it.

"Not you as much as me. You didn't even want to have a child, yet you kept going along with my wishes, suffering in silence."

"I just wanted you to be happy, Charlotte. I still want you to be happy."

She took a step back and met his gaze again, tentatively reaching out to touch a hand to his cheek.

"I know you do, Sean, and I appreciate it."

The longing in his wife's eyes sparked anew the heat that had never quite stopped smoldering in Sean's loins. Before he could take the time to consider the possible consequences, he bent his head and claimed her mouth in a kiss meant to convey all the desire for her that he'd forced himself to ignore for the past six months.

He sensed immediately that he'd startled her, but he didn't ease up the pressure of his lips and teeth and tongue, becoming more gentle when she opened to him, melting against him with the equally fervid and well-remembered response he craved.

Not until he was desperate to draw a breath did he finally ease away from her, though he still kept her close in a firm embrace.

"Jeez, Charlotte…" he muttered as he struggled to regain some small hold on his slipping composure. "You have to know that I've only ever wanted you to be happy."

"Yes, I know, Sean, and you've made me so happy by agreeing to help me with the adoption."

Responding as he likely would have if she'd dumped a bucket of cold water on his head, Sean let go of Charlotte, then took a determined step away from her.

That was all she could say to him after the kiss they'd shared—*you've made me so happy by agreeing to help me with the adoption…?* Left unsaid, but still echoing in his head were the words she could have added—*and then divorcing me.*

What had possessed him to think that conceding to and apologizing for treating him badly six months ago constituted a change of heart on her part regarding either the adoption or the divorce issues they faced? He couldn't have been more naive if he'd tried.

Charlotte might regret that she'd hurt his feelings. But she still had a one-track mind where having a child was concerned, and she didn't really give a damn if he wanted to be on that track with her or not. In fact, she didn't seem to care about being a wife anymore now that she was finally going to have the chance to be a mother.

"Hey, that's me—always glad to be of service," he drawled, allowing an edge of sarcasm to coat his words. "Do you want more milk?"

She eyed him with the same mixture of hurt and confusion he'd seen on her face earlier. It was as if she hadn't the slightest clue why his mood had shifted, but didn't care enough to ask. He could always tell her, of course, but why bother?

She was happy getting what she really wanted from him—a child to love and care for. If, in the process, he occasionally responded to her in a prickly manner, she'd just have to deal with it the best way she could.

"No, I've had enough," she replied, all but shoving the mug at him, her tone indicating that she was talking about more than a cup of milk. "I'll just leave you to your contract."

Sean fumbled with the mug, almost dropping it as Charlotte swept past him, her head held high, her shoulders straight, her spine stiff.

"I'd like to get a reasonably early start in the morning," he called after her, forcing himself into businessman mode once again.

"I'll be down by eight o'clock, unless that's later than you have in mind," she assured him as she started up the staircase at a brisk pace.

"Eight o'clock is fine with me."

The silence that followed the none-too-polite slam of the guest-room door was deafening, and for Sean, unaccountably demoralizing. He sagged onto the chair his wife had just vacated, gripping the empty mug in his hands, and stared at the plush Oriental carpet beneath his bare feet.

Once more, it seemed to him that all he'd done was make a series of fatal-to-his-marriage missteps with Charlotte. Though how a shared kiss that had been heartening beyond belief to him could have been wrong, he certainly didn't know.

Sitting alone in the dark, he wondered why the hell he'd kissed her in the first place. What had he thought he would gain by it—leverage of some sort that might help to win her over to his way of thinking?

In all honesty, Sean had to admit that during those moments when Charlotte had clung to him and kissed him with such passion, hope for them and for their marriage had been reborn in him. But she hadn't seen it that way at all. To her it had merely been a thank-you for giving her what she really wanted—the adoption of a child and finalization of their divorce to follow.

He shouldn't have been either surprised or hurt that she'd been so single-minded, but of course he had been. And then, he'd gone on the defensive, surprising and hurting her in return.

Why did it seem that he could no longer talk to Charlotte without constantly feeling the need to retaliate in some way?

Always in the past, she had brought out the best in him, even when they'd argued about something. But starting six months ago, it seemed that during every exchange he had with her he ended up resorting to cynicism and snide comments. Then she would look at him as if he'd mutated into some kind of monster, making him feel even worse than he had to start.

There was just no way he could win—at least not in any way that would make victory sweet. Bottom line, Charlotte was more interested in becoming a mother than in staying married to him. The wisest thing he could do under the circumstances was accept what he obviously wasn't going to be able to change, and do what he could to make the next few months as pleasant as possible for both of them.

Winning wasn't everything, after all—especially not when it meant hurting the one person you truly loved.

He had offered to help Charlotte, and from now on, he would do so without any expectations of his own. He really did want her to be happy. Why not make her happiness *his* happiness, as well? Surely that would be a whole hell of a lot better for both of them than continuing to attempt to inflict his misery onto her.

Feeling much better, and nobler, than he had in the past half year or more, Sean stood and made his way to the kitchen. There he rinsed Charlotte's mug and stowed it in the dishwasher. He debated the wisdom of pouring a glass of whiskey to take upstairs with him, but decided against it. He was going to need a clear head to look over the contract.

Briefcase in hand, he climbed the staircase to the third floor yet again. He piled the pillows against the mahogany headboard of the bed and began to read. He was about halfway through the document when his eyes started to close. Sure that he would only doze a few minutes, he set the contract aside, but didn't bother to turn off the lamp.

Against all odds, Sean was soon sound asleep, and when he awakened as usual just after dawn, he was amazed at how rested and relaxed he felt. Maybe there was something to be said for taking the high road, he mused. After a decent night's sleep, he was more than ready to put that old adage to the test.

Chapter Five

At exactly five minutes till eight the next morning, Charlotte left the guest room and headed slowly down the staircase to the first floor of the town house. She dreaded having to face Sean again after their unsettling encounter in the living room the previous night, especially in her current state of mind. The sleep she had needed so desperately had eluded her completely despite the warm milk and whiskey tonic, leaving her just a mite testy, if not downright snappish.

She would have been so much better off if she'd simply stayed put in the guest room last night, or at least returned there immediately with her hot drink in hand. But no, she'd allowed herself to be lured to her favorite retreat without taking the time to consider how such an old familiar habit would inevitably trigger old familiar memories.

Of course, she hadn't thought that she would have to worry about meeting up with Sean again. Even having him appear in the living room so unexpectedly wouldn't have been a problem either, if only she'd had sense enough to scurry up the staircase before she'd had the chance to crumple into an emotional muddle. Not only teary-eyed, but also filled with regret, she had been much too easy a target for his kindness and concern.

Reminded of just how attentive and how caring he could be when he put his mind to it, Charlotte had wanted nothing more than to make peace with Sean, to tell him she was sorry for all the misunderstandings that had come between them in the past. She had wanted, too, to wipe the slate clean as best she could so they would be able to start fresh as partners of another kind as they embarked on their journey through the adoption process.

But her emotions as well as Sean's had quickly spun out of control.

So close had she been to her husband in the darkness of the night, his hands on her in such a well-remembered way, enveloped by the warmth of his body and his masculine scent, that she hadn't been able to either deny or hide the ache of physical desire that had overwhelmed her with such startling intensity. Instinctively she had known that she couldn't have stopped him kissing her if she'd tried. But once his mouth had claimed hers, she hadn't wanted to do anything except kiss him in return.

The heated flare of passion that had arced between them like wild lightning had stolen away not only her breath, but her willpower as well. Even after he'd finally released her, Charlotte hadn't been able to think straight. Nor had she known quite what to say in response to his vow that he only wanted her to be happy.

But then, evidently, not to mention unwittingly, she'd

said absolutely the worst possible thing—at least to Sean's way of thinking.

His shift from tenderness to biting sarcasm had cut Charlotte to the quick. She had floundered badly in her search for some clue as to what she had said to set him off. Unable to think of what else he might have meant besides the adoption when it came to her happiness, she had been at a total loss.

There was nothing else he could or, more to the point, *would* do for her now except help her to become a mother, so why pretend otherwise?

Angry and uncertain, Charlotte had returned to the guest room where she'd spent the rest of the night tossing and turning. One minute cursing herself for once again alienating the one ally she really needed now, the next minute cursing Sean for coming on to her in a way that had played with her deepest feelings, only to turn cold and cynical. She had been unable to get any real rest at all.

Pausing at the foot of the staircase, Charlotte caught the aroma of freshly brewed coffee and the spicy sausages Sean loved. Obviously he had been awake for a while, and busy. Despite her less-than-pleasant mood, she—and her rumbling tummy—were grateful that her husband had chosen to prepare a hearty breakfast.

Now if only she could find a way to look just a little less…pathetic.

Charlotte eyed her reflection in the oval mirror that graced one of the entryway walls and wasn't the least bit pleased with what she saw. She'd done the best she could, considering she'd been totally unprepared for an overnight stay, but her appearance was still rather pitiful.

There were no wrinkles in her gray wool pants and turtleneck sweater since she'd been able to hang them up overnight. Her panties, bra and black tights, rinsed out the previous night, were fresh and clean, as well. She'd also managed to tame her wild curls with the brush in her purse.

In the way of makeup, however, she'd had only a lipstick in a pale shade of rose. She had tried smoothing a little dab of it on the ridges of her cheekbones, but that had only accentuated how pale her skin was otherwise, while also emphasizing to a downright scary degree the dark circles under her eyes.

Realizing that she'd be late if she lingered any longer in front of the mirror, ruing her appearance, Charlotte turned away from the mirror and walked resolutely through the living room and dining room to the doorway that led into the kitchen.

How she looked wasn't going to make nearly as much difference to Sean as how she behaved. Instead of worrying about something she could do nothing about, she'd be better off concentrating on how best to smooth over any hard feelings he might still be harboring as a result of the exchange they'd had last night.

Pale, after-the-rain sunlight shone through the window above the sink, bathing the kitchen in a mellow morning glow. Normally such a positive change in the weather would have automatically brightened Charlotte's mood. But in her current frame of mind she had no intention of allowing herself to be so easily cheered. She and Sean had important matters to discuss—serious matters that would best be handled in an equally serious manner.

"Hey, I was just about to come looking for you," Sean said in an amazingly hale and hearty voice, drawing her attention to where he stood by the six-burner gas stove.

He was freshly showered and shaved, his face sans any shadow of a beard, his hair still the slightest bit damp. He was also dressed for the office in black suit pants, a starched pale blue dress shirt and a pair of expensive black leather Italian loafers. He hadn't put on a tie yet, and he had his shirtsleeves rolled to his elbows. But it would take only a few minor adjustments and he'd be ready to walk out the door every inch the president and CEO of his own very profitable business.

Charlotte had seen her husband looking just that way many times in the past, and she had always experienced the same throb in her heart as she noted how handsome, authoritative and distinguished he could so easily appear to be. What caught her off guard this particular morning was how chipper he also seemed, considering how they'd left things between them the previous night. Unlike her, Sean had obviously enjoyed a good night's sleep, and also unlike her, he had quite obviously gotten up on the *right* side of the bed.

"It's only just eight o'clock now and we did agree to meet at *eight*, didn't we?" Charlotte asked, her own tone prim and proper as she waved a hand at the clock on the kitchen wall.

"Yes, but the sausages and eggs were cooking a little faster than I'd expected." Sean smiled at her sheepishly, then nodded toward the counter.

"Help yourself to coffee and take a seat. Breakfast is just about ready."

Charlotte had to force herself not to gape at her husband in open astonishment. What the heck had gotten into him since midnight? Or maybe the better question had to do with what exactly he'd been busy cooking up besides scrambled eggs and patties of spicy sausage.

She walked over to the coffeemaker, her gait a bit stiff-legged, shooting a wary glance back at Sean along the way. He was definitely in a cheerful mood that seemed to be totally at odds with the behavior he'd displayed just eight hours earlier.

What had happened to turn Dr. Jekyll into Mr. Hyde—or was it Mr. Hyde into Dr. Jekyll? As she poured coffee into a mug and added cream and sugar to the dark brew, Charlotte wasn't completely sure she wanted to find out.

"Would you like toast, too?"

So engrossed in her musings had she been that Charlotte hadn't realized Sean was right behind her until he spoke. Startled, she jumped just enough to splash coffee out of her mug onto the countertop, then almost dropped the mug itself when he put a gentle hand on her shoulder.

Likely he had only meant to steady her but her nerves jangled all over again.

"Are you okay?" he asked, now solicitous.

"I'm fine," she snapped back, feeling even more at a dis-advantage as she mopped up her spill with a paper towel.

"Toast, then?"

"No… No toast for me."

She eased away from her husband and slid onto her usual seat by the island counter. Woven mats, napkins and silverware had been set out already, and with a flourish Sean deposited two plates of hot food, one across from the other, in the appropriate places.

Eyeing him suspiciously as he returned to the coffee-maker to refill his mug, Charlotte still wasn't sure exactly what he was playing at. Did she dare lower her guard enough to trust his newfound beneficence? She didn't want to set herself up for another round of ruinous rejection. But neither did she want to alienate him by responding to his seemingly friendly overtures in a petulant manner.

"I hope you were able to get some sleep," Sean said, glancing over his shoulder at her and catching her in mid-stare.

Embarrassed, Charlotte ducked her head and made a great show of positioning her napkin squarely in her lap, mentally cursing the blush that suddenly made her cheeks burn.

Sean had always had such an easy time reading her facial expressions. Happy or sad, angry, hurt or confused— he always seemed to know exactly how she was feeling. In the past, that had often seemed to be a good thing. But now she wasn't sure she wanted him trespassing so casually into her soul's private territory.

"Some," she said, crossing the fingers of the hand she hid in her lap.

Not a total lie—she might have dozed a few minutes here and there, and surely that counted as *some* sleep.

"We never did try out the bed in the guest room, did we?" Sean asked, his tone lightly teasing. "I hope it's reasonably comfortable."

Charlotte almost choked on the bite of sausage in her mouth as he sat on the stool across from her. Of all the subjects he could have brought up over breakfast, that had to be one of the least…tasteful.

The guest-room bed was actually one of the few places she and Sean hadn't made love in the town house. They had even graced the island countertop with their wild and crazy presence once or twice, as Charlotte had half a mind to remind him. But she wasn't about to give him the satisfaction of knowing how badly he'd rattled her with his sexually shaded comment.

"The bed is very comfortable," she said, forcing herself to look him in the eye as blandly as she could.

"I was just wondering…because you look a little tired."

Any amusement in his voice was now coupled with concern.

"I *am* a little tired, but I'm sure I'll perk up after I've eaten, especially if I have another cup of your coffee," she demurred. "The eggs and sausage are delicious, by the way."

"I know you prefer bacon, but I didn't have any on hand."

"I haven't had sausage for a long time, so it actually tastes pretty good to me today."

Having navigated successfully through what could have been potentially dangerous waters, Charlotte focused on her food, and thankfully Sean did likewise.

They ate in reasonably comfortable silence for several minutes. Sean got up once to put another slice of bread in the toaster and refill their mugs, but it was only as he finished his second piece of toast and Charlotte, her plate clean, was sipping coffee that he spoke again.

"I was thinking that maybe we could go through the paperwork from the adoption agency together first, then put in a call to set up an appointment. I tried the number in the telephone book just before you came into the kitchen and got a recording that said the agency hours are nine to six, Monday through Friday."

"That's fine with me. I'll run upstairs and get the envelope."

A few minutes later, with a second pot of coffee brewing, they sat across from each other at the island counter and took turns reading over the various documents sent to them by the Robideaux Agency. Meticulous as always, Sean also made a list of questions to ask their counselor, as well as another list of things to do to assure completion of all the paperwork in a timely manner.

At five past nine, he called the agency and very politely but also very insistently wrangled an appointment for them at one-thirty that afternoon.

Listening to how smoothly her husband handled the agency receptionist, Charlotte had to smile. She wished she were even half as good as he was at getting people to come around to her way of thinking while also giving them the impression that it was actually their idea all along.

But then she wouldn't have had any problem at all convincing Sean that becoming a father would be one of the best things he could ever do, she reminded herself with a wry twist of her lips.

"Okay, we're all set to meet with our counselor at one-thirty." Sean checked off the first item on his to-do list. "We also have to sign several of these forms and have them notarized. Why don't you come to the office with me and we can have Elizabeth do that for us since she's a notary?

"We also need some passport-size photographs to include with the paperwork in our dossier and a set of fingerprint cards to include with the agency's requests for criminal background checks. We can have the photos done at a shop on Canal Street and we can have the fingerprint cards made at our friendly neighborhood police station. We should be able to get the photos and cards before our appointment and still have time for a bite of lunch, but we'll have to stop all the lollygagging over coffee."

"Aye, aye, sir! Anything else, sir?"

Charlotte slipped off her stool, stood at attention and saluted her husband with a straight face. Her heart was humming, though, with a mixture of excitement and joy.

Whatever had transformed Sean from the previous night's grouch to gratifyingly cooperative, not to mention this morning's playful partner, she didn't really care. She was just happy to have her husband back in a way she recognized from better days in the not-so-distant past.

He had obviously decided to go all out in helping her with the adoption, and to do so as pleasantly as he possibly could. She was smart enough to accept her good fortune without asking any questions.

"I'll let you know if anything comes to mind," Sean replied with a sexy smile.

He reached across the counter and gave one of her errant curls a gentle tug, surprising her with the once-familiar and endearing gesture. Then he picked up their empty mugs and turned away.

"I'd better go up and get my coat and my purse," Charlotte said, feeling unaccountably shy in the sudden silence surrounding them.

"Meet you in the living room in say…ten minutes?" Sean asked, glancing back at her.

"Ten minutes, it is."

The next few hours flew by for Charlotte in a whirlwind of activity. She was amazed at all they accomplished and knew that she had Sean and his organizational abilities to thank for it. While she could have handled things on her own if she'd had to, she was truly grateful that she didn't.

As the day progressed, she was grateful, as well, that Sean's good humor continued.

Their first stop at his office in the French Quarter's business district produced a round of surprised but friendly greetings directed Charlotte's way, as well as Sean's, from his staff, followed by hearty congratulations when the reason for her presence in New Orleans was revealed.

Had she not known better, Charlotte would have assumed from his behavior that her husband was actually looking forward to the prospect of becoming a father. But then, Sean had never been one to air dirty laundry in public. He would never have revealed by word or action any inkling of their private strife in front of his employees if he could help it.

Thanks to his stellar business reputation and security contacts, Sean was also able to smooth their way at the police station. After only a short wait, they were able to complete the paperwork and obtain the certified fingerprint cards necessary to set the criminal background checks in motion.

They were off to get their passport-style photos next, but only after a quick stop in one of the department stores in the French Quarter where Charlotte bought foundation, blush and mascara. Official photographs were rarely flattering, but she preferred not to look like too much of a wraith if she could help it.

Lunch was a fried oyster po'boy sandwich at the Acme Oyster Bar where they sat at a tiny table crammed among other tiny tables full of other hungry people, all seeming to be talking at once.

"To be honest, I could use a cold beer right about now," Sean said. "Nothing washes down fried oysters quite as well. But we can always celebrate with a drink after our meeting with Ms. Herbert."

"That would be nice, but I'd better not plan on it," Charlotte replied. "I have to drive back to Mayfair, you know."

"Maybe another time, then," Sean said with a chilly shift in his tone.

Lowering his gaze, he drizzled hot sauce over the mound of fried oysters nestled in a bed of shredded lettuce and tomato on crispy French bread, his expression almost as detached as his voice had become.

He had to have known that she'd be going home later that afternoon, Charlotte thought, taking a bite of her own sandwich. She'd meant only to remind him, but her breezy air must have seemed like a brush-off to him, especially after the renewed sense of camaraderie they'd been sharing so easily all morning.

But then, he was the one who intended to file for divorce in a few months. How friendly could he expect her to be toward him with the end of their marriage looming in the not-so-distant future?

Charlotte wished she could think of something more to say that would dispel the sudden tension that had settled between them. But she felt as if she was walking on eggshells, and she didn't want to risk making bad matters worse. Having a serious discussion would also be really hard amid the steady din in the restaurant.

Halfway through her meal, Charlotte finally glanced in Sean's direction and caught him looking at her, his gaze just a bit quizzical. Taking a chance, she offered him what she hoped was an encouraging smile.

"They still have the best fried oysters in the city here, don't they?" she ventured, holding up what little remained of her sandwich.

"Still worth the crowds and the noise?" he asked with a slight smile of his own.

"Well worth it. Thanks so much for suggesting it."

"You're very welcome."

Again his tone had changed, warming several degrees

this time, causing Charlotte to utter a quiet sigh of relief
as she polished off the last few bites of her sandwich. She
might not always be able to understand the cause of Sean's
mercurial mood shifts, but dealing with them was a small
price to pay for his cooperation.

After lunch, they had to walk back to Sean's office to
retrieve his SUV from the parking garage, then drive east
of the city to the suburban neighborhood where the Robideaux Agency's office was located. Traffic was unusually
heavy, making it necessary for Sean to concentrate on his
driving. Charlotte didn't mind riding along in silence. In
fact, she was glad to have the time to collect herself before
the meeting with their counselor.

Though they had been matched with a child now
deemed by the orphanage in Kazakhstan to be ready for
adoption based on information already collected and
analyzed by the agency, she knew that they would still be
under scrutiny by both the Robideaux Agency and the orphanage personnel. Only after the foreign court system had
approved the adoption with the orphanage's recommenda-
tion, and the child had been admitted to the United States
as a citizen would they be able to believe that she was really
their daughter—well, *her* daughter, at least.

Until they'd started the drive to the adoption agency,
Charlotte had managed not to think about the false picture
of marital bliss she and Sean were about to present to their
counselor at the agency. She had always considered lying
a despicable act—dishonesty of any kind had always been
a deal breaker for her. Yet here she was, about to pretend
to be something she wasn't—a happily married wife—in
order to become the loving, caring, devoted mother she
knew without a doubt that she was meant to be.

But did the basic selflessness and purity of her deepest desire balance out the lie she and Sean were about to tell?

In her initial joy upon realizing she would finally be able to have a child of her own to love and nurture, she had thought any means would be worth the end. But for them to pretend to be something they no longer were—

"Hey, you look like you're a million miles away."

Sean's gently chiding voice and the touch of his hand on her arm drew Charlotte from her guilt-ridden reverie. Blinking once, she saw that he had pulled the SUV into a parking space on the lot behind the agency's office.

"Having second thoughts?" he continued when she looked over at him, unable to hide her consternation.

She could tell him what she'd been thinking. She could also tell him she just wasn't going to be able to lie about their situation. Only then she'd lose not only Sean to the divorce he'd already said he wanted, but also her one chance to live up to the expectations of her mother and grandmother by raising a child with the same care and devotion with which they had raised her.

"Just a little nervous, I guess," she answered at last. "They could always change their mind about allowing us to adopt if they suddenly decide that we're…unsuitable for some reason."

"Why would they decide that we're unsuitable at this late date? We've already been selected as suitable parents for a child. We've provided them with excellent references, we're still financially solvent, we can still provide the child with a safe and loving home. We certainly don't have criminal records to worry about, either."

"But you and I…we're not really…"

Charlotte looked at Sean sadly, then quickly looked away again as she saw understanding dawn in his pale gray eyes.

"Whatever is going on between us as a couple is not going to affect our ability to care for a child. Biological parents divorce and their children adjust. It's not like we're going to be estranged from each other or fighting a bitter, angry battle of any kind. You'll never have to struggle financially, either. I can definitely guarantee that."

"But what if something happens to us?"

"We've already had to name legal guardians for the child in case something happens to us," Sean reminded her. "You know we can trust Ellen and Noah to be there for the child."

"Yes… Yes, of course, they will," Charlotte agreed.

"Any other concerns you want to discuss before we meet with Ms. Herbert?"

Charlotte still wasn't happy about keeping the true state of their marriage a secret, but she understood and accepted the need to do so if she wanted to go ahead with the adoption; and she wanted that more than anything else.

Well, more than almost anything else, she amended, risking a sideways glance at her husband as they crossed the parking lot, avoiding several puddles left by the rain along the way.

What she wanted most of all was for them to be a real family—mother, father and beloved child. The encouragement Sean had given her to set aside her doubts when he could have just as easily used them as an excuse to call a halt to the whole business had given her a tiny ray of hope in that direction.

But then he had used the word *divorce* in such an offhand manner, as if it were already a fait accompli, and her heart had ached all over again.

"Ready?" Sean asked, pausing with a hand on the door handle, his gaze steady.

"As I'll ever be," Charlotte replied, looking back at him dolefully.

"Then tip your chin up and smile, sweetheart," he chided softly. "Let them see how well they've done choosing a mother for one of their orphans this time around."

He was right, of course. Now was not the time to allow her uncertainty to show. The Robideaux Agency wanted secure, confident, self-possessed people to parent the children they placed for adoption. She was all of those things and more, and she'd do well to let it show. There was Sean's endearment, too—*sweetheart*—said with real warmth and tenderness.

"Aye, aye, sir. Anything else, sir?" she quipped as she had earlier in the day. She smiled at last, as well, just as he'd instructed.

"That'll do it for now," he assured her.

He tweaked her on the cheek, opened the door and escorted her to the reception desk where a middle-aged woman with a kindly face waited to greet them.

The meeting with their counselor went extremely well. Once again Charlotte was grateful for Sean's masterful ability to focus on the most pertinent issues. He might not intend to take on the role of full-time father, but nothing in his manner or his attitude betrayed that fact in any way.

Bethany Herbert was pleased that they were able to produce the various forms they'd already completed, signed and had notarized at Sean's office, the passport-style photographs and the fingerprint cards for the criminal background checks. She was also very helpful regarding the travel arrangements they would have to make within the next few weeks.

She recommended the airline with the best connection to Almaty, the city where the orphanage was located, as well as several hotels near the orphanage that other adoptive parents had used and found suitable.

Ms. Herbert advised them that they should have approval from the Kazakhstan government, a travel visa and an official invitation from the orphanage to adopt one of their children in approximately four to five weeks. That meant they would have to plan to leave the United States by mid-February at the latest.

They would need to take clothing and diapers and perhaps a few small toys for the child, she also advised, handing over a typed list of suggested items. Since the winter months were normally quite cold in Kazakhstan, they should include warm clothes, boots, hats and gloves for themselves, as well—things not often needed in the more temperate climate of southern Louisiana.

Their counselor had questions for them, too, mostly to do with affirming that their primary residence and their places of employment hadn't changed in the months since they'd last talked. Much to Charlotte's relief, Sean answered her without hesitation, as matter-of-fact as always.

By the time they left Ms. Herbert's office, carrying what seemed like twice as much paperwork as they'd brought with them originally, Charlotte was beginning to feel over-whelmed by the information overload.

She found herself wondering about what, exactly, they were getting themselves into, traveling halfway around the world to an extremely foreign country to adopt a totally unknown child. The thought that maybe this kind of adoption hadn't been such a good idea after all entered her mind.

"It certainly sounds like we're in for an adventure," Sean said, his tone both rueful and, unbelievably, eager as they crossed the lot to the SUV, again dodging puddles.

"I can only hope that's not an understatement," Charlotte replied with a wry smile.

Sean's upbeat manner instantly made her feel better.

"It's not too late to change your mind," he said.

He eyed her seriously as he unlocked the passenger-side door and swung it open.

He was right about that, Charlotte acknowledged. She *could* change her mind, but what then? She would not only be giving up her one chance to have a child. She'd also be giving up the chance to spend a few weeks with her husband while he was still her husband.

"Actually, a little adventure would be nice for a change," she answered him at last, sliding into the SUV.

"And here I thought you liked the quiet life in Mayfair."

"Lately it's been much too quiet even for me," Charlotte admitted.

"Well, that won't be the case much longer, will it?"

Sean quirked a funny kind of smile at her, more sad than happy. Then, not waiting for her to answer, he closed the door, walked around to the driver's side and climbed behind the steering wheel.

"Speaking of Mayfair, I'm guessing you're wanting to head back there before it gets much later," he continued, now matter-of-fact.

Now that the time had come, Charlotte realized that she didn't really want to go back home. She had enjoyed the day spent with Sean more than she'd enjoyed anything for at least the past six months. Neither did she want to stay in the guest room at the town house for another long, lonely, sleepless night, but that she couldn't bring herself to admit aloud.

"I would like to be home before dark," she said, keeping her eyes on the traffic ahead of them as Sean steered the SUV onto the highway.

"We'll head back to the town house, then, so I can drop you off at your car."

No plea for her to stay, but had she really expected one?

Not *expected*, but *hoped*, she thought, although she didn't say as much. But then, she had been the one to blow off his offer of a celebratory drink at lunch.

Sean did ask if she wanted to go inside the town house to freshen up before she started the drive back to Mayfair. But he seemed ready to have her gone—something about having to go back to the office for awhile to finish reviewing the contract he'd mentioned the night before. So she said a polite "no thank you" and climbed into her little car.

He didn't back away immediately, however, after she turned the key in the ignition. Noting the slight frown on his face, she realized that there must be more he wanted to say to her.

Rolling down the window, she looked up at him and asked politely, "Anything else?"

"Just that I thought we could talk again in a few days, if that's okay with you." Sean propped an arm on the roof of her car and eyed her through the open window. "That will give me time to get started on our travel arrangements."

"That's fine with me. I can start shopping for the things we'll need to take with us."

"I don't mind helping with that, too, if you'd like."

Charlotte's first instinct was to insist that she could handle the shopping on her own, but she stopped herself just in time. So far, Sean had been much more than a distant and resentful participant in the adoption process. Discouraging him in any way, especially by refusing any offer of help he made, would not only be selfish on her part but also a foolish mistake.

She didn't want her husband feeling that he was expendable again because he most certainly wasn't. She needed him as much now as she had ever needed him in the past, perhaps even more so.

"That would be wonderful," she said, sending a wide, appreciative smile his way. "I'll go over the list and divvy it up. There are sure to be lots of things you'll have an easier time finding in New Orleans than I would in Mayfair."

"So we'll talk again in a few days?"

"Yes, please. I'm always home in the evenings, you know, so just call whenever you can."

"Drive safely, then…and Charlotte…" He hesitated a moment, then added quietly, "Call me when you get home, okay? So I know that you made it back to Mayfair without any problems."

"I'll be fine," she began, then noted the frown furrowing his brow. "But I *will* call you as soon as I get home…I promise."

Sean tapped the roof of the car once in final farewell, then stepped back. Feeling strangely bereft, Charlotte gave a little wave of her hand, shifted the car into gear and pulled away from the curb. She knew that it was best to go back to Mayfair on a high note. Yet leaving Sean was much more difficult than she'd anticipated.

All that day he had behaved like the man she remembered

from the early years of their marriage. Though she'd warned herself that it wasn't wise, she hadn't been able to stop herself from falling in love with him all over again. Only by acknowledging that he was being kind to her out of a gentlemanly sense of duty had she been able to behave sensibly.

A glance in the rearview mirror a few moments later as she came to the cross street and signaled a left turn, however, gave Charlotte a small jolt of surprise. Sean still stood in the street, watching her drive away, and the look on his face could quite easily be described as forlorn. For a man who had seemed rather anxious to see her go so that he could return to his office, he wasn't moving especially fast in that direction.

Shifting her gaze to the street ahead once again, Charlotte was tempted to think that her husband was actually as sorry that she was leaving as she was. Perhaps he had enjoyed her company as much as she'd enjoyed his. Despite all his comments about the pending divorce, she took that as a positive sign and her spirits lifted noticeably as she sped down the highway.

She had a lot to do when she got home. Call Sean first, of course, because he really did care about her well-being. Call her best friends, Ellen and Quinn, with the good news about the adoption, too. Then she had shopping to organize and a room to prepare for her little girl. And it would probably be a good idea to read up on the faraway place to which they'd soon be traveling.

For the first time in a long time, Charlotte was filled with a sense of exuberance as well as an important sense of purpose. The child waiting for her in Kazakhstan was going to bring about many changes in her life. Who was to say that one of those changes wouldn't be a change of heart for Sean?

In her current frame of mind, Charlotte wanted to believe anything was possible and so, she decided, smiling to herself, she would.

Chapter Six

Over six months had passed since Sean had last driven the narrow country road that would eventually take him to Mayfair. Midway through a seasonably cool but sunny Saturday morning in late January, he passed only a few other vehicles, all heading in the general direction of the interstate, making the trip an unexpectedly quick and pleasant one for him.

He hadn't planned on going to Mayfair that weekend. In fact, the decision had been so spontaneous that Charlotte didn't even know he was currently on his way. He supposed he could have called her before he'd left the town house in New Orleans, or even once he was on the road. But he hadn't wanted to risk the possibility that she would tell him not to come.

He had half a dozen other things he could have been doing that Saturday. But he'd awakened just after dawn with a restless edge riding on his shoulders and the knowledge that only by seeing Charlotte again would the subtle hum of agitation in his gut begin to ease. So he had loaded up the back of the SUV with all the gear he'd bought for the child, the delivery of which he'd decided to use as his reason for showing up at the house in Mayfair unannounced.

Ten days had passed since the stormy night Charlotte had appeared on the doorstep of the town house—ten long days and nights when he'd rattled around the place feeling unexpectedly lost and lonely. After only one night together, though they'd really spent more time *apart*, her essence still lingered in the sunny kitchen and the shadowed living room, not to mention the guest room where she'd slept.

Considerate woman that she was, Charlotte had tidied the room and changed the linens on the bed before she'd left, and that was a good thing. Otherwise, Sean acknowledged, in those moments when he'd felt most forlorn, he might have been tempted to curl up on the bed where she'd slept.

Jeez…how maudlin would that have been?

Sean had talked to his wife on the telephone, of course, more times than she probably liked. He had first used a discussion about the somewhat complicated arrangements he was making for their mid-February trip to Kazakhstan as an excuse. Then he'd wanted to confer with her, on the various items he'd bought on the shopping expeditions that had filled quite a few of his evening hours the past week or so.

Shifting his gaze from the road ahead to the pile of boxes and bags stacked in the back of the SUV, he admitted that he'd probably gone just a tad overboard on his buying sprees. He told himself that his main intention was to save Charlotte as much time and money as possible. But in all honesty he'd had a surprisingly good time choosing things for the little girl waiting for them in an orphanage halfway around the world.

No, for *Katie*, he amended, making an effort to use the name Charlotte had chosen for the child with his agreement. It was an Americanized version of her given name of Katya, finally provided by the adoption agency just a few days ago, along with a favorable update on the status of their dossier's progress toward completion.

Sean had arranged to have the furniture he'd purchased—a bed, dresser, chest of drawers and rocking chair—delivered by the store directly to the house in Mayfair just as soon as Charlotte finished painting and papering the room they'd long ago chosen as a nursery. But the other things—a high chair, a stroller, an old-fashioned wooden rocking horse, a bright pink tricycle and at least half a dozen stuffed animals of all sizes and shapes—he wanted to deliver in person.

He thought he could also lend a hand with the painting and papering, as well. He'd even packed his overnight bag in case he could think of a good excuse to stay in Mayfair until Sunday night, or even early Monday morning.

A glance at the bright blue sky assured him there was no chance of stormy weather on the horizon. But if he got busy helping his wife prepare little Katie's room and accidentally lost track of time, then surely Charlotte would insist that he wait to make the drive back to the city until the next day.

There were more vehicles on the road as Sean entered the Mayfair city limits, typical of a sunny Saturday morning. While not an especially large town, Mayfair's population had grown enough to support its fair share of national chain stores tastefully built in a couple of retail centers on the main north-south route along which he was traveling.

The more historic, renovated town center, which had been spared by Hurricane Katrina, drew tourists practically year-round, as well. On such a nice day, Sean wasn't surprised to see people walking on the narrow sidewalks along which small shops, restaurants and a popular French bakery had thrived for the past couple of decades.

More and more of the old homes on Mayfair's quaint residential streets had also been restored as couples with small children sought a quieter, more family friendly place to live that wasn't too far from the city. Several of the larger houses had been converted to bed-and-breakfast retreats that helped the local economy thrive.

Not much had changed in the six months that he had been gone, though. Continuing south out of town, he passed the top-notch high school where Charlotte worked, and then, a mile farther down the road, the small, but highly rated regional medical center. Mayfair was still a lovely place to live, and still, as far as he was concerned, one of the best places to raise a family.

Two miles past the medical center Sean came to the turnoff for their house, and as he slowed and signaled, he experienced a first flutter of uncertainty. He really should have called Charlotte to let her know he was on his way to see her; he owed her that small courtesy. No matter how cordial she'd been to him each time they'd talked on the telephone, he didn't have the right to assume that she'd be glad to actually find him standing on her doorstep without any advance warning.

Of course, the house was still legally his property. By leaving it, and Charlotte, the way he had, though, he had, to his way of thinking and probably Charlotte's, also given up certain liberties such as coming and going as he pleased.

But driving through the avenue of century-old live oak trees, with dapples of sunshine and shadow playing on the hood of the SUV, Sean also had a sense of homecoming. It strengthened even more as he turned onto the gravel drive and caught his first glimpse of the old house up ahead, perched on a small bluff that overlooked a narrow river channel.

Originally a small but flourishing plantation, the property, like the New Orleans town house, had belonged to Sean's father's family for several generations. All that had remained under his father's ownership during Sean's childhood, however, had been the house and three acres of land.

Sean had only lived in the house until he was five years old. Then his father had begun traveling more frequently for the drilling company that then, as now, provided the bulk of the higher paying jobs in the area.

His mother had never really liked living so far from her native New Orleans, especially in an old house in a place she'd always referred to as the middle of nowhere. Using her loneliness as an excuse, and Sean's need for a more sophisticated education than she thought he would get in the town's small elementary school, she had insisted on moving to the town house in the city.

The house in Mayfair had become mostly a summer place where Sean and his father had retreated on the rare occasions when he wasn't out of town on business. By the time Sean had graduated from high school, he had visited the old house so infrequently that it had become little more than a dim, though happy, memory to him. Years later, when he'd inherited the place following his father's death, he had graduated from West Point, served in the military for eight years, then returned to civilian life to start his own business in New Orleans.

Sean had finally ventured to Mayfair on a Saturday afternoon in October for the sole purpose of assessing the property's value so that he could put it on the market for sale. But that weekend he had run into Charlotte, literally, as she'd come around the veranda, head down, camera in hand, and walked smack into him.

She had been so embarrassed and so apologetic for trespassing. She had also been so damned charming as she'd tried to explain that she rarely gave in to her curiosity so casually. But she'd been intrigued by the house ever since she'd begun her job at the high school that September. She'd finally decided to do a little exploring, she'd admitted, and wasn't it sad that such a lovely old home had been so neglected by its owner?

She had turned an even brighter shade of red when he had introduced himself as the neglectful owner. She had offered to leave immediately. By then, though, Sean would have only let her go if he'd had no other choice. So he'd invited her to see the inside of the house, and she had accepted, and seven months later—after many trips to Mayfair just to see her—they were married.

Together they had restored the house to its original beauty. They had become a part of the community, they had put down roots and they had made friends. Though Sean had used the town house in New Orleans on an increasingly regular basis as his business had expanded, the house in Mayfair had been the place he'd considered his home...or rather, *their* home together.

Pulling to a stop on the curve of the drive that led to the

detached garage, once an old barn, Sean saw that the house looked just the same as he remembered it—warm and welcoming. The white-painted wood rocking chairs on the veranda were empty, though, and on such a sunny day there weren't any lights shining in the long, tall windows on the first or second floor. But Charlotte's sporty little car was parked on the drive, and unless she'd gone off with a friend, she should be at home.

Sean parked the SUV on the drive, as well, headed slowly up the wide brick walkway and climbed the equally wide wooden steps that led to the veranda. He paused in front of the gleaming double front doors, inset with oval panes of beveled, opaque glass, his heartbeat accelerating just a little.

He knew that he had no reason to feel so nervous, yet he did. Even when he'd given her good reason to be hurt and angry, Charlotte had always chosen to respond in a polite and quiet manner.

Of course, there had been times that night she'd come to the town house to ask for his help with the adoption when she hadn't been especially polite or quiet. But it wasn't the possibility of another flare of temper on her part that had him hesitating on his own front porch that sunny Saturday morning.

He was more concerned that she would retreat into that cool and distant place of hers, leaving him to feel as if he were about to fall off a tightrope into an insurmountable abyss.

Why should that matter to him now, though? Charlotte wasn't going to be his wife for much longer, and he'd really only come here to do her a favor. He didn't have to worry about her being appreciative. That was part of her gentle, caring nature.

Only he wanted more from her than simple gratitude, Sean realized with a jolt of astonishment.

Suddenly frustrated by the convoluted pattern of his thoughts, Sean finally stabbed a finger into the button that rang the doorbell. The one thing he knew for sure as he waited as patiently as he could for his wife to come to the door was that he didn't know exactly *what* he wanted anymore, at least where Charlotte was concerned.

Birds twittered in the sprawl of live oak trees surrounding the house and a cool breeze rippled across the lawn, but otherwise all was quiet on the veranda. Hands in the pockets of his leather jacket, Sean fidgeted from one foot to the other. If Charlotte happened to be in the midst of a project upstairs, it would take her a few minutes to answer the door. But if she happened to be out with one of her friends—

The sound of footsteps on the wood-plank floor of the entryway followed by the snick of the bolt lock just before the door swung open gave a mighty lift to his spirits. He shouldn't be quite so glad that his wife was home; merely relieved that he hadn't made the journey all for nothing.

But, damn it, he was happy, Sean admitted, smiling as Charlotte appeared in the doorway, dressed in faded jeans and a ratty, paint-spattered red sweatshirt that made her fair skin glow becomingly.

"Hey, I hope I haven't caught you at a bad time," he began by way of a greeting.

Charlotte gazed at him, the look on her face first one of surprise, then confusion as she ran a distracted hand through the impish tangle of her shiny, dark curls.

"No...this isn't a bad time," she replied. "But...was I supposed to be expecting you?"

Still staring at up him uncertainly, she continued to stand half-inside the doorway.

"I know I should have called to let you know I was on my way, but once I decided to make the drive down here, I wanted to pack up the SUV and get on the road before the weekend traffic got too heavy. I…I hope you don't mind too much…my just showing up…."

Lame, really lame, Sean thought to himself, all but holding his breath as he waited for Charlotte's response. She could very well mind, and with good reason.

"No problem…no problem, at all," she said after a last moment of hesitation. Finally she returned his smile with one genuine enough to set his mind at ease and stepped back, opening the door wide and waving a hand in invitation. "This is still your house, you know, and actually, you're timing is excellent. I've been trying to put up some shelves in the nursery and I can't, for the life of me, seem to get them to hang straight. Would you like to give me a hand?"

"I can't think of anything I'd like to do more."

"That is so good to hear." She paused to close the door, then glanced at him again. "Have you had lunch yet?"

"Actually, I haven't even had breakfast," he admitted.

"I was just about ready to take a break to heat up some tomato soup and maybe make a grilled-cheese sandwich for myself. It's no problem to make enough for two."

"A bowl of tomato soup and a grilled-cheese sandwich sounds really good to me," Sean assured her, his smile widening into an appreciative grin.

"Let's eat, then."

Charlotte's smile widened, too. Then she turned to lead the way to the kitchen. Following after her, Sean noted that she hadn't made any changes, at least to the rooms on the first floor of the house, in the half year he'd been gone. Not that he would have protested if she had. To his way of thinking, the house was hers now, to do with as she pleased.

The only stipulation he would make for the future was the right to have first refusal is she ever wanted to sell it. Though he couldn't foresee that ever happening. Charlotte loved the town of Mayfair, in general, and the old plantation house, in particular, so much that he doubted she would ever choose to move anywhere else, at least of her own volition.

A long hall extended from the entryway to the back of the house with a narrow staircase to the second floor set off to the right. On either side of the hallway at the front of the house were the living room and study. At the back of the house, again on either side of the hallway, were the dining room and the kitchen with half bath, laundry room and sunroom added by them during their renovations. All four bedrooms and two full bathrooms were located on the second floor.

Though much smaller in scale than most of the old plantation houses in southern Louisiana, theirs still offered more than enough room for a growing family.

"Need any help?" Sean asked, pausing in the middle of the sun-bright kitchen as Charlotte continued on to the refrigerator.

Like the kitchen in the town house, this one was also outfitted with high-quality modern appliances. But the cabinets, wood molding and wood-plank floor were all original to the house and much more rustic. A round, mahogany gate-legged table and six matching cottage-style chairs with seats upholstered in rose-and-green striped fabric were tucked into a small dining alcove built into the sunroom.

"You can start the soup if you'd like," Charlotte replied, setting a plastic container of her homemade tomato-basil soup on the counter.

"Pots and pans still in the same place?"

"Oh, yes."

Sean took off his jacket and hung it on a chair back, then opened the lower cabinet door nearest the stove and retrieved a copper-bottomed pot. As Charlotte plugged in her treasured griddle pan and began buttering slices of whole-grain bread for the sandwiches, he filled the pot with soup and set it on the stove to heat. Without asking, he found bowls, plates, silverware and napkins and set the table before returning to the stove to stir the soup.

"So you were hanging shelves in the nursery?" he asked, glancing at his wife to gauge her mood.

The silence they'd been sharing as they'd worked at the lunch prep had seemed companionable enough to him, but he'd occasionally been wrong on that account in the past.

"*Trying* to hang some shelves," Charlotte emphasized with a wry smile. "It looked simple enough in the do-it-yourself book I found at the library. But what looks straight to me, close up, keeps turning out to be just a little crooked at a distance."

"That's because the house is so old and the walls have settled a lot over the years. Remember what a hard time we had initially when we replaced the cabinets in the upstairs bathrooms?"

"I did remember that, but only after I'd messed up my first attempt with the shelves."

"I think hanging them will be a lot easier if one of us holds them up and the other one stands back and determines where to place the screws."

"Me, too."

With the soup and sandwiches finally ready, Charlotte poured glasses of iced tea for them. Then they took their usual places at the table and began to eat.

"You mentioned something about packing the SUV before you headed here, didn't you?" Charlotte asked, eyeing Sean curiously once they'd had time to take the edge off their hunger.

"I thought since it was such a nice day I might as well deliver the stuff I bought for the…for Katie."

"But didn't you decide to have the store make a delivery?" Charlotte frowned in confusion. "In fact, I called them yesterday afternoon to set up a day and time. They've promised to be here next Thursday at four o'clock in the afternoon."

"They're only going to deliver the furniture. I bought a few more things in the meantime."

Sean listed the items packed in the SUV for Charlotte as she eyed him with a mixture of amazement and delight.

"Wow! You've been busy," she acknowledged. "I feel like such a slacker by comparison. Although I have bought some clothes and shoes and the cutest little snowsuit and a hat and tiny wool mittens for her."

"But you've been doing all the work on the nursery yourself. I actually thought that maybe I could help you with the painting today, too. Sounds like you've about finished with it, though."

"There's still a lot to do, and I can certainly use any help you have to offer," Charlotte assured him.

Sean thought he saw the faintest hint of wariness in her eyes just before she ducked her head and dipped her spoon into her bowl of soup. But there had been no hint of hesitancy in her response, and so he chose to count himself as welcome here, at least for the time being.

"I never was much good at hanging wallpaper, but I seem to remember being pretty good with a paintbrush."

"I decided against wallpaper except for a six-inch border along the top of the walls, and I've finished that already. We still have to paint the closet, though—walls and ceiling. I saved it for last so the furniture could be delivered. There are the shelves to hang, too, and the floor needs to be waxed before we put the rug down."

"We definitely have our work cut out for us, then."

"Good thing you wore jeans and an old shirt."

"Like I said—I planned to help you with whatever we still needed to do to have the nursery ready before we leave for Kazakhstan."

"And I'm glad you did," Charlotte said, her voice soft and sincere as she met his gaze again.

"Sure you're not upset that I didn't let you know ahead of time?"

"I admit such spontaneity is a little out of character for you, but finding you on the veranda, ready, willing and able to help me with those blasted shelves, was a very nice surprise."

"Hey, I can be spontaneous," Sean protested in an aggrieved tone belied by his rueful grin. "Sometimes…"

"Yes, sometimes."

Charlotte stood to clear the table and Sean followed suit. He considered arguing with her about his ability to act with abandon, but knew that he would lose the battle. Hell, he'd spent at least two hours going over and *over* and over the pros and cons of showing up on her doorstep unannounced before he'd even started loading the SUV.

Which reminded him…

"Do you want me to get the stuff I brought with me out of the SUV before we start on the closet and the shelves?"

"Let's do as much as we can with the room first, then I'll help you move everything into the house."

They were on their way up the staircase when Sean thought he heard the sound of a car pulling up on the gravel drive. Pausing, he glanced back at Charlotte.

"Are you expecting anybody?" he asked.

"No, not really."

As curious as his wife, Sean walked back down the staircase with her, then stood beside her in the entryway as she opened the door.

A tall, slim young woman dressed in black pants, long-sleeved black T-shirt, black boots and a bright red puffy vest, her long blond hair caught up in a sassy ponytail was climbing the steps to the veranda. She paused and looked up at them, obviously startled.

"I've always said you're psychic, Charlotte, but this is ridiculous," Ellen Herrington observed with a wry smile.

"We heard your car pull up on the driveway," Charlotte replied, stepping onto the veranda to give her friend a hug.

"We?"

Ellen glanced past Charlotte, caught sight of Sean lurking just inside the doorway and made no effort to hide her astonishment.

"Well, hello, stranger," she said in a neutral tone.

Still standing beside Charlotte, one arm around her waist in what Sean determined to be a protective show of sisterhood, his wife's best friend eyed him steadily. He had no idea how Charlotte had explained his absence for the past six months, but Ellen likely knew the real reason for it, and just as likely didn't approve of his behavior. But obviously she thought too much of her friend to direct any overt animosity his way in front of her.

"Nice to see you again, Ellen," he said, equally detached. "How's Noah doing?"

A shadow crossed the woman's lovely face at his mention of her husband's name, but it was gone in an instant as she offered him a bright smile.

"Just fine, at least as far as I know. He was home for the Christmas holidays, but he's gone back to Indonesia again to start supervising another drilling project for his company."

"We were just about to finish up some work in the nursery," Charlotte said. "Come in and see how it looks, then stay and have some coffee with us."

"I'd love nothing better, but I have half a dozen errands to run, then I have to get back to the shop," Ellen replied, referring to Passages, the popular store where she sold antiques, many of which had been acquired when she'd traveled overseas with her husband. "I just stopped by to invite you to lunch tomorrow afternoon—say one-ish. I had a spur-of-the-moment wild hair to cook for a change, and it's no fun doing all that work just for myself. You're welcome to come, too, Sean—if you'll still be in town."

Again Ellen eyed him steadily, something in her look gave him a nudge of sorts. Charlotte, on the other hand, blushed prettily and ducked her head.

"I'd love to come for lunch tomorrow," she began. "But—"

"No buts about it," Sean cut in heartily. "We're not missing one of Ellen's famous home-cooked meals. Would it be too much to hope that your chicken-and-sausage gumbo will be on the menu?"

For the first time since she'd arrived, Ellen Herrington shot him an approving, not to mention grateful, look.

"Why, yes, as a matter of fact, it is," she said, then to Charlotte she added, "About one o'clock, then?"

"Sounds like we'll be there."

Charlotte glanced up at Sean, still a little uncertain.

"Yes, definitely."

"Can we bring anything?" Charlotte asked.

"Just your delightful selves." Ellen flashed another of her bright smiles, then turned to leave. "See you *both* tomorrow."

"Well, that was nice," Charlotte murmured as her friend climbed into her truck, then drove away with a wave of her hand.

"Very nice, especially since she makes the best gumbo I've ever tasted," Sean agreed. "Although I'm surprised she included me, too. I got the feeling that I might be persona non grata around here, at least in her estimation."

"Why would you think that?"

Charlotte looked back at him curiously as they walked into the house again.

"I haven't exactly been here for you the past six months."

"You and I *agreed* a separation would be good for both of us," she reminded him quietly. "That's what I told my friends in June and I certainly haven't been playing the injured party since then. Ellen and Quinn and my friends at the high school know about the adoption, too. I've told them you're going to Kazakhstan with me, but I haven't said anything about our…divorce, at least not yet.

"I will, of course, when the time seems right, and I promise not to paint you as the bad guy because you aren't. In fact, if you want to tell Ellen about the divorce tomorrow, it's okay—"

"Charlotte…sweetheart…" Sean caught her by the hand at the foot of the staircase and turned her to face him. "Let's just focus on what we need to do to get through the adoption process, at least for the time being. Okay?"

"Okay."

"We can sort out everything else and advise our friends accordingly once you and Katie are settled here in Mayfair. Okay?"

"Okay."

"Now let's get that closet painted and those shelves hung on the wall."

"So you don't mind staying over until tomorrow?" Charlotte ventured as they started up the staircase once again.

There was an odd tremor in her voice, but Sean couldn't see her face clearly enough to determine if it signaled a positive or a negative shift on her emotional scale.

"Not at all…although maybe I shouldn't have assumed it would automatically be all right with you. It's not my intention to insinuate myself into your…space."

"Actually, I'm glad you don't mind staying over. That way we don't have to hurry to get everything done today."

"Ah, so it's my brawn you're after, is it?" he teased as they reached the top of the staircase.

"Well, there is *that*," Charlotte demurred, her own tone suddenly light and playful.

"Yes, there certainly is."

The hallway at the top of the staircase bisected the second floor of the house much the same as the first-floor hallway did. They had always used the two front bedrooms on either side of it as offices. The larger of the two back bedrooms that overlooked the river channel was theirs, and the other had always been meant to be the nursery.

As far as Sean could see, Charlotte hadn't made any changes on the second floor, either. His office looked just as it had the last time he'd used it, although sans the paperwork that usually lay scattered across the desktop. Charlotte's office was as cluttered and cozy as always.

Sean only allowed himself a quick glimpse into their bedroom, though. He couldn't afford to be overwhelmed by all the memories lurking there. The possible temptation to say or do something both he and Charlotte would likely regret might be too great.

"So, what do you think?" she asked. Pausing just inside the doorway of the nursery, she glanced at him expectantly.

"Oh, wow, it looks great, Charlotte, just great. You've done a really, really good job," Sean said, the praise coming honestly and easily to his lips as he walked around the bright and cheerful room.

"I didn't want it to be too…girlie, but I did want it to look pretty," Charlotte admitted.

"Well, you certainly succeeded."

She had painted the walls a lovely buttery shade of yellow that set off the white wood window and door frames perfectly. The wallpaper border up near the ceiling featured fuzzy teddy bears wearing yellow and green flowered dresses. On a table in the center of the room Charlotte had also laid out a patterned quilt with a matching bear in the center panel. There was also an area rug, rolled up and stashed to one side of the room that had pale yellow and green flowers woven into its pattern, as well.

"You like it, then?" she asked with hushed expectancy.

"Oh, yes, I like it a lot. The furniture is really going to look good in here, too."

"I was never especially fond of pink when I was a little

girl. Of course, Katie may love that color, and if she does, we...um, I can always repaint the walls."

"She'll probably be so delighted with the room the way it is that we won't have to redecorate until she's a more sophisticated five or six."

"That would be nice." Charlotte smiled at him gratefully, then gestured to the can of paint, brushes, tarp and ladder at the ready by the empty closet. "I guess we'd better get busy, huh?"

"How about if I work on the ceiling while you start on the lower half of one of the walls?"

"Sounds good to me."

They worked together companionably for the rest of the afternoon, much as they had years ago when they had renovated the house. Luckily the closet was large enough that they could both paint inside of it without too much bumping and thumping into each other...not that Sean minded at all when they did.

They didn't talk much at first, each of them still a little hesitant as they felt their way along the boundaries of their new and ever-changing relationship. Eventually, though, Charlotte seemed to relax, and that, in turn, helped Sean to let loose of his lingering tension, as well. But a certain amount of anticipation—not apprehensive but rather expectant—remained, riding deep in his belly throughout the rest of the afternoon.

Sean couldn't say that he was surprised by it. Charlotte was still the most attractive woman he'd ever known, physically and emotionally. He would have been truly worried if a few sparks hadn't flared, sharing such close quarters with her as he was after a half year of celibacy.

They might not be on the same page when it came to

parenthood, but that didn't mean he no longer found his wife desirable. He had never had any trouble being Charlotte's husband; his hang-up resulted only from the prospect of becoming a father.

"I've been doing some reading about Kazakhstan," Charlotte ventured after a while, brushing buttery-yellow paint on one wall of the closet with long, methodical strokes.

Sean had been meaning to do the same, but had only gotten as far as asking Elizabeth, his assistant, to do some research on the Web and print out the most pertinent information available. She had compiled a file folder full of data that he hadn't yet reviewed.

"Have you found out anything interesting?" he asked as he ran the roller-brush over the ceiling one last time.

"Quite a lot, actually. Kazakhstan was part of the Soviet Union until 1991 when the country declared its independence. It's located mostly in west-central Asia, and for hundreds of years the Kazakh people were mainly herders of sheep, camels, cattle and horses. Now their chief products include natural gas and petroleum. They also now have a parliamentary government with a strong president."

"You've certainly done your homework, haven't you?"

"I wasn't the least bit familiar with the country, but since it's our daughter's homeland…"

Charlotte shot a smile his way as he started painting another of the closet walls.

"I was interested, too," Sean admitted, returning her smile. "I had Elizabeth do some research for me, but I haven't had time to read through it yet."

"Too busy shopping, huh?" Charlotte teased.

"Well…yes."

"Let me finish up the quick course for you, then. The city

of Almaty where the orphanage is located is the country's largest city, but the capitol is Astana. Social life is family-centered, and most of the people can read and write because the government requires children age six to seventeen to attend school. Kazakh is the official language, but many people, especially in urban areas, also speak Russian."

"We'll definitely need an interpreter, then," Sean said.

"We'll need warm clothes, too. The winters are bitterly cold, just like Ms. Herbert advised us."

"The travel agent who's making our airline and hotel reservations told me the same thing."

"Do we have a definite date for our flight to Kazakh-stan yet?" Charlotte asked.

"Reasonably definite. But our departure will depend completely on when we get final approval to enter the country and our visas are issued. On the advice of Ms. Herbert, I have us booked to leave New Orleans on February 15 with our return to the United States scheduled for March 20, just in case it takes longer than the antici-pated four weeks for us to get the Kazakh court's approval of the adoption."

"Wow…February 15." Charlotte stopped painting and turned to face Sean, the look in her eyes equal parts ex-citement and trepidation. "That's less than three weeks away. I can't believe how fast everything seems to be falling into place."

"At least so far, but we could still run into a glitch or two," Sean cautioned quietly.

He didn't want her to be too disappointed if they had to postpone their departure date for some unforeseen reason.

"Yes, I know," she agreed matter-of-factly. "But, still…"

Charlotte smiled a dreamy smile that shot straight

through Sean's heart. He loved seeing her so animated and so obviously happy again. He also didn't mind being somewhat responsible for the decided lift to her spirits.

"Even if there's a delay of some sort, it shouldn't be for more than a week or two," he said.

"And then we'll be home again before we know it with our daughter...just think of it, Sean...*our* daughter, *our* Katie."

"Yes, well, time does have a way of flying by." He gestured to the two still-to-be-painted closet walls with his brush. "So we'd better finish up here while we have the chance."

"Yes, we really should."

Looking just the slightest bit crestfallen, Charlotte turned away to dip her brush into the paint can, then silently went back to work.

Aware that he had rained on her parade big-time, Sean mentally cursed himself for not at least trying to share his wife's exuberance. Or more to the point, expressing his own increasing beguilement with the child they would soon be traveling half a world away to make a very special part of their family.

He could tell himself that the shopping he'd done, and the trip to Mayfair to lend assistance with the preparation of the little girl's room, were meant only to help Charlotte. But deep inside of him, Sean couldn't deny that he wanted the best of everything for their daughter.

The day-to-day routine of fatherhood might not be for him, but he knew how to be a good provider for those in his care and that included not only Charlotte, but Katie, too.

They finished up the painting and hung the shelves, white-painted wood to match the furniture. They also used the buffer Charlotte had rented to polish the wood floor. Then they headed downstairs to unload the SUV. Sean suggested that they stow the high chair, stroller, rocking horse and tricycle in the sunroom and take everything else up to the nursery.

Charlotte was delighted with the rocking horse. She also insisted on arranging the stuffed animals on one of the shelves.

"They'll be too sad if we leave them all cooped up in that shopping bag for the next six weeks," she said, smiling whimsically as she positioned each one just so.

Finally satisfied with her handiwork, she turned to Sean, a slight frown furrowing her forehead.

"I suppose we'd better think about fixing something for dinner now. It's after five, you know. I just wish I'd thought to take some steaks out of the freezer earlier."

"I was actually wondering if you might want to drive down to T-Bone's, drink some beer and eat some boiled shrimp." Sean eyed her hopefully. "I don't know about you, but I think we deserve a treat after all our hard work this afternoon."

"Oh, T-Bone's," Charlotte murmured, smiling once again. "That would be wonderful, especially since we don't have to dress up. Just let me wash my face and hands real quick and change into fresh jeans and a sweater, and I'll be all ready to go."

"Don't take too long. You know how crowded it gets there on a Saturday night."

"Five minutes, max—I promise."

With Sean driving the familiar bayou back roads south of Mayfair, they made it to T-Bone's, a huge old, wood-frame roadhouse-style restaurant built up on stilts along the river, in record time, arriving right before the dinner-hour rush. They were able to secure a table far enough away from the band and the dance floor to be able to talk without shouting. Yet they were also close enough to watch all the action once the live band began to play their toe-tapping Cajun music.

They ordered icy cold bottles of beer and a platter of spicy boiled shrimp served with small red potatoes and cob corn, and wasted no time digging into their meal. The tables all around them filled quickly with locals and tourists alike, all eager for guaranteed good food as well as a good time.

Some of the locals, acquaintances of Sean and Charlotte's, waved to them or called out greetings. There were hints of surprise on some of their faces, Sean noted, likely a result of seeing him with his wife after such a long time away—a reminder that they had once been regulars at T-Bone's on many a Saturday night.

"This was a wonderful idea," Charlotte said after a while, wiping her fingers on a paper napkin, her hunger obviously sated. "Thanks so much for suggesting it."

"I didn't think you'd feel much like cooking a meal tonight. I know I didn't," Sean admitted with a wry smile.

"No, I didn't, either." Charlotte drained the last of the beer in her bottle and set it aside, then shot him a look that spoke of her satisfaction.

"Want another beer?" Sean asked.

He wasn't sure if she was ready to head home again now that they'd finished eating. Given a choice, he wouldn't mind staying a while longer, especially since the band had started to play.

They had always enjoyed not only listening to the music, but also dancing to it in the past. But so many things had changed between them that tonight he wanted the decision to be hers and hers alone.

"I'll have one if you have one," Charlotte replied. "Unless you're ready to go…"

"I don't mind staying if you don't," he assured her, both slightly annoyed and amused by their overly polite, not to mention totally out-of-character, exchange.

"I'd really like to stay," Charlotte said, her smile soft and sweet and sexy as hell, her tone as decisive as the faintly challenging way she met his gaze and tilted her chin.

"Yeah, me, too," he admitted, grinning at her, then signaling their waitress for another round of drinks.

With their table cleared of the remains of their meal and two icy bottles of beer in front of them, Sean settled back in his chair to enjoy the rousing music. Beside him, Charlotte tapped a toe on the floor, smiling as she watched several couples whirling on the dance floor.

Suddenly emboldened by the faint buzz of alcohol in his system and his wife's apparent good mood, he took her by the hand, stood and pulled her to her feet.

"May I have this dance, ma'am?" he asked, using a teasing tone to cover his uncertainty at making such a move.

They had always danced together at T-Bone's—*always*. More than anything, he wanted to dance with Charlotte again that night. He wanted to feel her supple body in his arms and see her smile up at him as he guided her into the fast, familiar pattern of steps they had learned together years ago and still knew so well.

She hesitated only a moment, then nodded her head in eager agreement. Clutching his hand, she followed him along the narrow path between the tables, then slipped into his arms naturally as they reached the dance floor.

The wild music had them spinning around with the other couples, but they only had eyes, and smiles, for each other.

They were equally quick and lithe, meshing so well, one with the other, and with the rhythm of guitars, fiddles and accordion as one rousing tune led to another and then another.

By the time the music slowed and the lights lowered provocatively, they were both breathless. But instead of leading Charlotte back to their table as she seemed to expect, Sean pulled her closer, holding her firmly against him. She seemed to hesitate, but then she relaxed with a soft, barely audible sigh, her head resting on his shoulder.

Sean smiled just a little, bent his head and nuzzled her cheek as he'd done so often in the past. And just as she had done so often in the past, Charlotte lifted her face to him, her smile as dreamy as the look in her eyes, her luscious mouth too inviting for him to ignore.

Chapter Seven

Charlotte couldn't say that she had been caught unawares by Sean's kiss. She had invited the intimacy as she had so many other times when they had danced together just so at T-Bone's. But she hadn't opened herself to the shared intimacy only out of habit.

She had wanted her husband's kiss, needed it with a soulful longing that had built within her as the afternoon and evening had progressed. Her initial surprise and confusion at finding him on her veranda that morning had quickly turned to a gently humming sense of pleasure at having him there with her in Mayfair once again.

His shopping spree for Katie as well as his offer to help her finish the painting in the nursery had come as an especially nice surprise. Such consideration on his part had also been immensely heartening for her.

How could a man who claimed to be so opposed to

taking on the role of fatherhood also be so willing, so *eager* even, to do so much on their soon-to-be adopted daughter's behalf? Could it be that he was actually having second thoughts?

Sean had also agreed to stay overnight in Mayfair. Granted he'd done so at Ellen's none-too-subtle urging. But he *had* done it, and without any obvious sign of resentment. Surely that had been a positive signal on his part, as was his suggestion that they have dinner at their favorite place.

Why would he take her to T-Bone's, why would he ask her to dance, then kiss her so thoroughly, if there hadn't been some shift in his intentions toward her, and toward Katie, for the future?

And, oh, how thoroughly Sean was kissing her, Charlotte thought, opening her mouth to him and pressing closer still to his hard, muscular body without the least bit of embarrassment. He was her husband after all, and this wasn't the first time he had kissed her with such fervor on the dance floor at T-Bone's, either. Nor were they the only couple to have ever indulged in such a show of affection in the intentionally dim lighting that always accompanied one of the band's slow, sexy tunes.

The knowledge that Sean still wanted her, as evidenced not only by his kiss but also by the noticeable thrust of his masculinity against the softness of her belly, gave Charlotte a renewed sense of hope, as well. She had never desired any other man the way she desired her husband. And the fact that he still desired her had to count for something.

The music began to fade and slowly, lingeringly, Sean broke off their kiss. With the lights still low, Charlotte gazed up at him, her eyes meeting his as she tried to fathom the shadowy depths of his expression. She was sure that she saw longing there. But was there also regret in the thinning of his lips and a distancing in the shift of his pale gray eyes to a place somewhere just beyond her shoulder?

"We'd better get back to our table before somebody else claims it," he said, moving his hand from her shoulder to her elbow as he took a polite step back.

With a sharp stab of disappointment twisting through her, Charlotte nodded in agreement, then turned to leave the dance floor as the lights came up and the tempo of the music increased once again. Sean knew as well as she did that they could have danced all night without any real concern about losing their table. But he'd obviously needed an excuse, any excuse, to end the intimacy he'd initiated.

What else could she do but go along with him? She had never been the type of woman to cause even a mild scene in public. Nor had it ever been her style to cling to a man when he seemed to no longer want her company.

Back at the table, Charlotte perched on the edge of her chair and took a last, long swallow of her beer as Sean fished his wallet from the pocket of his jeans and thumbed out a couple of twenty-dollar bills to pay their check. Apparently he was now ready to head home and, Charlotte admitted sadly, so was she.

By withdrawing from her, even as politely as he had, he'd taken the fun out of their evening together at T-Bone's and left in its place an uncomfortable measure of uncertainty.

"Ready?" he asked, not quite meeting her gaze, as soon as he'd settled up with their waitress.

"Yes, of course."

She stood quickly and slipped into her jacket, giving him no chance to help her with it.

They made the drive back to Mayfair in virtual silence.

Charlotte didn't know about Sean, but she was plumb out of ideas, not to mention the energy, for polite conversation. She also sensed a thread of tension in her husband, evidenced in the tighter than normal grip of his hands on the steering wheel and the unusually rigid line of his jaw. No sense attempting to resume their earlier camaraderie, she thought, sure that a rebuff would be his only response.

The old-fashioned gas lamps on either side of the front door flickered in warm welcome as they rolled slowly up the gravel lane at last. But instead of feeling relieved that she was home again, Charlotte experienced yet another wave of uncertainty that had her tummy roiling nervously.

The one thing she hadn't yet allowed herself to think about that evening was where, exactly, Sean intended to sleep. Granted, she had flirted with the issue mentally for a few moments after he'd accepted Ellen's invitation to come to lunch on Sunday afternoon. The sofa in his office folded out to make a full-size bed. He could always sleep there.

But they had worked together so companionably all afternoon and then had gone to T-Bone's much as they had on so many past Saturday nights that she'd been lulled by a pleasant sense of déjà vu. His kiss had also heightened the old familiarity between them. For a few moments at least, Charlotte had seen that sexual overture as an acceptable prelude to a deeper, more sensual intimacy to come.

However, Sean's hasty emotional retreat as their last dance had come to an end had, to Charlotte's way of thinking, negated the possibility of anything more between them except the quiet murmur of good-night she would offer him in a few moments.

"Tired?" Sean asked as he pulled to a stop and switched off the SUV's engine.

"Yes, actually, I am," she admitted.

Frustrated, too, she thought to herself. But how could she even begin to explain that without revealing her need for more of him than he seemed willing to give?

Though why he had made a point of kissing her with such passion twice already if *he* didn't want or need more from *her*, Charlotte couldn't, for the life of her, guess. Not only that night at the town house, but again on the dance floor at T-Bone's his desire for her had been more than evident.

Had he simply been caught up in the familiarity of the moment both times? Had his behavior been spurred only by fond memories? Or was he maneuvering her toward the kind of sexual fling—a very final fling—that some divorcing couples considered a means to attaining closure within their relationship?

"Let me grab my overnight bag off the backseat, then we'll get you inside the house and straight up to bed," Sean said, his tone ringing with forced heartiness to her ears.

Overnight bag? We coupled with *straight up to bed?*

Charlotte opened the passenger door of the SUV and stepped onto the gravel drive, her thoughts whirling even more feverishly. No wonder her husband had accepted Ellen's invitation so graciously. Apparently he had planned all along to stay the night in Mayfair. Ellen had simply given him the excuse he'd needed, but for what? That little fling she had just considered?

Her heart pounding and her face burning, Charlotte dug her key from her pocket as she set foot on the veranda, Sean following after her a few steps behind. She thought of how tenderly he had always made love to her, even those times when conceiving a child had been their—*her*—major goal. She remembered how deftly he could pleasure her with the tease of his tongue, the gentle nip of his teeth, or the subtle press and stroke of a well-placed hand.

How considerate a lover he had always been, and how safe she had always felt with him in those most vulnerable of moments when she gave herself up to his ministrations and all control slipped away.

At that moment, more than anything, Charlotte wanted to surrender to her husband all over again, to give herself up to his hot embrace, to his wild kisses and sweet caresses. She wanted to lure him into their bedroom, into their bed, into her own hungry arms, and she had no doubt that she could do it.

She hadn't imagined either the intensity of his kiss or the hard length of him pressed against her as they'd swayed slowly to the music at T-Bone's. Why *plan* to spend the night with her unless he meant to spend the night *with* her in the bed they'd shared for the past ten years?

But not necessarily because he still loved her and wanted to share his life with her again, Charlotte reminded herself with brutal honesty. Men had physical needs, after all. Why not take care of those needs with someone you knew almost as well as you knew yourself, especially if that someone seemed willing?

And she had been willing, hadn't she? Quite willing to share a slow, deep, sexy kiss with him, not once but twice already.

But the one thing Charlotte wasn't willing to do was service her husband sexually simply for old time's sake.

"You've been awfully quiet," Sean noted, putting a hand on her arm to halt her flight across the entryway as he dropped his bag on the floor and closed the front door.

"Like I said, I'm tired, and you've been quiet, too."

Her gaze focused on a spot just over his shoulder, Charlotte tried not to notice the sudden warmth and tenderness of his hand against her skin.

"I was wondering if maybe you're angry about something, too. You seemed to be in a hurry all of a sudden to get inside the house."

"No, not angry," she said after a moment's consideration. Then, opting for honesty, she looked him in the eye at last. "Confused is more like it."

"Confused about what?" Sean prodded, frown lines appearing on his forehead.

"About what exactly you're after, coming here the way you did this morning, planning all along to stay the night, kissing me at T-Bone's. None of that meshes with the fact that you have every intention of divorcing me a few months from now, at least not in my mind."

Sean released his hold on her arm as if he'd been stung.

"I came here to deliver the things I bought for the child and help you finish painting the nursery, and oh by the way, hang some shelves for you, too. I packed a bag in case we ran late with the work or…whatever," he said, hands braced on his hips, his voice now edged with anger. "As for kissing you…hell, Charlotte, it's not all that easy to just turn off my feelings for you. You're an attractive woman—"

"Attractive enough to kiss now that we've been forced to spend some time together again. But not attractive enough to stay married to if it means that you'll have to help me raise our daughter," she cut in, now angry as well.

"I've told you how I feel about being a father, and why. I have no problem providing for you and the child, but I'm not prepared to do anything beyond that. How I feel about you is another issue altogether. Your well-being matters to me more than anything."

"Her name—our daughter's name—is Katie, and what she's going to need from you as she's growing up is something your money can't buy," Charlotte pointed out in a heated rush. "As for me, I'm perfectly capable of looking after my own well-being, thank you very much. Especially if your idea of looking after me includes a little recreational sex to cap off the evening."

For a long, breathless moment Sean stared at her, looking as if he'd just been slapped across the face. Then he bent, picked up his overnight bag and squarely met her gaze again.

"If it weren't so late and I wasn't so damned tired I'd put your mind at ease and drive back to New Orleans tonight. But I'm going to pretend that I didn't hear what you just said, go on upstairs and bed down on the sofa in my office the way I'd planned to do all along."

In the blink of an eye, Charlotte's anger turned to dismay. Her wild imaginings had not only led her to the worst possible conclusion but also to speak without really considering how hurtful her words might be to the man she still loved.

It had been one thing to point out what their daughter would likely need from Sean and what she, herself, wouldn't. It was something else altogether to accuse him of having ulterior motives simply because he'd kissed her in the heat of the moment on the dance floor at T-Bone's.

"Sean, wait, I'm sorry—I didn't mean to—" she began as he brushed past her on his way to the staircase.

Without stopping, or even glancing her way, he said very quietly, "You're not the only one who's sorry, Charlotte. I'll be gone first thing in the morning. We can talk again next week. You can also rest assured that during any future dealings we have regarding the adoption I'll treat you just like any of my other business partners. That's a promise, and you, of all people, should know that I always keep my promises."

"But you said you'd go with me to Ellen's house tomorrow," Charlotte called after him, grasping almost desperately for a way to smooth over the serious upset she'd caused him with her thoughtlessness. "She'll be so disappointed if you don't, and…and so will I."

"I'm not sure that would be a good idea under the circumstances."

"Sean, please—"

"Good night, Charlotte. Sleep well."

With those last words, spoken in a tone heavily laced with finality, Sean disappeared from view at the top of the staircase. A few moments later, the sound of his office door closing with a firm, no-nonsense thud echoed through the house.

"Well, fine. Have it your way," Charlotte muttered, angry all over again at having her apology so thoroughly tossed aside.

Maybe treating each other as business partners was the best way to proceed through the remainder of the adoption process. That would certainly go a long way toward eliminating the emotional roller-coaster ride upon which she seemed destined to embark every time they were together. She really didn't need to continue allowing her hopes to build up, only to have them dashed all over again.

Surely it would be much easier for both of them if she stopped thinking that Sean would, or even could, change his mind about fatherhood. As painful as it was for her to bear, she owed it to him to respect the decision he'd made. She also owed it to him to treat him as the forthright and undeniably honorable man he had always been.

Sean had never dealt with her in any way that wasn't truthful. Accusing him of trying to get her into bed for the sport of it had been on a par with calling him an unfeeling bastard. He had never given her reason to think so lowly of him, and she should have known him well enough by now to believe that he never would.

With a quiet sigh, Charlotte locked the front door and turned out the light in the entryway. Her heart heavy, she walked up the staircase, moving slowly past the closed door of Sean's office. She was half tempted to go to him and ask for his forgiveness. But in the end, she decided her mea culpa would be better left to another time and place.

Charlotte was sure that she'd have a hard time falling asleep in her big empty bed, especially knowing that Sean was so close by, yet so very far away. But an afternoon of painting followed by a couple of beers and several rollicking swings around T-Bone's dance floor had left her too exhausted for more than a few minutes of dreaded wakefulness once her head hit the pillow.

She slept soundly, too, her dreams neither good enough nor bad enough to leave any lasting impression. And by the time she awoke, early morning sunshine was teasing its way through the wide slats of the blinds on the bedroom windows.

Schooling herself not to hope too much that Sean had changed his mind about leaving, Charlotte showered and dressed as usual, though in about half the normal time. Wearing black pants and a sweater, her dark hair brushed into a glossy tumble of curls, she ventured into the hallway and saw immediately that Sean's office door was open.

It was only when she walked into the starkly empty kitchen that she accepted the fact that her husband had been as good as his word. He hadn't even bothered to make coffee before he'd gone. Nor had he left even a scrap of a note for her.

So be it, then, Charlotte told herself as she measured beans into the coffee grinder and set it whirring. He had said he would call her later in the week and she would wait for him to do so. She would be businesslike as he'd requested, and she would focus completely on becoming a mother since being a wife no longer seemed to be one of her options.

With the coffee brewing, she slipped into her jacket for the walk down the drive to retrieve the Sunday paper. To her surprise, though, she found it sitting on the veranda, in all its plastic-wrapped glory, just outside the front door. Unexpectedly, a rush of tears stung her eyes.

Sean, she thought, stooping to pick up the paper. Only Sean, angry with her as he'd likely been, would have known how much such a gesture, small as it was, would mean to her. But it was also a quiet reminder of how she'd misjudged him, making her even more ashamed of her behavior toward him the night before.

The last thing Charlotte wanted to do that afternoon was go to Ellen's house for lunch. She even considered calling her friend to beg off. There was a good chance that spending the afternoon with Ellen would serve as a much-needed tonic for her spirit, though. She would have to explain Sean's absence, but then she would also be able to seek advice from her trusted friend and confidante.

Not a bad idea since she didn't seem to be doing all that well thinking for herself lately.

Charlotte arrived at Ellen's house on a quiet side street a couple of blocks from Mayfair's downtown business district at a little past one o'clock and parked her car at the curb. She thought she spotted Quinn Sutton's car parked across the street and smiled. Spending time with both of her best friends would definitely cheer her up.

No-nonsense Quinn, especially—an attorney with a busy family law practice, happily single at forty with no desire at all to be either a wife or a mother—had little time or sympathy for spouse-related self-pity. Her motto was love and be loved by them or move on, sister.

Odd, though, that Ellen had invited Sean to join them. Unless she and Quinn had assumed that the situation between her and her husband had changed for the better. They had been surprised at how willing he'd been to help with the adoption, and had considered each effort on his part—duly reported by her—as a good sign.

"Hi," Charlotte said, dredging up a smile for her friend when Ellen opened the front door in response to her knock.

"Hi, yourself." Ellen stepped out onto the porch and gave her a quick hug, then asked the dreaded question. "Where's Sean?"

"He headed back to New Orleans early this morning. We had a little...misunderstanding last night."

"Oh, Charlotte, I'm so sorry."

Ellen gave her another hug, then looped arms with her and drew her into the house.

"I almost didn't come myself," Charlotte admitted.

"Good thing you're here or I would have come looking for you."

"Is Quinn here, too? I thought I saw her car parked across the street."

"Yes, actually she is." Ellen shot her a tender smile, then added as they walked into the living room where at least a dozen women awaited them, "Along with a few of your other friends."

"Surprise!"

Everyone called out the greeting in unison as Charlotte's eyes widened in amazement. Pink paper streamers hung from the ceiling, a cardboard stork holding a baby bundle stood at attention on the mantel over the fireplace and clever bouquets of pink helium-filled balloons decorated the tables on either side of the sofa. A stack of gaily wrapped packages towered on the coffee table, as well.

Deeply touched, Charlotte found herself blinking back a blur of tears for the second time that day.

"A baby shower?" she asked, turning to look at Ellen. "Oh, how wonderful…"

"Enjoy," Ellen said, giving her arm an encouraging squeeze. More softly, for her ears only, she added, "We'll talk later."

"Yes, thanks." Charlotte shot her friend a grateful smile. "For all of this, too."

"My pleasure, sweetie. Now come and sit in the place of honor and let's see what's hidden inside all of these pretty packages."

"Yes, please—let's do."

Perched on the burgundy red, upholstered wingback chair that Ellen indicated, Charlotte smiled and said hello to the other women happily crowded into her friend's living room. Almost all were on the staff at the high school in one capacity or another, but there were a few old friends of the Fagan family, longtime Mayfair residents, as well.

Quinn sent her a satisfied smile coupled with a teasing

wink that eased the last of Charlotte's earlier unhappiness. Quinn had obviously been in on the planning of the baby shower and Charlotte made a mental note to thank her specially just as soon as she could.

In the meantime, however, she dug into the pile of gifts, opening first one then another, amazed at all the lovely, thoughtful things that had been chosen for her little girl. There was just about everything she would need, from a year's supply of disposable diapers from ever-practical Ellen to a pale yellow cashmere sweater, hat and delicately knitted receiving blanket from ever-extravagant Quinn.

Her friends also offered lots of advice as well as recommendations on reliable child care and a trustworthy pediatrician who had been in practice in Mayfair for many years. Lunch included Ellen's famous gumbo along with her tarragon chicken salad on crusty French rolls, a Caesar salad, strawberries and cream, and Charlotte's favorite triple-layer chocolate cake with chocolate-cream cheese frosting.

Busy as Charlotte was enjoying herself, she had several moments during the afternoon when she dearly wished that Sean could have been there with her, too—as Ellen had obviously intended. He might have felt a little uncomfortable at first among so many women. But Charlotte was sure he would have enjoyed being a part of the celebration in honor of their soon-to-be-adopted daughter.

By four o'clock, only Charlotte, Quinn and Ellen remained, and as Charlotte expected, her two closest friends drew her into the kitchen for the talk they'd had to postpone.

"It's not too early for us to have a glass of wine, is it?" Ellen asked, already removing the cork from a bottle of their favorite cabernet.

"Not as far as I'm concerned," Quinn said as she and

Charlotte sat on tall stools at the raised counter overlooking the work area.

"Count me in, too."

Charlotte smiled at Ellen as her friend set a glass in front of her and filled it with the rich red wine.

"So, were you surprised?" Quinn asked.

"Very surprised," Charlotte admitted. "And very grateful to both of you. You couldn't have done anything nicer for me…and Katie, if you'd tried."

"Now for the question I've been dying to ask all afternoon," Ellen said, sliding onto the vacant stool next to Charlotte.

"And what would that be?" Charlotte asked with a wry smile.

"What happened to Sean? He sounded fairly agreeable when I invited him to join us for lunch today."

"Just the fact that he was here in Mayfair again seemed like a really positive sign to us," Quinn added, swirling the wine in her glass before taking a sip. "We thought it would be really good for him to attend the baby shower and see for himself how happy everyone is for both of you."

"Yes, well…" Charlotte hesitated, more than a little ashamed of how she'd spoiled that possibility with her rush to judgment. "I jumped to some conclusions and said some things that I shouldn't have said last night and sort of…ran him off."

"Do you want to tell us about it?" Ellen asked. "Although we'll both understand if you'd rather not."

"I don't mind talking about it."

Charlotte gave them a shortened version of the past evening's events and the verbal altercation that had unfortunately resulted. She also revealed the fact that Sean planned to divorce her after they returned to Mayfair with Katie. Ellen and Quinn murmured sympathetically, but neither of them seemed surprised by her husband's behavior.

Finished with her monologue, Charlotte eyed her friends hopefully, ready to take any advice they had to offer her.

"Did you ever consider that Sean might have been angry because he *had* intended to have sex with you for the exact reason you stated? Men often express guilt as anger, especially when they get caught not only doing something they're not proud of, but even just thinking about it," Quinn pointed out with an attorney's practicality.

"Well, no, I didn't," Charlotte admitted. "But now that you mention it, that is a reasonable possibility." She paused, frowning, then looked first at Quinn, then Ellen. "Maybe that was the real purpose of his trip to Mayfair. Maybe delivering the things he bought for Katie and helping me with the painting were just excuses to…to…"

"I don't think he would have showed up on a Saturday morning if all he'd wanted was sex. He would have rolled into town about dinnertime and whisked you off to T-Bone's. That would have been the easiest thing for him to do," Ellen said. "I saw him yesterday and he looked like he'd come to the house ready to work. One thing just led to another, and he did say he's still attracted to you, Charlotte. I'm also wondering if you would have been upset if he *hadn't* made a pass at you."

Charlotte's frown deepened as she eyed her friend. She *had* enjoyed Sean's kiss. In fact she had welcomed it quite enthusiastically, all things considered.

"I suppose I could have sent out the wrong signal…" she murmured reluctantly.

"Not necessarily a *wrong* signal," Quinn interjected. "A

signal based on certain hopes about the health of your relationship that he aroused with *his* behavior towards you. Why wouldn't you assume that he might be having positive second thoughts about the adoption with all he's already done for you and Katie? He certainly seems to be acting like a proud father-to-be. And the only reason he's given you for wanting a divorce is that he doesn't want to be a daddy."

"That's true," Ellen agreed. "Just seeing him at the house yesterday made me think that he'd had a major change of heart."

"Maybe he actually has." Quinn touched Charlotte's arm encouragingly. "But you've been so fixated on becoming a mother. It's understandable that he's come to believe that he's not equally important to you. Maybe he's just too scared to admit how he really feels, either to himself or to you."

"Then I ran him off with false accusations," Charlotte said, her tone suddenly as defeated as her spirit.

"Oh, no, you didn't," Ellen hastened to assure her. "You just made him take a good, hard look at himself that he didn't much like, and at the same time, you let him know that you aren't going to sell yourself short just to please him. He has to understand that you and Katie are an all-or-nothing package. Either he has it in his heart to love both of you, or he doesn't. And if he doesn't, you're better off finding that out now."

"Yes, well, I suppose I have."

"Don't be so sure," Quinn said with another touch of her hand to Charlotte's arm. "Two weeks ago you were amazed that he'd even considered helping you go through the adoption process. Since then, he's bought enough stuff for your little girl to put most doting parents to shame, and he made a special trip down to Mayfair just to help you paint a closet, put up shelves and buff a floor. He's a good and decent man, Charlotte. I'd say there's still hope for him, a whole lot of hope."

"But you're going to have to let him know that as much as you believe that you're meant to be a mother, you also believe that you're meant to be his loving wife," Ellen added.

Much later, as Charlotte carried the last of her shower gifts up to the nursery, she remembered her friends' encouraging words. Only time would tell if they were right about Sean.

For the past two years she had been fixated on only one goal. She had been so determined to fulfill one aspect of what she'd believed to be her destiny that she had disallowed the stellar achievement she'd already attained with her marriage to Sean.

She realized now what a mistake she'd made. But errors in judgment could be rectified. In the days ahead she intended to focus on plans for the future, plans that would center on the month or more she and Sean would be together in Kazakhstan.

There she would finally have a chance to show him that being a mother wasn't going to negate in any way her ability to love and honor him as her husband. A daunting task, she admitted with a wry smile. But she had achieved so much already in her lifetime. Failure now was not an option.

Chapter Eight

Sean tossed aside the weekly news magazine he had been trying to read, shoved out of his chair in the town house living room, shot back the sleeve of his black turtleneck shirt and checked the time yet again. Just past noon, he noted with a disgruntled sigh.

He found himself wishing, as he had all morning, that he'd been a lot more insistent about chauffeuring Charlotte to New Orleans. Then she would be with him already instead of still on her way. Of course, he would have had to make the trip down to Mayfair the previous afternoon, and that, in turn, would have meant that they would have had to spend the night together, one place or another.

Considering the angry accusations—Charlotte's—and the hurt feelings—his—that had flared between them the last time they'd slept under the same roof almost three weeks ago, Sean had been more than a little gun-shy about even suggesting it. Especially when Charlotte had made a point of telling him that she had accepted Ellen Herrington's offer of a ride to New Orleans.

Ellen had wanted to see them off, Charlotte had explained. He would also be saved the long drive to and from Mayfair just a day before they were scheduled to begin a longer, even more tedious journey, first to Frankfurt, Germany, then on to the Kazakhstan city of Almaty.

Though not exactly to Sean's liking, he'd agreed to go along with the plan that had apparently already been made to Charlotte's satisfaction. He hadn't wanted to rock the boat. They were going to be sharing a hotel suite in Almaty for the next four weeks—the one-bedroom suite he had requested because they were supposed to be happily married. He could think of nothing worse than getting off on the wrong foot with his wife before they'd even left the country.

Well, nothing except missing their flight altogether, he amended as he headed for the kitchen, although they didn't have to check in at the airport for their flight until three o'clock.

Now that it was past noon, Sean figured he could justify drinking a beer, and even if he couldn't, he was going to do it anyway. He filled the frosted glass he took from the freezer with icy brew, found the can of cashews he'd stashed in the pantry and sat on a stool by the island counter.

Telling himself that he didn't have to start worrying about Charlotte for at least another hour, he tried to rein in his impatience. The worst that could happen was that they'd be forced to take a later flight, and that would be Charlotte's screw-up, not his.

He wouldn't lose any of the good-guy points he'd gained over the past few weeks unless he allowed his annoyance to show. Since he was already mellowing out thanks to the beer he was drinking, he doubted that was likely to happen.

Sean hadn't actually seen Charlotte face-to-face since he'd left Mayfair in a huff three weeks ago, unless he counted the few minutes they'd spent together on a recent Saturday. She had driven to New Orleans with her friend, Quinn Sutton, ostensibly to do a little shopping. But they had also stopped by the town house to drop off two of the four large suitcases they would be taking with them overseas.

Charlotte had packed them full of the things they would most likely need for the child as suggested by Ms. Herbert at the Robideaux Agency. Apparently the director of the orphanage in Almaty also wanted to see for herself that the American couple could provide clothing, shoes, toys and even treats for the child they intended to adopt.

He and Charlotte had talked several times before that Saturday, and again several times afterward. All they had done, though, was exchange polite, reasonably friendly conversation centered on the progress of their adoption dossier through the necessary channels as well as their upcoming trip to Almaty. But today would be the first day they'd be spending any real time together since that night in Mayfair when she had accused him of coming on to her for the sole purpose of enjoying a little sexual sport.

Sean had been both hurt and angry that his wife of ten years had thought that he could be so callous. But he had experienced more than a twinge of guilt that night, as well. The desire to take Charlotte to bed and make love to her had grown into a very real need by the time they'd left T-Bone's and arrived back at the old plantation house.

His intentions hadn't been dishonorable, though. He

would have never *used* Charlotte simply to assuage his physical needs. She meant too much to him to treat her as a sexual object, or to use her as a means to an end, however pleasurable that end would have been for him.

Only that was exactly what he would have been doing for the very reason she had pointed out to him, he'd realized as he'd driven away from the house before dawn that Sunday morning. As tired, frustrated and angry as he'd been after a miserably sleepless night on the fold-out bed in his office, he had still been able to be honest with himself on that account.

No matter how hard he'd tried, Sean hadn't been able to stop loving Charlotte, nor had he stopped wanting her in the most physically intimate way possible. He also believed that she still loved him and wanted him, too. The kisses they'd shared, raw and passionate, had assured him of that fact.

But Charlotte needed the love and desire they had for each other to be a part of a commitment that included more than just the two of them. She needed their love and desire to be the foundation of a family that included the child they would soon be adopting. She needed to be a mother as well as a wife while he was satisfied being only a husband and, as he'd told her, a good, dependable but distant provider.

The ring of the doorbell, intruding so rudely on his reverie as it did, almost caused Sean to knock over his beer glass. He took a deep breath to calm his momentarily rattled nerves and glanced at the clock on the kitchen wall. Not quite one o'clock yet, he noted with relief. They would be able to get to the airport with time to spare.

Both Charlotte and Ellen stood on the front doorstep and offered him almost identical, not to mention rather sheepish smiles as he looked from one of them to the other.

Despite the mild February weather, Charlotte was dressed in layers of winter clothing—dark gray wool pants, white knit-turtleneck shirt and gray wool cardigan—and carried her long black wool coat, ready for the subzero cold awaiting them when they finally exited the plane in Kazakhstan. Ellen, on the other hand, was casually comfortable in her usual jeans and T-shirt, long-sleeved today since the air was still just a bit cool.

"I hope you weren't getting worried about us," Charlotte said.

"And if you were, I'm sorry," Ellen added hastily. "It was my fault that we were running a little behind schedule."

"I figured we could always catch a later flight if we didn't make it to the airport on time," Sean replied, waving them into the house. "Did you have a problem on the road?"

"Actually a customer of mine who lives here bought an old chest to the store on Saturday. I had the bright idea that I could deliver it to her today and kill two birds with one stone. I forgot how much she likes to talk—and talk and *talk*—so it took us a little longer to get away from her than I'd anticipated."

"No harm done," Sean assured her. "We still have lots of time to get to the airport. I can always call a taxi, too, if you're anxious to get back to Mayfair."

"The airport isn't that far out of my way. I'm in no hurry to go home to an empty house, and I really do want to see you safely on your way."

During his exchange with Ellen, Charlotte had stood by quietly, her coat over her arm, her hands clasped in front of her. Stealing a look at her, Sean noted that her face appeared pale, her eyes tired. He'd expected her to be buzzing with excitement, or at least a little more animated than she seemed to be that afternoon.

For the briefest moment, he wondered if she was having serious second thoughts about the adoption. But just as quickly he dismissed that possibility. Not only had Charlotte wanted to have a child so much for so long, she also had to know that adopting little Katie was the right thing for them to do—because, surprisingly enough, now that they were about to start their journey, *he* knew that it was.

"Do you mind if I use the powder room?" Ellen asked.

To Sean's relief, she seemed to sense his need for a few minutes alone with his wife before they left for the airport.

"Not at all. You remember where it is?"

"Just off the kitchen, right?"

"Right."

Sean waited until Ellen had disappeared through the kitchen doorway, then he reached out and gently touched his wife on the cheek.

"How are you doing?" he asked.

She met his gaze, her lovely eyes wide and just a tad woeful.

"I'm okay," she murmured, her smile obviously forced.

"Not having second thoughts about the adoption, are you?"

"No… Yes…I don't know…." With a shrug of her shoulders she looked away. "I guess I'm just having a hard time believing it's finally happening, and I'm wondering if it's really the right thing for me to do."

"Do you want to adopt that little girl, Charlotte? Do you want to bring her into your life and love her and care for her and raise her as your child—your little Katie?"

Charlotte looked away for several long moments, her

brow furrowed thoughtfully. Then she gazed up at him again, her smile now radiant as her eyes danced with undisguised delight.

"Oh, yes. Yes, I do."

"Then you are doing the right thing, and in the end, when we're home again and you've settled into motherhood, you won't have any doubts at all that you've made the right choice."

"You sound very sure about that."

"Only because after ten years of marriage I know you so well. You are a kind, generous, loving woman, Charlotte Fagan, and you've always been meant to share your kindness, your generosity and your love with a child. You've said so yourself many times."

"I've said it about you, too, Sean."

"Only because you don't know me quite as well as I know myself."

"Don't be too sure about that," Charlotte countered quietly, taking any sting out of her warning by offering it with a considering smile. "The knowing that goes with ten years of marriage also goes both ways."

"Trust me on this, Charlotte. You're going to be a wonderful mother, but I'm just not cut out to be a father."

"We'll see."

Her smile widened in a way that made Sean feel more than a little nervous. What kind of scenario was she imagining in that inventive mind of hers? More importantly, how could he discourage her from entertaining false hopes without…*discouraging* her?

"Seriously, Charlotte—"

"Hey, you two," Ellen interrupted, making a show of looking at her watch as she joined then in the living room once again. "We'd better get busy and load up the rest of your luggage so we can head for the airport. Check in for international flights takes quite a while these days and I don't want you to miss your plane."

"Let me just make a quick trip to the powder room myself, and I'll be ready to go," Charlotte said, already on her way.

"I need to run upstairs and grab my suit jacket and overcoat, too. Then we can shift the suitcases from the entryway to the back of your truck," Sean added, grateful for the reprieve, however temporary it would likely be.

He and Charlotte were going to have more than enough time to talk, thrown together 24/7 as they'd be in the days ahead. There was no sense browbeating his wife with his determined stance against fatherhood when she was wavering a bit herself on the threshold of the huge life change that motherhood was going to be.

She was doing the right thing, adopting little Katie, and she deserved all the support he could give her through these last weeks of the necessary legal process.

"You will take care of her, won't you Sean, and yourself, too, of course?" Ellen asked as they carried the suitcases to her truck.

"Yes, and the child, as well," he assured her. "I'm not an ogre, you know."

"I never said you were." Ellen shot him an amused glance. "Just a little misguided on occasion."

"It's not like I've been the only one," Sean pointed out defensively.

"Again, that's not what I said," Ellen chided him gently. "Charlotte knows that she's taken some wrong turns during the past year, too. But I'm thinking now that you both seem to be on the same track again, it might be a good idea to just relax and enjoy yourselves and see where you finally end up."

Before Sean could argue the wisdom of Ellen's well-intentioned advice, Charlotte called out to them from the doorway of the town house.

"Is there anything else we need to load into the back of the truck?"

"We have all the big stuff," Sean said, leaving Ellen to lock up the enclosed cargo area. "I just need to get my carry-on bag and then set the alarm."

They made the drive to the airport without incident and arrived with time to spare despite the heavy afternoon traffic on the freeway. Sean commandeered a porter to help with the luggage. Then, with the trolley loaded, he and Charlotte took turns hugging Ellen and saying their goodbyes.

"I'll check on the Mayfair house every day," Ellen promised.

"We'll call when we can and send e-mail," Sean assured her.

He gestured toward the laptop computer he'd brought along so that he could stay in touch with the office, as well as his assistant who would also be looking after the town house for him in his absence. Sean had done his homework and found out that wireless Internet service was available at the hotel where they'd be staying.

"That would be great." Ellen turned from him to Charlotte and drew her into a last embrace. "Just think, sweetie. Next time I see you, you'll be a mother."

"That's pretty amazing, isn't it?" Charlotte gazed at her friend in wonderment.

"Yes, it is. Now get going, you two, and don't forget to have fun."

"Take care, Ellen," Sean said, putting a hand on Charlotte's elbow and turning her toward the entrance to the terminal.

"Yes, take care," Charlotte called out with a last wave of her hand. "Have a safe trip back to Mayfair, and thanks again for everything."

"You take good care, too—both of you."

On their own at last, Sean and Charlotte made their way through the busy terminal. They quickly found the check-in counter for the international airline on which they were scheduled to fly to Frankfurt and quietly joined the line of people already waiting there.

Thirty minutes later, with their first-class seats confirmed, their luggage checked all the way through to Almaty and their boarding passes in hand, they proceeded to the security checkpoint, then on to the gate area. With time on their hands, they browsed the gift shop where they bought magazines to supplement the books already packed in their carry-on bags.

Finally they found a table in a quiet corner of the bar where they could wait until it was time to board their flight. Each of them also ordered a beer to go with the sandwich Sean suggested they share since neither of them had eaten lunch, and dinner wouldn't be served on the plane until they were well on their way.

Charlotte had been much less talkative than usual since Ellen had dropped them off. But then so had he, Sean reminded himself as the waitress set their beers and the sandwich on the table along with the extra plate he'd requested.

While he wondered if she was still having second thoughts about becoming a mother, he didn't want to broach that particular subject again. Of course, there were lots of other things they could discuss, just as they'd been doing ever so politely for the past three weeks.

But the last thing Sean wanted to do that Wednesday afternoon, sitting in a bar in the New Orleans airport, was make small talk with his wife. Or, he amended, maybe that was the second last thing he wanted to do. Introducing any issue that might lead to any sort of volatility would be even worse.

"It's so strange, sitting here together, about to embark on the journey of our lives, and not even talking to each other," Charlotte murmured unexpectedly, seeming to read his mind.

She had eaten only a few bites of her half of the sandwich and her beer glass was still almost full. Looking at her as closely as he could in the dimly lit bar, Sean was sure he detected more than a hint of sadness shadowing her dark eyes. Certainly he had heard the unusually bleak tone of her voice as she'd spoken.

"I was thinking the same thing." Smiling ruefully he reached across the small table and touched her hand. "But I've also been thinking that I've had a tendency lately to always say the wrong thing to you when we're together, and I don't want to do that again today."

"Neither do I." Smiling as well, Charlotte turned her hand palm up so that she could hold onto him, strengthening by several degrees their tentative connection. "But it's worse just sitting here like a couple of strangers." She hesitated a long moment, then added, "Do you think we could call a truce of sorts? Maybe agree not to dredge up any past issues or engage in any potentially heated discussions about the future until we're home again?"

"I could definitely agree to those conditions," Sean replied, his smile widening.

"Then we can take each day as it comes, good, bad or indifferent, as friends as well as partners."

"Because we *are* friends as well as partners, aren't we?"

"I'd like to think so."

"Yes, so would I." Sean gave Charlotte's hand a quick squeeze that she returned. "Deal, then? We're going to live for the day from now until we're home again, without bringing up the past or the future, and have fun doing it."

"Yes, it's a deal."

Smiling at each other like conspirators, they shook hands. Then just a little self-consciously, they released their grips, and Sean, at least, sat back in his chair and relaxed.

"So, Sean, that couple at the bar," Charlotte said, tipping her head slightly to indicate the direction in which she wanted him to look. "Husband and wife or illicit lovers on a secret rendezvous?"

Gladly joining in the game they had played on so many past trips, Sean glanced at the man and woman sitting together at the bar.

"Illicit lovers, definitely," he said, relishing the joyful sparkle now lighting his wife's eyes. "They're too well dressed and having way too much fun to be an old married couple."

"Oh, I don't know about that. We're well dressed and we're having fun together," Charlotte pointed out.

"But we're also wearing wedding rings and they aren't," Sean said, holding up his left hand for her to see.

Charlotte seemed momentarily taken aback, and Sean feared that he'd somehow said the wrong thing after all. But then she looked at her left hand, still adorned with her square-cut diamond engagement ring and diamond circlet wedding band, and smiled.

"Yes, we are, aren't we? Both of us," she murmured. Looking up again, she gazed at him in playful challenge. "Okay, your turn."

"The man in the black leather jacket, torn jeans and designer Italian loafers with three days' growth of beard on his face sitting near the doorway."

"Ah…drug runner or corporate spy?" Charlotte queried.

By the time they were settled in their seat aboard the aircraft and the plane was lifting off the runway, any lingering strain between them had disappeared. They were definitely friends again, talking and laughing together lightheartedly and living in the moment. Sean couldn't speak for Charlotte, but he was enormously relieved.

They had very serious, life-changing business ahead of them. But they could, and would, handle it just as they had handled almost every other issue they'd faced in their life together—as a team.

Later in the evening, after dinner had been served and the first movie was being shown, Sean lifted the armrest between their seats, put his arm around Charlotte's shoulders and drew her closer to his side. With a soft sigh of obvious contentment, she snuggled against him, and after a while, her breathing slowed and deepened, and Sean knew that she was blessedly asleep.

His own sense of peace increasing as well, he, too, relaxed in his seat, stretched out his legs and closed his eyes. Cocooned together as if in their own private world, they slept side by side for the first time in over six months. Hours later, they awakened to sunlight peeping through the shades on the windows and the flight attendants moving through the cabin offering coffee and juice, omelets and croissants and sweet rolls, and the dawn of a new day.

Chapter Nine

Late in the afternoon on the second day of their journey to Almaty, Sean and Charlotte finally arrived at their hotel in the Kazakhstan city. Despite the few hours of sleep she'd managed to catch on the overseas flight, Charlotte was exhausted.

Due to a delay caused by bad weather in Frankfurt, they had spent longer than anticipated at the German airport awaiting the departure of their connecting flight. Clearing customs in Almaty had taken quite a while, as well.

But their interpreter—a fresh-faced young woman in her mid-twenties, Marta Kozolshy—had been waiting to greet them in the airport terminal as arranged by the adoption agency. Once they'd collected their luggage, she had led them out to a car staffed with a driver that had also been assigned to them for the duration of their stay in the city.

Sean's calm, steady presence throughout the long,

tedious day buoyed Charlotte's spirits enormously. But by
the time they'd left the airport, sitting together on the
backseat of a severe black sedan in the waning daylight,
she'd been too numb to pay much attention to the city
sights that Marta so eagerly pointed out to them.

The Hotel International was housed in an old but very
ornate building in the city center, conveniently located
near shops and restaurants and only a few minutes drive
from the orphanage. It was too late to meet with the
director that day, Marta explained, but she hoped they
would be able to keep the ten o'clock appointment she'd
made for them the following day.

With their room key in hand and the luggage already on
its way up to the suite they'd been assigned at the hotel
desk, Sean assured the young woman that they would be
waiting for her in the hotel lobby at nine-thirty sharp the
next morning. Then he put an arm around Charlotte's
shoulders and led her to the bank of elevators, one of which
they boarded for the ride to the fifth floor.

"Well, we made it this far," he said, hugging her a little
closer as the elevator rose slowly. "How are you doing?"

"I'm not sure," Charlotte admitted a tad ruefully. "I'm
actually feeling a little spacey right now."

"It's the jet lag. I'm starting to fade myself. But if we
try to stay awake until eight o'clock tonight we should be
able to sleep through the rest of the night and wake up in
the morning feeling reasonably refreshed."

"But that's almost three hours from now. I'm not sure
I can stay awake another three *minutes*," she retorted,
making no effort to hide her chagrin as she gazed up at
her husband.

"You'll feel better after a hot shower. Trust me," Sean

urged, smiling at the skeptical look she shot his way. "Then we'll go down to the hotel restaurant and have dinner."

"I *am* hungry," Charlotte conceded.

"So am I. It's been a while since we had those sausage sandwiches at the Frankfurt airport."

"I'm glad you insisted we eat something there. In fact, I'm just really glad that you're here with me. I'm not sure I could have managed nearly as well on my own, especially with the delay in Frankfurt."

"Hey, there's nowhere else I'd rather be than here with you…partner." Sean hugged her close again as they stepped off the elevator on the fifth floor and started down the quiet hallway, then he added, "Here's our room."

The bellboy was waiting for them just inside the open doorway, having deposited their luggage in the suite's bedroom. Sean tipped him with the Kazakh currency he'd had the forethought to buy at his bank before they'd left New Orleans. As had been the case in Frankfurt, where he'd produced a handful of euros to purchase their sandwich, Charlotte was not only impressed, but also even more grateful to have him with her.

When Sean had promised that he would take care of everything involved in arranging their trip to Kazakhstan, he had meant *everything*, and he had kept his word. Even during their unexpected delay he'd made every effort to guarantee her comfort. She could have told him, and eventually she *had* told him, that just having his company made any inconvenience they encountered of minor importance. Had she been there on her own, she was sure she would have not only been bone-weary, but also a frazzled mess.

The suite was not especially large, but it was very clean and quite cozy. The living room held an array of heavy antique wood furniture including a desk that obviously met with Sean's approval, a small upholstered sofa and two comfortable chairs. In the bedroom there was more heavy antique wood furniture—nightstands, dresser and chest and a bed that was much smaller than she was used to seeing in a hotel.

Had she not been so exhausted, Charlotte might have considered more intently the intimacy inherent in sharing such a bed with Sean. But the little twinge of dismay she experienced was sidelined almost immediately by her delight at finding a deep old-fashioned claw-footed tub—rigged to make showering possible as well—not to mention a heated towel rack, in the bathroom.

She hadn't been sure what kind of home away from home she would have for the next four weeks in such a distant and foreign place. She should have known that Sean would be able to find the best possible accommodations for them even halfway around the world.

"Do you want to bathe first?" Sean asked, shrugging out of his overcoat as he joined her in the bedroom.

"I'm afraid once I do I'll be too tempted to curl up on the bed and fall asleep," Charlotte admitted. "Why don't you shower first while I unpack our bags?" She waved a hand at the suitcases the bellboy had placed near the dresser. "Having something to do will help me to stay awake."

"That's an offer I can't refuse." Sean smiled gratefully. "A hot shower and a change of clothes is going to feel damn good, especially after spending almost twenty-four hours in either airports or airplanes. I promise not to take too long, though."

Keeping his vow, Sean was showered and dressed in fresh jeans and a navy blue sweater in less than thirty minutes. Charlotte had used the time well, storing their clothes in the dresser drawers and the small bedroom closet, and arranging the few personal items they'd brought with them around the room to give it an even cozier feel. To her relief, the physical activity after so many hours of sitting in airline terminals and on airplanes also helped to revive her.

Much as she would have loved a long, leisurely soak in the bathtub, she was suddenly too hungry to dawdle. She opted for a quicker, more efficient shower, instead. Then, dressed in jeans and a sweater, too, she found Sean sitting at the desk in the living room, busily at work, sending e-mails on his laptop computer.

"I hope everything is all right at home and at the office," she said.

Pausing beside the desk, she put a hand on his shoulder without really thinking, just as she'd done so often in the past.

"Everything is just fine," Sean assured her. "I wanted to let everyone on our e-mail list know that we've arrived safely." He glanced up at her and smiled as he touched her hand. "Ready to go down to the restaurant and have some dinner?"

"Yes, please."

"I thought we could check out the hotel dining room tonight and explore farther afield when we're not quite so tired."

"Sounds good to me. I'm not sure I'm up to much more than a ride down to the lobby in the elevator."

"I know what you mean. I'm starting to feel a little spacey myself now, too," he acknowledged, closing his laptop computer and standing slowly. "But trust me—if we stay awake just a couple more hours we'll have a better chance of getting over our jet lag within the next couple of days."

"I do trust you."

Caught up in the new sense of closeness they'd shared since their talk in the bar at the New Orleans airport, Charlotte put her arms around him and gave him a hug. Seemingly surprised, Sean hesitated for a long moment, then embraced her almost fiercely.

"I won't let you down, Charlotte—not ever."

"I know, Sean...I know."

At such an early hour, by European standards, at least, the hotel dining room was almost empty. But Sean and Charlotte were greeted cordially and shown to a table near a fireplace where gas logs glowed intimately.

The menu was considerately printed in several languages, making it relatively easy for them to order a hearty and delicious meal of roast chicken, potatoes and vegetables that included carrots and cabbage. They chose not to have coffee, but they did indulge in a rich pastry filled with sweet chocolate cream for dessert.

At eight o'clock on the dot, with the restaurant beginning to fill with a mix of people—mostly European and Asian—and the trill of languages foreign to their ears, Sean and Charlotte thanked their waiter and finally headed back to their fifth-floor suite.

Charlotte made the mistake of leaning against the back wall of the elevator and closing her eyes as it made its slow ascent. Had Sean not been there to rouse her as the elevator doors opened, she was sure she would have spent the night standing upright, sound asleep.

She made it down the hallway to their room only with his strong arm around her shoulders for support. Thanks mainly to his tender help, she managed to shuck her jeans and sweater and pull on the warm flannel pajamas she'd so wisely brought with her.

Next thing she knew, she was tucked between crisp linen sheets under a layer of wool blankets and a down comforter that was as light as a feather, but also incredibly warm. The last thing she remembered before she dropped into a deep sleep was curling up against the solid length of Sean's body—her own safe harbor—his arms secure around her, his breathing slow and steady and ultimately reassuring.

The thought that perhaps such physical contact between them might not be a good idea flitted at the edge of her mind. But she wouldn't have given up the comfort of lying so peacefully in his strong arms for anything—not anything at all.

Sleeping as soundly as she did, it seemed to Charlotte that one minute she was drifting off and the next minute Sean was gently shaking her shoulder, urging her to wake up. Blinking her eyes in the soft glow of light from the lamp on the nightstand, she saw that he sat on the edge of the bed, already showered, shaved and dressed for the day in black suit pants and a gray turtleneck sweater.

"What time is it?" she asked, sure that it had to still be the middle of the night.

"Almost eight o'clock," he replied.

"I can't believe I slept almost twelve hours."

"I would have let you sleep longer, but we have to meet Marta in the lobby at nine-thirty so we can be at the orphanage by ten o'clock," he reminded her. "I thought we'd better have time to eat breakfast before then, since I'm not sure what our schedule will be for the rest of the day."

The muzziness muddling Charlotte's mind lifted slowly as she realized where she was and then why. In just a few hours, they would be meeting with the director of the orphanage. Perhaps they would even have the opportunity to meet little Katie, as well.

She sat up in bed and eyed Sean with a mixture of excitement and trepidation. She had waited for this day for so long and she'd traveled so far to get here. It didn't seem possible that she might finally be able to hold her precious little girl in her arms at last.

"Oh, Sean…I'm scared," she said, her voice quavering as she took hold of his hand in both of hers.

"Of what?" he asked, his voice gently teasing. "We've been vetted and found acceptable as adoptive parents by no less than the Kazakhstan government. We are also genuinely good and decent people, as the director of the orphanage will immediately see for herself."

"Yes, I know. But crazy as it will probably sound to you, all of a sudden, having the child I want finally seems *real* to me instead of just a dream. Going through all of the initial steps of the adoption process was one thing—coming here and beginning the final stage is something else altogether."

"First, I don't think there's anything crazy about how you're feeling. But are you sure what you're experiencing right now is actually fear or is it something more akin to excitement?"

Sitting up in bed, Charlotte thought about Sean's question. The two emotions *did* cause similar physical reactions—a quickening of the pulse, a nervous flutter in the stomach, a slight tremor in the hands. The word *fear* held such a negative connotation, too, while excitement always seemed to bring with it a certain degree of upbeat exhilaration.

"You know, I think you're right," she said, smiling at Sean with sudden, joyful anticipation. "I'm much more excited than I am afraid, and that feels downright good to me."

"Well, then, do you think you could hustle up a little so we can grab something to eat before we meet with Marta?"

"Aye, aye, sir." Charlotte tossed back the mountain of bedcovers as Sean stood, then she scooted out of the bed. "I'll be ready in fifteen minutes, twenty minutes max."

Good as her word, Charlotte bathed quickly, dressed in black wool pants and a cheerful red sweater. Together she and Sean rode the elevator down to the lobby with several Asian businessmen. Then, with the help of the bilingual concierge, they found the hotel's smaller, much less formal café where American-style as well as Continental-style breakfast was being served.

Charlotte was amazed at how hungry she was considering the full and hearty meal she'd eaten the previous evening. But she didn't hesitate to order eggs and sausage and pancakes, orange juice and rich, dark coffee along with Sean.

"It's the bitter cold weather," he assured her when she worried that her appetite had grown so much in the space of a few days. "Your body knows it's going to need the extra calories to keep you warm."

"Really?" she asked, slathering real butter, thick and creamy, atop her stack of pancakes.

"Well, that's my story and I'm sticking to it," Sean replied with a teasing grin as he speared another of the half-dozen links of sausage on his plate with his fork.

They had just enough time to go back to their suite to freshen up a bit and grab their coats, hats and gloves before returning to the lobby. Marta arrived as promised at exactly nine-thirty sharp. Bundled up in several layers of clothing, with only her mischievous brown eyes to give her away, she was just barely recognizable among the multicultural crowd of people coming and going in the weekday bustle of activity.

Rudi, their driver, greeted them with a sedate nod of his head once they were seated in the car. Then he pulled into the daytime rush of traffic on the narrow street.

Much more awake, as well as aware, than she'd been the previous afternoon, Charlotte looked out the car window, trying to absorb the sights and muted sounds of the foreign city tucked into a Kazakhstan mountain valley. Marta pointed out the various government buildings on their route along with the theater where the Russian ballet and symphony orchestra held performances.

As they traveled farther from the city center, the road widened and the buildings became more modern and much plainer in appearance. Marta explained that many of the Almaty urbanites lived in the relatively new apartments they passed. Most of the people they saw on the streets also wore Western-style clothing that appeared to be of good quality.

Sooner than Charlotte had anticipated, Rudi slowed the car, then signaled a right turn into a driveway that took them through an open wrought-iron gate, then curved in front of a squat, square, three-story concrete building painted a dull off-white with small regimented windows set into its facade. Charlotte had noticed a small sign at the entrance to the driveway, but she had been unable to read the neatly painted combination of Cyrillic letters on it.

"We are here right on time," Marta announced from her place in the front passenger seat of the sedan. The smile she directed Sean and Charlotte's way was full of pride. "Madame Zhirkova will be very pleased."

As the car rolled to a stop, Charlotte looked at Sean. The lump that suddenly lodged in her throat made it impossible for her to speak. But he seemed to sense that her emotions were roiling again. He reached over and took her hand in his and gave it a reassuring squeeze.

"We're starting off with high marks in our favor for punctuality," he said softly. "That has to be a good thing."

"Oh, yes," Charlotte agreed, clinging to her husband's hand, her voice equally low.

"Now, if you could just do something about that deer-in-the-headlights look on your face, we'd be even more impressive to Madame Z."

The hint of teasing irreverence in Sean's tone did exactly what he'd likely intended it to do—made Charlotte giggle like a schoolgirl.

The moment of heartfelt good humor eased her nervous anticipation one hundred percent. She rested her head on her husband's shoulder for a long moment, overwhelmed by the gratitude blossoming anew deep in her soul.

"Thanks—I needed that," she murmured, looking up at him again.

"My pleasure," Sean replied, shifting on the seat beside her so that he could meet her gaze.

Something in his pale gray eyes—something soft and dark and intimately sweet, something well remembered and sorely missed—caught Charlotte completely off guard. For the space of several heartbeats they seemed to be alone in the universe, sharing a special bond that had suffered strain but had never yet been broken.

Sean, too, seemed aware of the electrifying current

that flowed between them. He shifted again, and almost in slow motion, claimed her mouth in a kiss that stole her breath away.

"We should go into the orphanage now," Marta said, sounding just the slightest bit censorious.

"By all means," Sean agreed. He gave Charlotte's hand another reassuring squeeze. "Ready to meet your daughter, Mrs. Fagan?"

"I am if you are, Mr. Fagan."

"Then let's do it."

They followed Marta through the ornately carved, heavy wooden door into a small, overheated reception area where an attractively dressed young woman sat at an old-fashioned metal desk. She greeted them with a slight smile, then directed her attention to Marta.

The two women cordially exchanged a few words of Russian. Then the receptionist picked up the handset on her telephone, pressed several buttons and spoke a few more words to the person who answered on the other end of the line.

Charlotte stood close to Sean, her heartbeat quickening. She was glad to have his steadying arm around her shoulders as the receptionist paused for a long moment, eyed them both critically, spoke again and finally cradled the handset. The young woman then spoke to Marta again, stood and gestured for them to follow her to the door to the left of her desk.

"Madame Zhirkova will be right with us," Marta explained.

They were shown into another small, overheated, windowless room filled with an assortment of overstuffed chairs and a small sofa, all obviously old, but as they soon discovered, also very comfortable. Otherwise, the room was empty, and once the receptionist had shut the door, leaving them alone there, it was also very quiet.

Charlotte wasn't sure exactly what kind of place she'd expected the orphanage to be. Now she admitted that it was much more severe and much more intimidating than the homey enclave—noisy with the chatter of small children—that she'd imagined back in Mayfair.

"Let me help you out of your coat, okay?" Sean offered, turning to Charlotte.

"Yes, thanks."

Their voices sounded abnormally loud in the small, enclosed space, and as they sat silently side by side on the small sofa, Charlotte's nerves began to jangle all over again. With each minute that ticked by, she found it more difficult to project poise and self-confidence. She also had to force herself not to keep checking the time on her watch.

After what seemed like an eternity, the door opposite the one through which they'd entered the waiting room opened abruptly. A tall, big-boned, matronly woman, extremely well dressed in an expensive brown wool suit, knee-high brown leather boots and an amazing array of chunky gold jewelry, walked toward them, her right hand extended in greeting. Her iron-gray hair was cut sensibly but stylishly short, and despite the stern line of her mouth, good humor as well as intelligence radiated from her bright blue eyes.

"Hah-lo," she said.

Her voice was deep and authoritative, but not unfriendly. Although she didn't smile, she shook hands firmly, first with Sean, then with Charlotte.

They said hello in return, and Marta quickly made the introductions in Russian, politely deferential to the director of the orphanage. She also explained to Sean and Charlotte that Madame Zhirkova spoke no English except for her obviously well-intentioned *hah-lo*.

The director waved them into yet another small, overheated room, this one apparently her office. Tastefully decorated, the room also had two wide windows overlooking a somewhat barren, snow-covered garden area bright with morning sunshine.

Sean and Charlotte took seats on the upholstered chairs facing the director's large mahogany desk while Marta stood off to one side, ready to perform her assigned task of interpreter. Sitting ramrod straight in her leather desk chair, Madame Zhirkova glanced at the array of papers spilling from the open folder in front on her, studied Sean and Charlotte for a minute or two, then spoke to Marta.

"Madame Zhirkova says that she is very pleased to meet you, Mr. and Mrs. Fagan. She is also pleased that you have come here to adopt one of the orphaned children under her care. She believes that you will find the child she's chosen for you—Katya—to be a suitable match."

"We are very pleased to be here," Sean answered for both of them, much to Charlotte's relief. "We are also very eager to meet Katya."

Another exchange between Marta and Madame Zhirkova took place, after which Marta assured Sean and Charlotte that they would be able to see Katya shortly. First, however, they must discuss the process established by the director and her staff to facilitate the bonding between the adoptive parents and the child.

They would begin the following morning by spending several hours with the child in one of the orphanage's special bonding rooms. They were encouraged to bring along toys to stimulate the child's imagination. They were also allowed to bring along treats for the child such as plain cookies and fruit yogurt available at the local shops.

Their time with the child would increase each day and after two weeks, they could begin to take the child on short trips outside the orphanage in order to prepare her for the longer journey she would be making with them to the United States. They would, of course, have to provide warm clothing for the child for those trips into the outside world, but Madame Zhirkova trusted they had been advised of that already by the agency in New Orleans.

There were also papers to be signed, printed in both English and Russian. One form was necessary to request a hearing from the local court to legalize the adoption. Another declared that they were willing to accept responsibility for the child's well-being while she was in their care, and another authorized them to receive copies of her birth certificate, medical records and personal file.

By the time they had finished with the instructions and paperwork—a tedious process made more so by the need for constant repetition—Charlotte's head was swimming. Sean, however, seemed none the worse for wear. But then, he was much more used to long, drawn-out business negotiations than she was.

Not surprisingly, the small room had grown stuffy, too, leaving Charlotte with what could very well become a splitting headache unless she found a way to surreptitiously dose herself with the aspirin she carried in her purse. Her stomach was queasy, as well, likely from a mix of tension and discomfort. She kept staring out the window, wishing she could slip away to steal a few moments alone in the fresh air of the barren but sunny garden.

No, not alone, she amended, but with Sean and Katie.

She imagined them bundled up against the frigid cold, tramping through the untouched snow, flopping on their backs, laughing as they made three side-by-side angels in the frosty white—

The sound of knuckles rapping sharply on the mahogany desk brought Charlotte instantly, and with some embarrassment, back to the moment at hand. She saw that Madame Zhirkova had closed the file folder and was now eyeing them expectantly.

"The director says that she can have the child brought in to meet you now that the preliminaries have been completed. You are agreeable to this?" Marta asked.

"Oh, yes—yes, *please*," Charlotte replied, speaking for the first time since they'd entered Madame Zhirkova's office.

Amazingly, she suddenly felt much better than she had only a few minutes earlier.

"Tell Madame Zhirkova that we would definitely like to meet Katya," Sean added.

Reaching across the space separating their chairs, he took Charlotte by the hand. Though she couldn't be absolutely certain, she sensed that his gesture was as much for his own benefit as for hers. Turning to look at him, she noted an air of expectancy about him that also matched her own.

Madame Zhirkova nodded and smiled, then pushed a button on her telephone. Within a minute, no more than two at the most, the door to her office opened and a young woman dressed in a neatly pressed, impeccably clean and tidy white blouse, black calf-length skirt, black stockings and soft-soled, serviceable black shoes entered the room. In her arms, the caretaker held a small child, smaller than Charlotte had expected. She recognized the little girl immediately, though.

Katya looked exactly like the child in the photograph Charlotte carried in her wallet—wispy dark hair, big brown eyes and pale porcelain skin. She was dressed in brown corduroy pants and a beige heavy-knit sweater, thick white socks and sturdy brown leather shoes. The pants and sweater appeared to be at least two sizes too big for her and much too masculine for her dainty, feminine features.

The little girl clung tightly to the young woman holding her, but she also gazed curiously at the strangers in the room, her eyes roving from one to another of them before finally settling rather thoughtfully on Sean.

"This is Elmira, Katya's caretaker," Marta said, repeating Madame Zhirkova's introduction. "She is the one who has been responsible for most of the child's care since she arrived at the orphanage."

Elmira smiled politely, nodding graciously in response to Sean and Charlotte's greeting as she moved farther into the room. Charlotte noted that the child's grip seemed to tighten on the woman's blouse, but her gaze didn't waver. Instead her dark eyes moved slowly from Sean to Charlotte as she shifted in her chair and sat forward eagerly.

Though Charlotte still clung to Sean's hand, she could barely control the urge to stand and close the distance remaining between herself and the little girl. Her heart ached with a new and breath-stealing emotion—love, yes, but a love unlike any other she had ever experienced; not greater than her love for Sean, but different and distinct. The empty place inside of her heart filled with new desires, as well— to hold, to coo, to cuddle, to nurture and protect.

Elmira spoke directly to her then, a question that Marta repeated.

"Katya's caretaker asks if you would like to hold your daughter, Mrs. Fagan."

Her daughter…her precious little girl…

"Yes…yes, please," Charlotte replied.

Letting go of Sean's hand at last, she started to stand. Immediately, the little girl turned her face away, shyly, Charlotte thought. Hoping that she hadn't frightened her, she paused and looked at the caretaker questioningly.

"Perhaps it would be best if you sat down and let Elmira bring Katya to you," Marta suggested.

"Oh, yes. I can do that," Charlotte readily agreed.

She sat in her chair again and glanced at Sean for a long, gratifying moment when he touched her arm and smiled encouragingly. Then she looked back at Elmira as the caretaker walked slowly forward, gently extricated the little girl's hands from the fabric of her blouse and quickly shifted her feather-light weight into Charlotte's outstretched arms.

For several silent moments, adoptive mother and precious daughter eyed each other with equally wide brown eyes, one looking just as startled as the other.

"Well, hello…Katie," Charlotte said at last, pitching her voice low and letting loose the smile in her heart. "It's so nice to finally meet you."

In an instant, the little girl's face crumpled and her whole body went rigid. With an ear-splitting shriek that turned into a heartbroken wail, she twisted in Charlotte's arms, and then to her dismay, reached out for the caretaker, desperately flailing her limbs.

Charlotte discovered at once that as small and fragile as the child appeared in the oversize clothing she wore, she was actually a very strong and sturdy little girl. Holding onto her was no easy task, and having no experience with small children, Charlotte was terrified that she would do something unforgivably wrong.

She shot a desperate glance at Sean as she gripped the squirming, wailing little girl, beseeching him wordlessly for help. To her utter amazement and dismay, the look on his face was one of amusement laced with a measure of what she could only describe as *approval*.

"Sean....?" she began, hurt and confused not only by Katie's reaction to her motherly embrace, but also her husband's all-too-obvious and not exactly supportive, assessment of it.

"I told you she looked like she had a mind of her own," he said, his voice tinged with pride. "But she's a little mite, too, barely more than a year old, and we're a strange and scary addition to her sheltered world."

"Perhaps it would be best to return Katya to her caretaker now," Marta suggested after some stern prompting from Madame Zhirkova.

With a surprising lack of reluctance, her own face flushed and helpless tears in her eyes, Charlotte did exactly that. Then she sat straight and still in her chair, her gaze fixed on her hands clasped in her lap as Elmira whisked the sobbing child out of the room with a soothing, unintelligible murmur of foreign words.

So much for her idyllic vision of herself in the role of mother, Charlotte thought with a mixture of disappointment and regret. She had always been so sure that she was meant to be a mother, yet she hadn't even been able to hold the child on her lap without making her cry.

"The director wants me to assure you, Mr. and Mrs. Fagan, that such behavior on the part of a young child is not altogether unexpected. The children here have very little contact with anyone except their assigned caretakers. In fact, it is very unlikely that they will ever have the opportunity to meet a stranger until they are introduced to their adoptive parents."

"Please tell Madame Zhirkova that we understand," Sean assured her.

"After you have had the chance to spend some time with Katya in the bonding room, she will be more at ease with you. That has always been the case."

Charlotte was tempted to ask what would happen if Katie *never* felt at ease with her, but she was still too mortified to speak. She also found herself wondering, as well, if perhaps *she,* not Sean, was the one who wasn't cut out to be a parent.

Weren't mothers supposed to know instinctively how to soothe a child's fears?

"What time should we be here tomorrow?" Sean asked.

Charlotte couldn't believe that he still sounded as cool and calm and collected as he had before Katie had started screaming and struggling to get out of her arms. But then, he hadn't been the one rejected by the little girl in a fit of fearful temper, had he?

"Madame Zhirkova asks that you arrive here at ten o'clock in the morning," Marta replied. "You can spend two hours with the child before it is time for her lunch."

"We'll be here then."

Charlotte sat silently in the back of the sedan on the drive back to their hotel. Huddled into her coat, she stared out the window without really seeing anything, trying desperately not to cry.

In the hotel lobby, Sean suggested that they stop at café

for a late lunch, but she said that she wasn't hungry. She didn't pause in the living room of their suite, either, but continued into the bedroom, shrugged out of her coat and stretched out on the bed. Understandably concerned, Sean followed her there.

"Hey, are you okay?" Sitting on the edge of the bed, he touched her shoulder with a tentative hand. "You've been really quiet since we left the orphanage. Are you feeling ill or is it just the jet lag catching up with you again?"

His voice was so gentle and so filled with concern that fresh tears flooded Charlotte's eyes.

"I'm sorry, Sean…so, so sorry," she murmured, without looking at him.

"For what?" he asked, sounding truly puzzled.

"For dragging you halfway around the world to prove that you're not the only one who isn't cut out for parenthood," she admitted, a sob in her voice. "It seems I've been wrong all these years. I'm obviously not meant to be a mother after all, am I?"

Chapter Ten

Sean gazed at Charlotte's prostrate form, her question echoing in his ear, and barely quelled the urge to laugh. His humor wasn't mean-spirited or vindictive, though. Instead, sympathy and tenderness for his lovely yet so unfortunately misguided wife had been the spur. In her present frame of mind, though, she could all too easily assume that he was delighting in her misery.

"Charlotte, sweetheart, you have to know that's not true," he said, putting a hand on her shoulder.

"But Katie screamed when I held her, Sean. The child looked at me and screamed and sobbed and wailed inconsolably," she reminded him tearfully as she finally turned to meet his gaze.

Her expression mirrored the desolation Sean heard in her voice, and for several silent moments, exasperation and affection warred in the depths of his soul. Affection won out, of course—he was an understanding man, after all, and he loved his wife despite her shortcomings.

He had also suspected that Charlotte had long harbored a romanticized vision of motherhood. Now faced with the reality of a living, breathing child—a little girl who very clearly had a mind and a will of her own—his wife had suffered a bit of a setback. Not one so great that she couldn't get past it with a little well-intentioned help, though.

Sean recalled the first moment he had seen their little Katie. Such a tiny mite, she was, but so fiercely and so obviously aware and intelligent. She had gazed at him with her big brown eyes, so much like Charlotte's, and something deep inside of him, something hard and cold, and until then, determined, had cracked and shifted.

He had realized that quite possibly his own view of parenthood might be just a tad…skewed. In the space of a few minutes, he had gone from cool and distant observer to fully engaged in a new desire to give the courageous little girl who would soon be his daughter all those things that no amount of money could buy.

Suddenly he'd understood as he never had before that love and guidance, companionship and consideration on a daily basis were what she would really want and need from him—just as Charlotte had told him that stormy night in New Orleans.

"Of course, Katie sobbed and wailed," Sean said. Holding her gaze, he stroked the tangle of dark curls away from his wife's tear-streaked face. "Wouldn't you have done the exact same thing if you'd just been handed off to a complete and total stranger by one of the few people who'd been a constant in your short life?"

"Well…yes…I guess I would," Charlotte admitted, shifting into a sitting position on the bed beside him.

"So would I." Sean handed her a tissue from the box on the nightstand and watched as she blotted the tears from her eyes. "Madame Zhirkova said that it's not unusual for a child who has led a very sheltered life to behave that way when first introduced to the adoptive parents. I doubt that you were any more inept than any of the other parents who've had the same thing happen to them. You didn't drop Katie on her head, or do anything else potentially harmful to her, did you?"

"Well, no, I didn't do anything like that," Charlotte acknowledged. "But I couldn't get her to stop crying, either. I'm sure I would have known how to ease her fears if…if—"

"You'd had years of practice like your mother and grandmother?" Sean cut in gently. "I doubt it—not in five minutes in a room full of strange people."

"I thought being a mother was something that would come naturally to me because I wanted it so much." Charlotte gazed at him, wide-eyed with confusion, her frustration evident in her tone. "For the past four weeks I've imagined the first time I held my daughter in my arms. I imagined hugs and smiles and cooing baby talk, not heartbroken sobs and wails loud enough to damage our eardrums."

"Charlotte, Charlotte, Charlotte," Sean murmured, tenderly cradling her face in the palm of his hand. "Taking on a new role in life is never easy even when we want it more than anything—perhaps because we *have* wanted it so much and our expectations are so high. I have no doubt that your mother suffered her share of disappointments and temporary setbacks when you were an infant, too, but she still enjoyed being a mother enough to recommend it highly.

"Just because Katie was a little frightened of us doesn't mean we're not really suited to be her parents. It just means we have to work a little harder than we anticipated. You know, as well I do, that working hard to achieve a goal makes the achievement even more rewarding, don't you?"

"Yes…"

"I'd lay odds that after a few days with us, our Katie won't be wailing loud enough to damage our eardrums anymore. She'll have had a chance to see by then that we're kind and caring people who have only the best intentions where she's concerned."

"Do you really think that will happen, Sean?" Charlotte asked, the first glimmer of renewed hope shining in her eyes.

"I certainly hope it does," he answered, finally allowing his humor free rein. "That little girl has a pair of lungs on her powerful enough to lift the roof off a house."

Charlotte eyed him with chagrin for several moments, but then the beginning of a smile brightened her expression.

"She does, doesn't she?" Her tone now held the faintest hint of pride, as well. "She's so small and dainty and she looks even prettier than she does in the photograph they sent us. But she's no pushover, is she?"

"No, she most certainly isn't," Sean agreed, unable to hold back a grin of approval. "But we wouldn't want her to be, would we?"

"No, definitely not." Charlotte's gaze turned serious as she looked up at him again. "Thank you, Sean. Thank you so much for believing in me when I was having trouble believing in myself. Thank you for understanding about Katie when I couldn't, and for caring about her, too."

"Of course I believe in you, Charlotte. I always have and I always will." He put his arms around her and drew her into a tender embrace. "And of course I care about Katie. How could I not? She's such a valiant little soul, just like her adoptive mother."

"I'm not sure I've been especially valiant today." Charlotte shifted in his embrace and met his gaze, smiling once more, then added softly, "But thanks for saying that about me."

"I wouldn't have said it if I didn't honestly believe it was true," Sean assured her.

The look of love and trust in his wife's dark eyes coupled with the feel of her lithe, strong body in his arms stirred a sudden longing deep within Sean's heart.

"You're actually the one who has displayed great valor lately," Charlotte acknowledged, leaning close to him and kissing him on the cheek. "You have truly been my hero."

Her whispered words, soft and sincere, and the brush of her lips, lush and warm against his skin, made Sean's heart beat a little faster.

"Shucks, ma'am," he drawled, only half teasing. "The pleasure is all mine."

"Oh, I wouldn't be too sure about that," Charlotte murmured, her face turned up to him, her dark eyes seeming to mirror the depths of his own barely restrained longing.

With his wife's mouth mere inches from his, so tantalizingly close that it seemed an open invitation, Sean's willpower began to waver. In that moment, he wanted her so fiercely his whole body ached with the strain of holding back.

He could have controlled his baser instincts, though, unwilling as he was to initiate a replay of the night in Mayfair when she'd accused him of wanting sex only to satisfy his shallowest needs. But then Charlotte put her hand against his face in such a tender, well-remembered way and the last of his control slipped from his tentative grip.

"Charlotte…"

He said her name in a voice that rumbled deep and low, half plea and half warning. Then he took her mouth in a ravishing all-or-nothing, no-holds-barred kiss. He meant to leave no doubt in her mind about what he wanted, what he needed from her. Yet somewhere in the back of his mind he was also prepared to beat a hasty retreat if Charlotte chose to fend him off.

He would never, ever bully her into making love with him, but in the space of a heartbeat she let him know that she was with him all the way. Sighing quietly, she clung to him, her arms now wrapped around his neck, her hands threaded through his hair, her mouth open to the tasting tease of his tongue.

A little hesitant yet, he moved his hand from her hip, splaying his fingers along her rib cage. But then, as she sighed again, he rubbed his thumb over her breast, seeking and finding the hard peak of her nipple through the layers of clothing she wore.

Charlotte moved again in his embrace, arching into his touch and returning his kiss with heightened fervor. Her hands moved busily, as well, clutching his shoulders, skimming down his back, tugging insistently on his shirt, freeing it from his pants so that she could slip her hands beneath the fabric and trail her fingertips over the bare skin of his chest.

Sean's heart pounded and his blood pooled deep in his groin, hot and heavy in a throb of desire, yet he had just enough control left to break off their kiss. Still fondling her breast, he gazed at Charlotte for a long silent moment, determined that the choice of where they went next would be hers.

"I want to make love with you, Charlotte—right here,

right now. Tell me to stop, and I will. Otherwise, I want you to take off your clothes," he said, his tone decisive.

The time for vacillation had long since passed. He wanted her to know that she had a decision to make and that the decision she made had to be hers alone so that any regrets she might have couldn't be laid at his door. Charlotte met his gaze for several long, steady moments, her dark eyes soft and luminous. Then ever so slowly she smiled.

"Would you move your hand, please?" she asked.

"Yes, of course."

The hint of humor in her voice just barely kept his heart from sinking as he sat back on the bed and did as she'd requested.

Gracefully she slipped off the bed and with a single, sultry move, pulled her sweater over her head and dropped it on the floor. Looking at him again, she arched a teasing eyebrow.

"You're welcome to take off your clothes, too, you know." She shivered slightly, her nipples taut under the silky fabric of her bra. Rubbing her bare arms, she added, "It would probably be a good idea to pull back the bedcovers, too. Otherwise we might catch a chill."

"Your wish is my command."

Sean smiled, too. His whole body tightening with anticipation, he stood and whipped off his shirt. Then shivering a bit himself, he adjusted the bedcovers as she'd requested. No more than a minute later they both lay together naked upon the cool, crisp sheets, huddled under the pile of blankets topped by the feathery down comforter.

Charlotte pressed close against him, making no secret of the fact that she sought his warmth and, with the touch of her hand on the rigid length of his manhood, something intimately and encouragingly more.

"You're so…warm and so…hard," she murmured.

"Because you warm me and you make me hard," Sean replied. "Only you, Charlotte…always…"

He captured her bare breast in the palm of his hand and teased at the nipple with subtle strokes of his thumb, eliciting a quiet catch in her breath. She arched delicately into his touch and lifted her face to him. Her dark, dreamy eyes and her lush red lips, slightly parted in pleasure, had him groaning low in his throat an instant before he claimed another deep, drugging, delicious kiss from her lips.

So began the dance of intimacy between them, the pattern of kisses and caresses comfortingly familiar, yet after so much time spent apart, new and exciting and enticingly erotic. They had learned how best to pleasure each other long ago. But during the months they'd lived separate lives neither of them had forgotten where to nip and lick and suck, where to tease with the light-as-a-butterfly touch of fingertips, or where to cup firmly and stoke with increasing intensity.

They moved together, whispered sighs deepening into guttural moans of abject, aching need. The weight of the bedcovers became too much for them to bear against their fevered bodies, now slick and sweaty.

With Charlotte's hands wrapped firmly around his manhood, Sean drew her nipple between his teeth. He applied a gentle yet insistent pressure that matched the equally gentle yet insistent pressure of his thumb against the tender place between her legs.

She arched her back again and cried out, signaling how close she was to the edge of total fulfillment.

"Do you want me inside of you, Charlotte?" Sean murmured, moving his hand to her hip, nuzzling her neck, tormenting her almost to the point of yearning misery.

"Oh, yes, Sean…yes, please…"

Her gaze locked with his, she rolled onto her back, taking him with her, wrapping her legs around his waist and guiding him to her hot, wet, womanly threshold.

Lost in the soul-searing depths of her dark eyes, Sean entered her slowly, then savored her gasp of delight as he finally sank his rigid length into her tight, waiting warmth. Breathing hard—as she was—he levered himself onto his forearms and forced himself to hold back just a little longer. Finally the deep inner pulsing that signaled her readiness began, making him want to howl.

He captured her hands in his and held them over her head, acknowledging the ancient, primal desire never to let her go that had lived in his soul since the first day they'd met. Then with swift, steady thrusts he claimed her, feeling her softness swell around him as her pleasure increased and listening to her quiet cries.

At last, unable to control his body any longer, he called out, too—her name like an entreaty on his lips—and spent himself completely in a rush of indescribable ecstasy.

For a long time afterward, Sean held his wife close in his arms. Their heated bodies cooled under the protective warmth of the bedcovers and their breathing began to slow. He allowed himself to drift in an endorphin-inspired haze, refusing to think beyond the moments spinning out in their hotel room, lit only by the dim sunlight of a winter afternoon.

Eventually, Charlotte stirred beside him and he tensed ever so slightly, weighing the possibilities of how they might, or might not, proceed. She had willingly made love with him. But had he merely caught her at a weak moment? Would she feel now that he had taken advantage of her in some way and resent him for it?

She didn't speak, but stretched like a big, languorous, leisurely cat, rubbing her warm, naked body against his with a casual sensuality that left him barely able to suppress a low moan at the sudden rekindling of his desire. Then she nuzzled his neck with her luscious lips and smoothed a hand over his belly, so close yet so far from his manhood, and finally murmured in his ear, her breath tantalizingly hot.

"I am *so* hungry."

With a snort of laughter, Sean caught her roving hand in his and held it still.

"For more of me?"

"Well, not just yet," Charlotte admitted in a coy tone. "I was thinking more of a hot meal first. It's been hours since we ate breakfast, and after the busy day we've had…"

"Yes, we have had a busy day, haven't we?" Sean acknowledged with a smile.

"And quite an afternoon," Shifting in his arms, she raised up enough on an elbow so that she could look directly at him. "I…I've missed you, Sean. I've missed you so much."

"I've missed you, too, Charlotte—more than you can imagine."

She held his gaze for a few minutes more, then snuggled against his chest again with a quiet sigh.

The slight frown furrowing her forehead—barely noticeable, but there all the same—had Sean wondering about the trail her thoughts might possibly be taking. But he figured it would be wiser not to ask her outright. No sense spoiling the special moments they had shared by starting a conversation that could all too likely end in recriminations about the past or implications about the future.

The past was over and done, and the future… Well, Sean wasn't quite as sure about how he saw his future as he'd thought he was four weeks ago. So surely it was better to go forward as he'd meant to all along, at least until he was certain about what he really wanted, and even more importantly, what he really *needed* in his life.

"I suppose we ought to crawl out of bed, take a shower, get dressed and go find something to eat," Charlotte said, obviously choosing to avoid engaging in any deeper conversation herself.

"That sounds good to me," Sean agreed. "Do you want to use the shower first?"

"We could use it together and save a little time."

"You really *are* hungry, aren't you?" he teased.

"Well, yes, but I also like the idea of sharing the shower with you. Unless you'd rather not—"

"Oh, I'd much rather shower with you," Sean hastened to assure his wife. "Don't blame me, though, if it actually take us longer to get out of here as a result."

"Really? What do you have in mind besides a good quick scrub?" Charlotte asked, trying but failing to look demure as she rolled away from him and slipped out of the bed.

"How about a nice *slow* scrub with special attention paid to certain special parts?" he countered, following after her and catching her in a hug just inside the bathroom doorway.

"That sounds like it might be fun."

"Lady, I promise you it will be a hell of a lot more than fun," Sean drawled, nibbling at her neck.

"You're not just getting my hopes up, are you, Mr. Fagan?" Charlotte asked, shivering in his arms.

"Oh, no, I most certainly am not, Mrs. Fagan."

Under the steaming spray of hot water, with Charlotte's mouth pressed to his shoulder to stifle her cries of delight, Sean kept his vow, and then some.

Chapter Eleven

Walking along the busy streets of Almaty within a few blocks' radius of their hotel, bundled into several layers of warm clothing and her arm linked through Sean's, Charlotte felt amazingly alive and energized.

She wasn't counting only the sexual intimacy they'd shared as the cause for the restoration of her confidence and good humor. Making love with Sean with such passion and intensity on both their parts *had* been a mighty salve to her debilitated soul. But his belief in her at the very moment when she had begun to doubt herself so seriously had been the real catalyst shooting her beyond apprehension and uncertainty into the much more welcome realm of poise and courage.

Making love with Sean had been truly momentous for her, but so, too, had his encouragement and enthusiasm regarding Katie. He hadn't attempted to hide the way his heart had warmed to the little girl. While *she* had retreated into a mass of insecurities, he, on the other hand, had calmly acknowledged one of the first realities of becoming the adoptive parents of a child beyond the earliest stage of infancy.

Had Katie been a tiny baby only a few weeks or a few months old, Charlotte's starry-eyed vision of love-at-first-sight, mother-daughter bonding might have been a possibility. But with an older child on the brink of becoming a toddler—especially a child who had already formed a one-on-one attachment to a kindly caretaker and had also led a fairly sheltered life—time would have to be taken. Loving care would have to be offered initially in a patient, gradual way, not to mention in small and careful doses.

"I think this is the place the concierge mentioned," Sean said, pausing outside the bow-front window of what appeared to be a European-style tearoom. "Want to give it a try?"

"Oh, yes," Charlotte agreed, relieved that the place looked warm and inviting.

Finally dressed and ready to have a meal, she and Sean had decided that a walk would also do them good. While the offerings at the hotel café and elegant dining room had been more than acceptable, they'd also wanted to explore the neighborhood surrounding the luxury hotel to see if any other restaurants were available.

Much to their delight, they had already passed a bakery with an array of delectable breads and pastries on display in the window, a wine-and-cheese shop, and a deli-style shop that offered meats and sausages as well as fresh fruits and vegetables for sale.

Sean had discovered that one of the end tables in the suite's living room opened to reveal a small refrigerator. That had given them the idea of buying some food, fruit juice and wine to keep on hand for quick meals those mornings or evenings when they didn't feel like dining more formally.

Even good restaurant food could lose its appeal after two or three weeks. They also wanted to be able to devote more time to Katie than to waiting for meal service three times a day, seven days a week.

Inside the tearoom—as warm and cozy as it appeared through the window—a friendly young waitress greeted Charlotte and Sean, then seated them in a snug corner away from the drafty doorway. Only three other tables were occupied, one by a group of twenty-something women, two by pairs of middle-aged women. All of them were sophisticated enough to merely glance at the American couple before returning to their own spirited conversations.

"I hope you don't feel too out of place in here."

Charlotte smiled at Sean over the top of her menu. Thankfully, it had been printed in English along with several other languages, obviously out of consideration for the many international guests staying at the nearby hotel.

"I've always wanted to eat in a tearoom," Sean admitted with a grin. "But I've never had the nerve to walk into one on my own."

Charlotte doubted that was true. Sean Fagan didn't have a shy bone is his body. But she chose not to press him on the issue.

"Some are better than others," she said instead. "The wonderful aromas wafting from the kitchen and the plate of pastries one of the waitresses just brought into the dining room have me thinking this one will be very good."

Her prediction proved to be more than accurate. Instead

of the more traditional tray of tiny sandwiches, they ordered hearty slices of hot meat pie filled with tender lamb and winter vegetables that tasted as good as they looked. The hot tea was sweet and lemony, and the plate of little cakes they shared for dessert added just the right finishing touch to their satisfying meal.

Lingering over a last bracing cup of tea, Charlotte realized that she and Sean had spoken very little during their meal aside from an occasional comment. She was comfortable with the long silences that stretched between them companionably. But she also found herself wondering if Sean had changed his mind about the future in any way at all during the oh-so-eventful day they'd just spent together.

She had no doubt about the sincerity of his tender, yet passionate lovemaking. The intimacy they'd shared had been not only physical, but also deeply and satisfyingly emotional—not one-last-fling sex, but rather a renewal of their marital commitment, one to the other. Charlotte's real question had centered on Sean's relationship with the idea of fatherhood.

Had the approval that he had expressed for little Katie been merely for Charlotte's benefit? Had he only wanted to lift her sagging spirits by accentuating the positive? Or was there a chink in Sean's armor now? Had Katie slipped into his heart with her bright, intelligent eyes, her stubborn little chin and her survivor instincts?

"The way you're frowning at that last cake on the plate, I'm afraid to touch it," Sean advised her.

Charlotte shifted in her chair and met his gaze with a sheepish smile, then pushed the plate a little closer to him.

"You can have it. I promise not to bite you on the hand."

"Thanks." He took the small square of pastry glazed

with chocolate and popped it into his mouth. "Good—very good. Now tell me why you were looking so serious all of a sudden."

Charlotte should have known that Sean would sense her change in mood, and call her on it.

"Just thinking."

She hesitated, looking away from the probing intensity of his gaze.

"About what?" he urged her quietly.

The touch of his hand on hers, so tender and so gentle, was all the encouragement Charlotte needed to be honest with him. Or at least as honest as she could be under the agreement they'd made in New Orleans not to talk about the past and not to talk about the future.

"You liked Katie, didn't you?" she began.

"I liked her a lot." Sean's expression softened noticeably. "She's a bright child and she reminded me even more of you in person than she did in the photograph the agency gave us."

"Was it the sobbing and the wailing?" Charlotte asked with a wry smile, keeping her tone light and playful.

Now was not the time to let her husband think that she was after anything more from him than first impressions.

"Hey, you're the one who said that, not me." Sean's smile elevated in wattage by several degrees, and the light in his pale gray eyes was as teasing as his tone. "Seriously, though, it was more the way she studied us when the caretaker first brought her into the room. She focused on us so thoughtfully, as if she were taking our measure. You do that, too, when you first enter a room full of strangers."

"You're right about that," Charlotte acknowledged. "But it's not because I'm feeling shy, just quietly curious."

"Again, that's how it seemed to be with Katie. Given a little more time before the caretaker handed her off to you, I'm sure she wouldn't have been quite so frightened. She certainly seemed to find us interesting enough at a distance."

"So instead of violating her space all of a sudden as I did this morning I need to take my time closing that physical distance until I see that she's starting to feel comfortable with me," Charlotte said.

She understood at last the mistake she'd made earlier in her eagerness to cuddle the fearful little girl. She also admired Sean's ability to pinpoint the problem. For a man who judged himself incapable of being a good father he was certainly in tune with Katie's feelings. He was also very wise about how best to handle a frightened child.

But Charlotte wasn't sure that it was time yet for her to express those sentiments to him. The last thing she wanted was to make him feel as if she were pressuring him in even the smallest way to change his mind about the future.

"It certainly can't hurt to try that approach when we go back to the orphanage tomorrow," Sean agreed, then waved a hand at her cup. "Would you like more tea?"

"No, thanks. I've had enough."

He glanced at his watch, pulled out his wallet and counted bills to pay the check the waitress had left on the table.

"We still have time to pick up a few things at the shops we passed on our way here," he said.

"Let's get some juice and rolls for breakfast tomorrow morning and order coffee from room service," Charlotte suggested, linking her arm with his as they left the tearoom. "Then we won't have to get up quite so early to have time to eat in the hotel café."

"I didn't realize you were so tired, Charlotte. You should

have said something sooner." Sean eyed her with concern. "Let me rustle up a taxi so I can get you straight back to the hotel."

"Oh, I'm not all that tired yet," she said, slanting a seductively sexy smile his way. "But I imagine I will be later, and so, I most certainly hope, will you, my dear husband."

"So the lady has plans for the evening ahead, does she?" Sean gifted her with a wolfish grin that nudged to life an ache of sensual longing deep within her. "I thought maybe you would be too...sore."

"I am...just a little," Charlotte admitted, shyly lowering her gaze. "But I know how gentle you can be with your hands and your mouth."

"It's a damn good thing I'm wearing an overcoat or the fair citizens of Almaty would be turning their eyes away in embarrassment at the American gentleman's obvious display of sexual need," Sean muttered, squeezing his wife's hand in gentle warning.

"So you won't mind having your way with me when we get back to our hotel room?"

"Not in the least." He paused on the sidewalk amid the bustling crowd and pulled Charlotte into a fierce hug. "Are you sure you don't want me to find a taxi for us?"

"I'd much rather take our time," she murmured in reply. "We can shop first and let the anticipation build."

"I'd accuse you of being a terrible tease, but I'm going to have you all to myself tonight. I can wait if you can, sweetheart."

Sean nuzzled her neck with his lips, bit her ever so gently, then laved the spot with his tongue, all in the space of a few seconds, and all achieving what he'd obviously intended.

Suddenly Charlotte was the one thinking a taxi ride back to the hotel might be a good idea. But Sean had her by the hand, laughing as he pulled her into the wine-and-cheese shop before she was able to gather her wits enough to speak.

With bags full of enough goodies to tide them over for the next few days, Sean and Charlotte finally arrived back at the hotel. Alone together in the small ornate elevator, they laughed softly and kissed deeply, taking care of certain preliminaries.

In the privacy of their hotel suite Sean stowed the juice and cheese they'd bought in the mini refrigerator, then joined Charlotte in the bedroom. Still dressed, she stood beside the freshly straightened bed.

"The maid must have tidied up while we were gone. She even left fresh towels for us in the bathroom," she said, her face warming with a faint hint of embarrassment.

They had left the bed a tumbled mess, indisputable evidence of the afternoon delight they'd so lustfully shared.

"Remind me to leave her an especially generous tip." Coming up behind her, Sean put his hands on her shoulders and pulled her against him. "I don't think I've told you lately how pretty you look when you blush, have I?"

"Why no, you haven't." Relaxing into his embrace, Charlotte smiled at the hard evidence of his desire pressed against the small of her back. "I never realized that I looked good in red."

"It's a very becoming color for you, especially when you're stretched out naked on clean, crisp white linen sheets."

With one hand still on his wife's shoulders, Sean reached around her, grabbed the bedcovers and pulled them back with a flick of his wrist.

"Are you sure about that?" Charlotte asked, slanting him a glance that was more sexy than demure.

"There's only one way to find out for sure."

He tugged her sweater over her head, dropped it to the carpeted floor and began to work at the back fastening of her bra with busy fingers. Moments later he had her on the bed, naked, and moments after that he joined her there, his fingers busy with another endeavor that soon had Charlotte begging him for release.

Looking up at her from where he'd positioned himself between her outspread legs, Sean smiled, saying softly, "Just so you know, sweetheart, I was right. Red *is* a good color for you—a very good color."

Then, as she smiled at his foolishness, he put his mouth on her tenderly, causing her to catch her breath in a gasp of pleasure as he slowly, skillfully teased her with his tongue.

The next morning Sean and Charlotte, along with Marta, arrived at the orphanage at the appointed time of ten o'clock. That day they had brought with them a diaper bag packed with a couple of small plastic toys suitable for a one-year-old child, a softly stuffed brown teddy bear with black stitched eyes and nose, a box of animal crackers and a carton of yogurt they'd purchased the previous afternoon.

As suggested in the agency brochure, they also included some disposable diapers, baby wipes, a small towel and washcloth. Optimistically, Charlotte also added a change of clothing—yellow corduroy overalls and a white long-sleeved knit shirt that she thought was not only serviceable, but also a lot prettier than the clothes Katie had been wearing the previous day.

They did not meet with Madame Zhirkova, but instead were led up the staircase to a small private room on the second floor of the building. To Charlotte's relief, there were a couple of windows in one of the walls that let in the morning sunlight.

There was a thick, industrial-grade, spotlessly clean carpet on the floor, an old-fashioned wooden rocking chair, a couple of upholstered easy chairs, an adult-sized dining table and two chairs, as well as a child-sized table and two child-sized chairs. Looking through an arched doorway indicated by the receptionist, Charlotte also saw a small bathroom with a toilet, a sink and what appeared to be a tall padded table suitable for changing diapers.

"Elmira will be here with Katya in just a few minutes," Marta explained. "Please make yourselves comfortable, Mr. and Mrs. Fagan."

After hanging their coats on the coat rack standing in a corner, Sean and Charlotte sat on the easy chairs, waiting expectantly for their daughter's arrival. The caretaker appeared in the outer doorway almost immediately, holding Katie as she had the previous day.

The child took one look at them, then hid her face against Elmira's sturdy shoulder.

Beside his wife, Sean chuckled softly and shook his head.

"So that's a good sign?" Charlotte asked quietly as the caretaker approached them.

"Well, she didn't start wailing as soon as she saw us. She's also peeking at us from the corners her eyes. She knows something's up and she's willing to find out what, but only as long as she feels safe."

"How do you know all that?" Charlotte eyed her husband with amazement.

"I can't say I know for sure," Sean admitted with a wry smile. "I'm actually just guessing."

Finally Elmira paused in front of them, then seemed to hesitate. Charlotte's stomach knotted with dread at the prospect of being rejected by the little girl all over again.

Should she stand and take the child from her caretaker? Wouldn't such an action on her part violate Katie's space in a way that hadn't proven helpful yesterday?

"Please ask Elmira to sit in the rocking chair with Katya for a few minutes," Sean said to Marta.

The interpreter eyed him quizzically for a long moment.

"But this is to be your time alone with Katya—"

"Yes, I know, but the child is frightened. I would like for her to see that we mean her no harm before she's left on her own with us," Sean explained patiently.

"Of course, Mr. Fagan. That is understandable."

Marta spoke to Elmira and the caretaker nodded in agreement. Still holding Katie, she sat in the rocking chair and gently set it moving rhythmically back and forth.

"What a good idea," Charlotte said to Sean, touching him on the arm in gratitude.

"We'll see," he replied, putting his hand over hers and giving it a reassuring squeeze.

Several minutes ticked past and finally Katie's curiosity got the better of her. She shifted on Elmira's lap and regarded Sean and Charlotte with her thoughtful brown eyes. Her attention focused on them, she waited to see what they might do next.

Remembering the teddy bear and the toys she'd packed in the diaper bag, Charlotte reached over slowly and pulled out a plastic car. Made up of large blocks and wheels in primary colors, it also sported a little man sitting in the driver's seat. It could be rolled on the floor, but it could also be taken apart, then put back together. With no sharp edges, all of the pieces were safe for a very young child to handle.

"That's a very wise move," Sean said approvingly as she set the car on the floor and pushed it across the carpet toward Katie.

The little girl eyed it with sudden interest and after another minute or two, wriggled out of Elmira's lap. On the floor, she crawled on hands and knees to the toy car. She sat on her bottom, touched the car tentatively with a fingertip and looked up at Sean and Charlotte. Then she eased the car a little closer to herself.

The caretaker stood from the rocking chair, nodded and smiled at Sean and Charlotte, and backed quietly out of the room. Marta followed after her, closing the outer door behind her with a soft click.

Watching Katie busily studying the toy car, Charlotte was about to allow herself a small sigh of relief. But the little girl seemed to sense the subtle change in the room.

Still holding the car in her hands, she looked back at the rocking chair where Elmira had been sitting until a few minutes ago. In the space of a heartbeat, the toy fell from her hand, and her lower lip began to quiver as she realized that her caretaker was nowhere to be seen.

Finally she looked back at Sean and Charlotte, and her little face crumpled as she began to wail.

"Oh, no," Charlotte murmured.

She started to stand from her chair, wanting only to comfort the sobbing child. Sean's hand on her arm kept her still.

"Remember what we discussed yesterday?" he asked her softly. "We don't want to force ourselves on her too quickly."

"Yes, but she's crying and we are the only ones here for her. We have to do something to comfort her."

Charlotte looked at Sean with a mix of panic and indecision.

Where was Elmira? Surely she could hear Katie crying. Why hadn't she returned to the room to soothe her little charge?

Katie had started to crawl away from them by then. To Charlotte's increasing dismay, she seemed to move as quickly as her little arms and legs could carry her across the floor, her destination the door through which her caretaker had disappeared.

"We have to do something, don't we?" Charlotte said, suddenly near to tears herself.

"Let's try sitting on the floor to start," Sean suggested. "That will bring us down to her size. Maybe then we won't look quite so scary to her."

Her gaze still locked on Katie, now weeping inconsolably by the closed door, Charlotte willingly followed her husband's lead.

"Here," Sean said softly, catching her attention by rolling the toy car over to her. "Now roll it back to me."

Charlotte was about to ask him how he could expect her to play with a toy when her daughter was so overwrought. But as the bright car bumped against her foot, Katie's sobs magically stopped.

"Go ahead, Charlotte. Roll it back to me," Sean urged her quietly once again.

Shifting so that she sat with her legs tucked under her, Charlotte did as he asked. From the little person by the door came a hiccup. Risking a glance from the corner of her eye, she saw that Katie was now sucking her thumb, her eyes following the movement of the car as Sean rolled it back to Charlotte's.

They continued to play with the car, moving incrementally closer to Katie until they were only a couple of feet away from her. They talked to the little girl, too, calling her Katie, referring to themselves as Mommy and Daddy, taking turns telling her all sorts of nonsensical things in an effort to get her used to the sound of their voices.

She watched them with interest, and listened to them, too, but she moved no closer. Every now and then, she looked at the closed door and her lower lip quivered yet she didn't cry again. And when Charlotte finally rolled the car to her at Sean's suggestion, the little girl touched it first with one tentative finger, then clutched it with a more possessive little hand.

Sean and Charlotte sat where they were, making no further attempt to move closer to her. They watched as she played quietly with the toy until the door slowly opened and Elmira, along with Marta, appeared once again.

Catching sight of her caretaker, Katie held out her arms and jabbered excitedly, asking to be picked up. Elmira scooped her up, gave her a hug, nodded to Sean and Charlotte and slipped out of the room again.

"It is time for Katya to have her lunch and a nap," Marta advised them. "You will return here again tomorrow at ten o'clock for another visit."

As Charlotte fetched the toy car and stowed it in the diaper bag, then let Sean help her on with her coat, she realized that she was exhausted. A glance at her watch revealed the fact that it was just past noon. She had spent only two hours with their daughter, but Charlotte was actually glad they wouldn't have to return to the orphanage until the following day.

"I don't know about you, but lunch and a nap sounds like a good idea to me, too," Sean murmured for his wife's ears only as they followed Marta down the staircase, then out to the car awaiting them on the drive.

"I'm so glad you said that," Charlotte replied with a slight smile. "I was thinking exactly the same thing. But then I started to wonder if a really good and caring mother wouldn't prefer to spend the afternoon with her child instead of in bed, asleep."

"I have a feeling that really *wise* mothers *and* fathers rest up every chance they get. That way they can enjoy the time they do get to spend with their children."

"Now that's a theory I can appreciate," Charlotte acknowledged with a smile.

"I think we're making progress with Katie," Sean said as they sat together in the backseat of the black sedan. "She didn't cry the entire time we were there, and she liked playing with the toy car."

"But she was so glad to see Elmira." Charlotte gazed out of the car window, suddenly sad. "Her little face just lit up when she saw that her caretaker had returned."

"I think it's actually a good thing that Katie is attached to Elmira. If she's capable of having a trusting and affectionate relationship with her caretaker, then she's capable of having a trusting and affectionate relationship with us, too, once she gets to know us."

"I hope so," Charlotte said.

"I know so." Sean gave her a hug. "Now lets decide where to have lunch, okay?"

"Yes, lunch, and then a nap...please?"

"Oh, yes. We'll definitely have a nap..."

Chapter Twelve

By their fourth day together with Katie in the orphanage's bonding room, Sean and Charlotte had begun to see favorable changes in the way the little girl responded to their overtures. They were now allowed to spend not only two hours with her in the morning, but also up to three hours with her in the afternoon following a two-hour break for lunch and the child's nap.

Sean was extremely pleased with the progress they were making in the bonding process. Overall, Charlotte seemed to be happy, too, though he sensed that she still had momentary bouts of disappointment and frustration.

Her expectations had been so high that she and the little girl would develop an instantaneous and mutually desirable connection. Charlotte understood now that love and trust had to build gradually between them and their soon-to-be adopted daughter.

But that didn't make it any easier for her to resist the constant urge to scoop up the child and shower her with hugs and kisses. Nor did it stop her from feeling sad each time Katie eagerly welcomed her caretaker's return with coos and gurgles and outstretched arms.

Have patience, Sean had said each time they left the orphanage, and he knew that Charlotte was trying. Surprisingly, she also sought his comfort and support, and respected his advice. Time and time again, Charlotte had also made a point of letting him know in subtle as well as none-too-subtle ways that his presence there with her and Katie was as important to her as it had become to him.

Sean had thought that he might resent devoting long hours every day to the wants and needs of a child. But watching Katie's mood shift from fearful to inquisitive had been a true delight. And coaxing that first smile from her had been a challenge that had reaped him a reward unlike any he had ever yet attained.

That particular Sunday afternoon, though, Katie seemed to have noticeably regressed more than a little. Charlotte had said that perhaps it was the weather. The day was dreary, the dark overcast sky promising snow, according to Marta. There was a chance that the little girl was teething, too.

For whatever reason, she wasn't particularly interested in any of the toys that had teased her imagination during other visits. She sat on the carpeted floor between them, grizzling and fussing. Several times already she had pushed the car she normally liked so much away from her with a forceful little hand. She had also thrown her big, brightly colored building blocks across the room in a small show of temper.

"I feel so bad for her," Charlotte said, gazing at her

husband with woebegone eyes. "She's so miserable and I don't have the slightest clue what to do for her."

"Do you think she's running a fever?" Sean asked.

"Maybe, although I don't think Elmira would have left Katie with us if she was ill. I wish I could pick her up and hold her," Charlotte admitted. "But she's so fussy already. I don't want to do anything that could make bad matters worse."

So far, they had limited themselves to sitting on the floor with the little girl, moving closer to her each day, as she seemed to become more accustomed to their company. Just then, she was less than an arm's length away from Charlotte.

"She might let you feel her forehead," Sean suggested. "Then you might be able to tell if she's feverish."

"Her little face is so red, but it's really warm and stuffy in here today," Charlotte murmured. Then, as if she couldn't hold back any longer, she reached out slowly with a tentative hand and brushed a dark, damp wisp of hair away from her daughter's face. "Poor Katie…you're just not feeling very well at all today, are you?"

Katie tipped her face up and locked her big brown eyes on Charlotte. Her gaze was as thoughtful as ever, and held no hint of fear. A full minute ticked by as Charlotte continued to stroke the little girl's hair ever so gently. Then, to both Sean and Charlotte's surprise, the child shifted onto all fours on the floor, slowly crawled over to Charlotte, climbed into her lap and popped her thumb in her mouth.

The look of amazement coupled with gratification on his wife's face made Sean's heart swell with pride and joy. The moment Charlotte had been longing for so desperately the past few days had finally come. The image of mother and daughter holding onto each other at last was a beautiful one to behold, and one never to be forgotten.

"Oh, baby girl," Charlotte murmured. Her arms around her daughter at last, she rubbed the little girl's back tenderly with one hand "Sweet, sweet little baby girl…"

"I wish I could risk capturing this moment on film—my two lovely ladies together, looking so serene," Sean said. "But I don't want to upset the little one by pulling out my camera just yet."

"She doesn't seem to have a fever," Charlotte advised him. "I think she's probably just tired."

"She's also obviously glad to have her mom holding her close," Sean added with a gentle smile.

"She does seem pretty content right now, doesn't she?" Quite satisfied with herself Charlotte returned his smile.

"Her eyes are starting to close," Sean observed. "Do you want to try to move to the rocking chair with her?"

"It isn't too bad sitting here on the floor."

"Maybe you could scoot back a bit so you have the wall behind your back," he suggested.

"I have a better idea." Charlotte's smile widened invitingly. "Why don't you grab a couple of cushions off the chairs, prop them up against the wall and sit with us, too?"

"Now there's a nice thought," Sean agreed. "But now that she's asleep, I'm going to take some photographs first."

Sean managed to click off half a dozen shots of Charlotte and Katie without waking the little girl. Then he built a nest with the chair cushions and sat among them. Drawing Charlotte against him so that she sat in the circle of his arms with Katie still sleeping peacefully in her embrace, he brushed his lips against her forehead.

"This is nice, isn't it?" his wife ventured after a few minutes, tipping her head back so that she could meet his gaze.

Her eyes had a soft, dreamy cast to them and her smile was so completely untroubled that Sean's heart soared anew. For the first time in a very long time all seemed to be truly right with his world, thanks in large part to a sleeping child.

Was this moment an aberration, or was it more a representation of what fatherhood was actually all about?

Sitting there together, the three of them shared a special closeness that spoke to him of family—mother, father and precious daughter—bound one to the other with threads of love and understanding, respect, kindness and consideration. Amazingly no sense of dread accompanied that realization in Sean's mind. Rather, what he experienced in those moments was more akin to a quiet sense of peace and heartfelt happiness.

"Yes, this is nice," he answered Charlotte at last, shifting slightly so that he could brush a chaste kiss upon her lips. "Very nice, indeed."

They sat together just so for maybe twenty minutes more. In that time Charlotte seemed as content as Sean was to sit in companionable silence. He wasn't sure about his wife, but he was happy just to savor this newfound closeness they shared, glad to be a welcome part of their very special circle.

All too soon, it seemed that the door opened and Elmira appeared to whisk Katie away for the evening. The little girl awakened almost at once and Sean sensed a subtle stiffening in Charlotte as she seemed to ready herself for the worst. But Katie merely sat up in his wife's arms and looked at her with sleepy eyes.

"Well, little girl, are you feeling better now?" Charlotte asked softly, the beginning of a tender smile tugging at the corners of her mouth.

In answer, Katie reached up with one tiny hand and touched Charlotte on the cheek.

"Bah," she said. "Bah...bah..." Then she shifted her dark eyes to Sean and added for good measure, "Bah, bah, bah..."

Obviously pleased with herself, she grinned at them as she rocked back and forth in Charlotte's arms and giggled.

"I guess I'll take that as a yes," Charlotte said to the child.

In the doorway, Elmira and Marta exchanged a few words, then Marta advised them regretfully that the caretaker must return her charge to the nursery so the child could eat her supper. Reluctantly, Charlotte shifted on the floor, lifting Katie out of her lap and holding her out to Elmira. The little girl went willingly enough, but she continued to smile at Sean and Charlotte, waving her hands and kicking her feet as the caretaker settled her on one hip.

"Bye, bye, baby girl. See you tomorrow," Charlotte said, then sat back on her heels as Elmira whisked the child away.

"You do not like the chairs?" Marta asked politely, making Sean smile.

He rearranged his legs and stood up stiffly, then offered his hand to his wife. She, too, seemed to be slightly the worse for wear after sitting for so long on the carpeted floor.

"The chairs are fine," he assured the interpreter. "It was just easier to stay on the floor with Katie this afternoon. She seems more at ease with us when we're on her level. I promise we'll start working up to the chairs, though— soon, if my creaking bones have any choice in the matter."

"That goes double for me," Charlotte said, then to Sean she added with a lopsided grin, "She let me hold her, *finally*."

"She not only *let* you hold her, she *asked* to be held," he reminded her.

"I wish you could have held her, too." Charlotte's smile was edged with the faintest hint of apology.

"Maybe she'll be ready to do that tomorrow or the next day. She's comfortable with us now, even when she's cranky," Sean replied, surprised by how much he wanted to share an even deeper parent-child bond with his daughter-to-be.

"She took a big step today, letting us comfort her."

"You did a mighty fine job of it, too."

"You helped quite a lot," Charlotte insisted as she gathered Katie's toys and tucked them into the diaper bag.

"How so?" Sean asked, slightly puzzled.

"You comforted me just by putting your arms around me and making me feel safe and secure."

"I was glad to do it," Sean admitted, then betrayed a bit more of his own realization. "It felt good to be…included."

"Of course you're included." Charlotte smiled up at him as he helped her into her coat. "You're the dad. We not only like having you here with us. We *need* to have you here with us, too."

True enough right now, Sean acknowledged to himself, fastening the buttons on his overcoat and digging his cashmere-lined leather gloves from one of the pockets. Charlotte's need of, and constant appreciation for, his presence there at the orphanage with her and Katie had been more than evident in the past few days.

She had made him feel like an important, not to mention instrumental, part of the bonding process. Alone with him in the dark of night, she also turned to him eagerly, willingly giving of herself and taking from him the pleasure he offered her in return.

Oddly enough, he had already proven to himself that he had the makings of a good and loving father.

But would Charlotte still want him to be there with her and Katie—still *need* for him to be there—when they were home again in Mayfair? Would he continue to be included once his wife had returned to familiar territory and her confidence as a new mother had increased? Would she still treat him like a lover and a friend, or would she start to view him as an annoying distraction that stole her time and energy away from the child she had waited so long to have?

"You *do* know how important you are to both of us, don't you, Sean?" Charlotte prodded, interrupting his reverie with a light touch of her hand on his arm.

"Yes, I know," he assured her, putting his hand over hers for a long moment as he met her gaze.

"Mr. and Mrs. Fagan—I am sorry to remind you that Rudi is waiting to return you to the hotel," Marta said.

Aware that they were keeping both their interpreter and their driver from their off-duty pursuits, Sean put an arm around Charlotte's shoulders.

"We'd better go, then."

"Yes, back to the hotel," his wife agreed, looking up at him mischievously. "I want to celebrate our achievement with a glass of wine, some bread and cheese, and *you*."

The look of promise in her eyes as she spoke had Sean's blood running hot despite the bitter cold and swirling snow they encountered as they stepped outside the orphanage. And though Charlotte had ordered her wishes one way, the wine and bread and cheese part of their celebration was postponed until much later in the evening by mutually eager agreement once they were alone again in their hotel suite.

More than happy to dwell in the present moment, Sean set aside his questions about the future. He wouldn't have any answers until they were back in Mayfair. He and Charlotte and little Katie still had at least three weeks together in Almaty. And he intended to enjoy every moment of their respite just as much as he possibly could.

The change in Katie's attitude toward them improved steadily in the following days. She reached eagerly for Charlotte when Elmira brought her into the bonding room. She always offered Sean a charming, flirtatious smile that melted his heart, as well.

As Charlotte had predicted, Katie was also soon crawling into his lap during their playtime and engaging in the games he devised for her, much to his wife's delight.

The little girl loved the treats they brought for her, too, especially the yogurt and animal crackers. Within a matter of days she was eating so well for them that they were allowed to begin giving her lunch. Then they would leave the orphanage for an hour or so to get something to eat themselves while their daughter napped in the nursery.

Katie was also fascinated with Sean's camera. After being surprised by the flash a few times, she didn't seem to mind at all having her photograph taken. In fact, Sean could have sworn she often posed for him specially.

Comfortable with them at last, the little girl proved to be as bright and cheerful as he had predicted. But she also had a stubborn streak that both amused and occasionally exasperated her adoptive parents.

One afternoon early in their third week together in the

bonding room, Katie achieved a milestone that had both
Sean and Charlotte grinning proudly. For days she had
been pulling herself up to a standing position, holding onto
either Sean or Charlotte's hands to stay steady. She refused
to take any steps, though, always dropping down to crawl
when she wanted to move about the room.

But that particular afternoon she started to take a step,
still holding onto Charlotte's hands. Stooping down a few
feet away, Sean held out his hands to his daughter and
offered her a teasing grin.

"Come on, Katie—come to Daddy," he urged. "You know
you can do it and better yet, you know you *want* to do it."

She giggled impishly and then to Sean and Charlotte's
surprise she let go of Charlotte's hands, took five toddling
steps and collapsed in Sean's arms, crowing with excitement and delight.

"That's my girl," he cooed, hugging her close.

"Oh, Sean, she took her first steps." Charlotte gazed at
him in wonder. "I wish I'd had the camera handy."

"Let's see if she'll do it again," he said, setting the little
girl on her feet once more and turning her to face his wife.
"Walk to Mommy now, Katie. Walk to Mommy."

The child toddled over to Charlotte and collapsed in
another fit of giggles, this time in her mother's arms. She
didn't stay put for long, though. Obviously thrilled by her
latest accomplishment, she was on her way back to Sean
almost at once.

Charlotte took a moment to dab the tears in her eyes
with a tissue, then grabbed the camera and captured a photograph as Katie started toward her yet again.

"I think we've created a monster," Sean declared
when his daughter wiggled out of his grasp, this time

heading for one of the chairs where they had left her teddy bear.

"I think you're right," Charlotte agreed. "But she's a cute little monster, isn't she?"

"Oh, yes…and lovable, too."

"Bah, bah, bah," Katie screeched.

She tried to pull herself onto the chair seat. Then, failing that, the little girl plopped onto her bottom, sat in surprised silence for several moments, then began to wail.

"Even those times when she's just a tad temperamental?" Charlotte asked, smiling at Sean as she set aside the camera.

"Yes, even those times," he assured his wife, crawling over to Katie and standing her on her feet again.

Immediately the little girl stopped crying, then smiled like a cherub as he handed her the teddy bear.

"You are *so* wrapped around her little finger," Charlotte accused.

A carton of Katie's favorite yogurt now in hand, she joined them on the floor.

"Like you're not," Sean retorted playfully.

"Okay, we're a couple of pushovers. What's so bad about that, Mr. Fagan?"

"Not a thing, Mrs. Fagan—as long as we nurture her a lot and only spoil her a little," Sean replied with a sage smile.

"Sometimes you amaze me with the depth of your wisdom," Charlotte acknowledged, half teasing.

"Only sometimes?" he countered with a grin.

"Well, you wouldn't want to be perfect, would you? That would be so boring."

"Trust me—I have no intention of boring my two special ladies."

"I don't think that could ever happen," Charlotte assured

him, her expression softening as Katie snuggled against his chest, still holding her teddy bear close.

"That's good to know," Sean replied, his gaze steady, his heart full, his soul wonderfully at peace.

Katie's newfound mobility coupled with her naturally inquisitive mind posed all new challenges for Sean and Charlotte. Most days, keeping up with the little girl could be exhausting, even with two of them looking after her. They were up to the task, of course, but some nights they were also happy just to fall into bed back at the hotel and go straight to sleep.

Sean was too tired in too good a way for too good a reason to feel even the least bit slighted when Charlotte's eyes closed almost the minute her head hit the pillow. She was always curled close in his arms, her deep, even breathing soothing him asleep before he had time to think about much of anything except how glad he was to have her there with him.

They had a meeting with the orphanage's pediatrician on the Monday of their fourth week in Almaty. He declared Katie fit to travel with them to the United States, gave them a copy of her medical history and immunization records, and wished them well.

Madame Zhirkova met with them on Tuesday to advise them about their meeting with the judge scheduled for Friday morning. She was pleased by their progress with the child and couldn't foresee any reason why the adoption wouldn't be approved and finalized then.

All of the necessary documents were in order and would be handed over to them by the judge at the conclusion of the court hearing. They would then be free to remove the child from the orphanage and would also be able to leave the country with her at their earliest convenience.

Sean was impressed by the director's handling of their case as well as her adherence to the time line that had originally been laid out by Ms. Herbert at the Robideaux Agency in New Orleans. Obviously both Madame Zhirkova and Ms. Herbert had coordinated enough adoptions to avoid all but the most unexpected delays.

Twice already Sean and Charlotte had run into other American couples at the orphanage also apparently there to adopt a child. But they had met only in passing at the entrance of the building and then just long enough to exchange only casual greetings.

Friday morning dawned clear and bitterly cold. So nervous had Sean and Charlotte been the previous night that neither of them had slept especially well, and they had both been wide awake well before their requested seven o'clock wake-up call.

"I can't believe we'll finally be on our way home with our little girl tomorrow," Charlotte murmured.

She was cuddled close to Sean's warmth under the pile of bedcovers as she'd been all night.

"It seems like we've been here forever, but also like we just arrived. Does that make any sense to you?" he asked, stroking a hand over her flannel pajama–clad arm, his fingers brushing against the side of her breast.

"Complete sense. I've been feeling the same way. It's as if we're in our own special world here and time doesn't seem to tick by in quite the same way that it does in real life."

"Are you ready to go home to Mayfair, Charlotte?"

"Yes…it's time," she answered after a thoughtful pause.

"We've had all the fun of getting to know our daughter without all of the 24/7 responsibilities full-time parenthood."

"I know what you mean. We've bathed her, and fed her, and changed her diapers. We've taken her to a park and to the tearoom, and we've brought her back to our hotel suite for a couple of hours at a time. But then we've always had to take her back to the orphanage."

Charlotte shifted in his arms and looked up at him with a tremulous-sounding sigh.

"Do you know that tonight will be the first and only night we'll spend with her on our own before we fly home?" she asked. "What if she misses Elmira and her bed in the nursery? What if she's so…bereft that she sobs her little heart out all night? What will we do then, Sean?"

"The best we can with what we have—each other and our loving, caring hearts and souls," he answered her with as much bravado as he could muster. "We're not strangers to Katie anymore. She's been happy enough to go on short expeditions with us, and she's been less and less agreeable about being handed back to Elmira at the end of the day. We've also proven that we have *some* parenting skills."

"Yes, we have," Charlotte agreed.

"We're going to have some challenges ahead of us, I'm sure," he continued. "We're also going to make some mistakes along the way. But overall, I'm absolutely positive we'll do right by our little girl."

"How did you get to be so wise and so confident?" Charlotte demanded in a teasing tone of voice.

"I don't think I'm any smarter than you are, sweetheart. I'm just not quite as panicky, so it's a little easier for me to tap into common-sense answers to your questions. I have to admit that there *were* times during the night when I had to talk myself off a mental ledge or two, though. Taking on the responsibility of a thirteen-month-old child is a scary thing. I wouldn't want to do it without you, Charlotte."

"I wouldn't want to do it without you, either, Sean," she murmured, ducking her head so that he couldn't read her expression. "You're a very important part of our family equation. You do know that, don't you?"

"I know that the past four weeks here with you and Katie have been really good for me." He tipped his wife's face up with a finger under her chin and kissed her deeply. "I hope it's been good for you, too."

"Oh, yes, being here like this with you… It's been more than good for me, Sean."

He heard the hint of wistfulness in her soft murmur, and her unexpected melancholy tugged at his heart. But then she moved her hands over him in an invitingly, erotically sensual way, and his body's response trumped the uncertainty in his mind.

"Do we have time to make love one more time?" she asked, trailing a line of kisses down his chest as she moved against him seductively under the bedcovers.

"More than enough time," he assured her, then gasped as her mouth closed over him in a delicate rush of warm and wet.

Chapter Thirteen

Her final day in Almaty flew by for Charlotte in a whirl-wind of activity, and to her way of thinking that was a good thing. Sean had calmed the worst of her fears about her ability to take complete responsibility for Katie. But had she not been so busy, she would have dwelled on the sadness that had lurked in her heart since he had left her in bed that morning to shower, shave and dress for their appearance at the court hearing.

Their lovemaking had been slow and tender and totally satisfying. Each of them had given as much as they'd received. But to Charlotte, at least, there had also been a sense of finality about their shared intimacy.

They would have Katie with them twenty-four hours a day, seven days a week, starting that afternoon. They would be starting their long journey back to New Orleans the following morning. She and Katie would likely be back in Mayfair Monday or Tuesday at the latest.

Her halcyon days and nights with Sean had come to an end. He would see her and Katie settled at home, and then…what? Would he distance himself from his wife and daughter and return to New Orleans? Would he hire an attorney, bid her to do the same, and go forward with his original plan to file for divorce?

Charlotte didn't want to believe that he could so callously set aside all that they'd been to each other, not to mention all that they'd shared during the past four weeks. But Sean had been so adamant about his intentions when he'd first agreed to help her with the adoption.

He hadn't yet *said* anything to indicate he'd had a change of heart. And Charlotte couldn't quite allow herself to believe that his actions since they'd arrived in Almaty spoke louder than his words to her two months ago.

Their hearing before the Kazakhstan judge took place not in a crowded courtroom but in an office Charlotte assumed was the judge's chambers. With Marta interpreting for them, they moved through the protocol at what seemed like a snail's pace.

The judge, a middle-aged man with heavy jowls, silver hair and a stern, no-nonsense manner, seemed to be vaguely bored by the proceedings yet in no special hurry to complete the process. Questions to determine their suitability as adoptive parents were asked and answered. Documents were studied carefully, stamped and signed in triplicate.

More than two hours after they'd arrived at the courthouse for their ten o'clock hearing, the judge finally nodded at them in apparent satisfaction. He gathered the paperwork into three separate piles, then inserted one into a plain brown envelope for Sean and Charlotte, and another into an envelope to be delivered to Madame Zhirkova at the orphanage.

They were also given the temporary passport that had been prepared for Katie, making it possible for her to leave the country with them and enter the United States upon their arrival in New Orleans. The judge then stood, congratulated them, still without cracking a smile, shook their hand, and sat back in his chair, effectively dismissing them.

"So that's it?" Charlotte asked Marta as they walked down the corridor outside the judge's chambers. "We're now officially Katie's parents?"

"Yes, Mrs. Fagan, you are now officially Katya's parents," Marta replied. "You will want to have lunch now, I'm sure. Then we will go to the orphanage. Madame Zhirkova has assured me that she would make sure the child is ready to leave with you by two o'clock this afternoon."

Charlotte didn't really want to have lunch first, but she knew they had no choice except to adhere to the director's schedule.

"Let's go back to the hotel," Sean suggested. "We can grab a quick bite at the café there, then finish packing so we won't be quite so rushed later in the day."

"Good idea," Charlotte agreed. "I'm not sure I'm going to be able to eat much, though. My stomach has been just a little queasy all morning."

"You aren't feeling ill, are you?" Sean eyed her with sudden concern.

"Not really. I think it's probably just nerves."

Charlotte managed to eat most of a bowl of hearty vegetable soup at the café. Then she and Sean returned together to their suite and quickly, efficiently packed everything except those items they thought they would need both that evening and the next morning. Not surprisingly, they were taking home many more items than they'd brought with them. Luckily they had planned ahead and hadn't filled their suitcases completely on the outward-bound portion of the journey so they had room to spare.

During the past four weeks they had purchased a variety of books filled with photographs of Kazakhstan and several dolls dressed in various native costumes to remind Katie of her birthplace in the future. They had also bought carved wooden boxes and small pieces of simple jewelry made by local artisans to give as gifts to Ellen and Quinn and to Sean's assistant, Elizabeth, who had proven invaluable at keeping him up-to-date on his business affairs.

Sean had also wisely requested that his assistant ship an appropriately sized car seat and collapsible stroller to them via air express. Inexperienced parents that they were, they had only realized a week earlier that they would need those two items to safely contain their very active little girl during their long journey home.

The time passed quickly and soon they were on their way back to the orphanage for one last time, copies of the court-approved and stamped paperwork in hand. As Ms. Herbert had suggested during their final meeting before their departure from New Orleans, Sean and Charlotte also brought with them the special gifts they had purchased in New Orleans for Madame Zhirkova and Elmira to show their appreciation. For the director they had chosen a chunky gold bracelet and for the caretaker a finely knit cashmere sweater.

They had gifts for Marta and Rudi, as well—a cashmere sweater for their interpreter and black leather gloves for their driver. But those gifts would be given at the airport the following day.

Rudi dropped them off at the orphanage just after two o'clock, and they were shown into Madame Zhirkova's office one last time. The director reviewed the paperwork sent by the judge and nodded with approval. She accepted the gift Sean offered her, opened it and beamed with satisfaction. Then she pressed the button on her phone to summon Elmira.

The caretaker entered Madame Zhirkova's office almost immediately, Katie in her arms. The little girl had been dressed in the clothing Sean and Charlotte had brought for her the previous day. She looked so very feminine and so very pretty in her pale green corduroy pants, green-and-white sweater, white socks and tiny, pale green, high-top leather shoes.

Her eyes bright with excitement, Katie looked first at Sean, then at Charlotte. She hesitated only a moment. Then, kicking her legs, she reached out to Charlotte, obviously eager for the hugs and kisses she knew that her mother would give her by way of a greeting.

The time had come at last for Charlotte to take her daughter home. But for a long moment all she could do was hold the child close as tears of joy pricked her eyes. Elmira, too, looked as if she were about to cry as she stood by silently, off to one side.

Sean stood and offered the young woman her gift.

"Thank you, Elmira," he said. "Thank you for taking such good care of our little girl. We'll make sure she never forgets how lucky she was to have you in her life."

Indeed, they had taken several photographs of the caretaker holding Katie to include in her baby book.

As Marta translated, Elmira clutched her gift and dabbed at her eyes. She nodded one last time to Sean and Charlotte, offering each of them her hand in farewell. She hesitated for a moment, then put a gentle hand on Katie's head and spoke a few words to the child. Then, tears on her cheeks, she quickly slipped from the room as Charlotte, biting her lip to keep from weeping, too, distracted Katie by helping her into her snowsuit.

Less than thirty minutes later, following final farewells to Madame Zhirkova, they were back at their hotel again. They would see Marta and Rudi one last time the next morning for the drive to the airport, but until then they would be on their own with their daughter.

Weaned from a bottle already and eating a wide array of soft table food, Katie was no problem to feed. Especially since they wisely decided to stay in their suite and order room service for their final night's dinner. She was also content to play with her toys in between toddling ventures around the suite to explore her new surroundings.

The hotel had provided them with a baby bed at Sean's request, and it had been set up in the bedroom. Bathed and changed into yellow fleece pajamas, her eyes starting to lower to half-mast, Katie didn't mind being put in the crib. But she protested vociferously to being left there alone, even with the small lamp on the dresser casting a soft glow around the room.

"It's understandable," Sean assured Charlotte. "This is her first night away from the orphanage."

"I know." Charlotte held the fussing child in her arms and paced slowly about the living room of their suite. "She's used to sleeping in a nursery with other babies nearby."

Much to her relief, she was no longer nervous about being Katie's primary caregiver. She was more than capable of tending to the little girls' needs, and she was also more than happy to do it. But her lack of sleep the previous night, the fast pace of their busy day and the return of that odd queasy feeling in her stomach had her wishing she could curl up in bed herself.

"Let me take her for a while," Sean offered as if reading her mind. "You look totally done in."

"I *feel* totally done in," Charlotte admitted as she gratefully handed off her daughter to her husband.

With a gurgle of contentment, Katie snuggled against Sean's shoulder, popped her thumb in her mouth and closed her eyes. Charlotte couldn't help but smile.

"What?" Sean asked, his gaze quizzical.

"I think she just might fall asleep now that she has her daddy dancing attendance."

"Right now I'd be willing swing from a trapeze if I thought that would get her settled down for the night," Sean admitted, a noticeably weary edge in his drawling voice.

"Do you mind if I take a shower?" Charlotte asked, eager to make good use of the reprieve she'd been given.

"Not at all, but then I want you to get into bed and try to sleep. You really do look exhausted."

"You're looking a little peaked yourself."

"I'll be all right for a while."

"Promise to get me up if you need me?"

"I will. Now take your shower and go to bed. We have two long days of traveling ahead of us, and I don't want you getting ill."

Charlotte did as Sean instructed. She showered, pulled on her flannel pajamas and crawled into bed. She was asleep almost as soon as her head hit the pillow. But she only slept for a couple of hours before she woke up again.

All was blessedly quiet in the suite, but Sean and Katie weren't in the bedroom with her. Concerned about them, Charlotte slipped out of bed and padded softly into the living room.

She saw the two of them at once and her heart melted at the picture of love and contentment they made together.

Sean was stretched out on the sofa with Katie on his chest. He held his daughter securely in his arms, one large hand splayed across her back, the other cupping her head. He had taken one of the extra blankets from the bedroom chest and used it to cover them, as well. Both of them were sleeping soundly.

Charlotte wondered if she should wake Sean and suggest that he put Katie in her bed, then come to bed himself. But she discarded that idea as soon as it came to mind.

Her husband was handling the situation in the best way possible. She wasn't about to question his tactics. After all, he *had* gotten Katie to sleep. Nor was Charlotte going to insinuate herself into the special dad-daughter space he shared with the little girl.

The only way Sean might begin to consider being a full-time husband *and* father was if he realized, on his own, how important his presence was to both Charlotte and Katie. There was so much he could offer their daughter that Charlotte couldn't. But only if—no *when*—he saw for himself that he was a wonderful and welcome father figure for Katie would he be able to have the necessary change of heart.

Sometime later in the night, Charlotte awakened again to find her husband curled close to her in bed, his arm around her waist, his breath a warm whisper against her cheek. Looking over at the crib in the pale glow of light from the lamp on the dresser, she saw Katie also sleeping peacefully. Settling back on her pillow, Charlotte smiled to herself.

How could Sean have ever thought he wasn't cut out to be a father? He might not have had the best experience with his own parents, but he had taken to caring for Katie as if he'd been preparing for his new role all of his life.

"Don't even breathe above a whisper," Sean cautioned her, his voice rumbling faintly just above her ear. "Unless, of course, you want to take a few dozen turns around the living room with her."

"Thank you, no," Charlotte murmured, turning in his arms and pressing a warm kiss into the hollow at the base of his throat.

"Nice…but there is no way…"

His words trailed off into a soft snore, causing Charlotte to chuckle quietly before she, too, drifted back to sleep.

The journey from Almaty to Frankfurt then on to New Orleans went as smoothly as Charlotte imagined any long, tedious journey made with a busy toddler in tow possibly could. There were occasional glitches along the way, but they had no major problems and thankfully no major delays.

Charlotte quickly discovered that as long as they made sure Katie was fed regularly and entertained, even by something as small as the lifting and lowering of the shade over the window next to her seat on the airplane, she was happy. Now that she could walk, she wanted to practice her new skill. Sure that the exercise would tire her out, Sean and Charlotte took turns holding her hand while she toddled around the airport terminal or up and down the aisle of the airplane.

They were generally successful in their endeavor, but they also learned that timing was everything. Trying to move an exhausted child down a crowded Jetway while juggling a car seat, an umbrella stroller, diaper bag and carry-on luggage proved to be a recipe for total meltdown.

Only as they waited in an interminably long line to pass through the U.S. customs checkpoint in New Orleans did Charlotte begin to lose her sense of humor. Almost as exhausted as the little girl, not to mention queasy for the third time in as many days, she was ready to offer a substantial bribe to anyone who could, and would, whisk her magically through the last barrier to being officially home again.

Had it not been for Sean's quiet, patient handling of both her and Katie, Charlotte wasn't sure how she would have managed until they were finally allowed to retrieve their bags and leave the airport terminal.

Their flight had been scheduled for arrival so late Sunday night that Sean had arranged for a limousine to pick them up. The driver was waiting for them just inside the baggage-claim area with a placard bearing their name. Under Sean's direction the man wasted no time loading their luggage onto a trolley. He then led them out to the curbside area reserved for such transportation.

"Is it still your intention that I take you to Mayfair tonight, sir?" the driver asked, once they were settled in the backseat of the limousine, Katie, tucked securely in her car seat between them, thankfully nodding off at last.

Charlotte glanced at Sean in surprise as she wiggled out of her heavy wool coat. The air outside the terminal had felt almost uncomfortably warm and humid to her after the month she'd spent in a much more frigid climate. But suddenly the noticeable difference in temperature became the least of her problems.

Although they hadn't discussed what they would do upon their arrival in New Orleans, Charlotte had assumed that they would go to the town house that night rather than straight back to Mayfair.

"Yes, take us to Mayfair, please," Sean answered the driver. Then to Charlotte he added, "I thought it would be best to get all of the traveling done at once, and also to get you and Katie settled at the house as soon as possible. I just assumed you'd feel the same way, too."

"I suppose it is a good idea to head straight home," Charlotte agreed, looking out the car window at the glow of lights brightening the night sky.

Katie *had* experienced a major upheaval in her young life over the past few days. Spending even a day or two at the New Orleans town house would only delay establishing a new and necessary routine for her. But Charlotte sensed something more than consideration for her and Katie in the tone with which Sean had explained his decision.

They had discussed everything to do with Katie the past four weeks, neither of them making any assumptions about the other one's thoughts or feelings. Now Sean seemed to be making choices solely on his own in a cool, practical and frighteningly detached manner.

Charlotte had become accustomed to once again having a husband who was also her friend and lover. His sudden retreat from the special closeness they'd shared for more than a month set off warning bells in her head. She couldn't have ignored them even if she'd wanted to.

Sean would have only one reason to start distancing

himself from her, Charlotte realized. Despite the love and tenderness, the caring and the consideration he'd shown her over the past four weeks, he must still intend to file for divorce now that the adoption process had finally been completed.

The lights beyond the windows of the limousine blurred as tears filled Charlotte's eyes. She blinked rapidly to keep them from trickling down her face as she dug a tissue from the pocket of her cardigan.

She had told herself so many times, and had rationalized in so many ways, that her husband must have surely undergone a change of heart during the weeks they'd spent with Katie in Almaty. But apparently she had been seeing only what she wanted to see, and had believed only what she'd wanted to believe.

Now dashed hopes and devastating disappointment were the price she had to pay for all those wonderful fantasies, and she had only herself to blame for the pain she had already begun to suffer.

Sean had never actually said that he had changed his mind about divorcing her once they were back in the United States. Nor had he ever said that he wanted them to live together as a family.

Charlotte wanted to protest that his actions had spoken louder than any words. But Sean's behavior toward her and Katie had been appropriate for the circumstances they'd shared in Almaty.

Certain major elements had changed now that they were almost home again. Most importantly, they were no longer isolated and dependent solely upon each other in a foreign environment. They were on the verge of stepping back into the lives they had led before they'd gone to Kazakhstan—lives they had led separately, and if she was reading

Sean's silence correctly, lives he intended for them to continue living separately.

Risking a sideways glance at her husband, Charlotte noted that he was staring out the window just as intently as she had been doing herself only a few moments ago. The expression on his face was somber, the line of his mouth grimly drawn.

Charlotte wished, more than anything, that she had even the vaguest idea of what he was thinking. Was he still weighing his choices, or was he merely contemplating more fully the decisions he'd already made? Had he just been playing a part for the past four weeks? Did her feelings matter to him at all?

And the true deciding factor—could Sean really walk out on her and Katie so easily?

Only if I let him...

The simple words spun through Charlotte's mind as she realized that her final question was the one over which she held some sway. She could allow Sean to leave her and Katie alone in the house in Mayfair just as she'd allowed him to leave her alone there in June. She could even save face by pretending that she was just as happy to see him go now as she had been that long ago summer day.

The only other alternative she had was to simply tell him, in no uncertain terms, what she wanted from him, what she needed from him, what she and Katie *deserved* from him. The worst that could happen was that she'd embarrass herself and Sean would leave her anyway.

Charlotte had made a fool of herself often enough in the past for embarrassment not to matter. So why not stand up to him and make a few demands and see how he responded?

Suddenly seeming to sense her calculating gaze on him,

Sean turned to look at her over the head of their sleeping child. His gaze was distant and obviously distracted.

"Are you all right?" he asked, his voice gruff.

"I'm very tired, but also very glad we'll be home again soon." Charlotte held her husband's gaze as she offered him a slow, sweet smile. "I can hardly wait to curl up with you in our own bed," she added in a low, sensual tone. "Lucky for us that our daughter is going to be too tired to do anything but curl up in *her* bed, isn't it?"

A startled look passed over Sean's face in the moments before he directed his gaze out the window again.

"I'm not so sure we're going to be that lucky," he muttered.

Bolstered by the simple fact that Sean had used *we*, not *you*, Charlotte chuckled softly, then murmured in reply, "Oh ye of little faith…"

Chapter Fourteen

Sean hadn't been sure what he'd do when they reached Mayfair. He had thought maybe it would be best to see Charlotte and Katie safely settled in the house, and return to New Orleans in the limousine.

With the end of their long journey to complete their daughter's adoption came the time for him to seriously consider his options for the future—at least to his way of thinking. Such deliberations, he'd learned in the past, were best done not only swiftly, but also on his own. He didn't want any outside influences to sway him as he made decisions that would be life altering for himself, for his wife and for his child.

Sean had thought long and hard about his ability to be a father prior to meeting little Katie. Spending the past four weeks getting to know her, as well as getting to know himself in a whole new way, had certainly put his doubts to rest on that account.

He was no slacker, nor a bumbling idiot, when it came to child care. He had quickly and easily learned how to feed his little girl, change her diapers, make her laugh and dry her tears. Giving up day-to-day contact with her, and with Charlotte, was not the choice he wanted to make—not anymore.

But that, along with filing for divorce, had been his intention when Charlotte had first asked for his help with the adoption, for reasons that still remained viable.

With the prospect of having his wife turn away from him to devote all of her time and attention to Katie looming large now that he'd seen her safely home again, wouldn't that choice still be the least painful one for him to make? As he had told himself at the outset of their venture, wasn't it better to walk away on his own than to wonder how long it would be until he was shut out of the circle of his wife's loving care?

Unfortunately, Charlotte had made it impossible for him to leave her tonight, at least in the quick, efficient way he'd contemplated on the drive from New Orleans to Mayfair.

Slowly turning his head on his pillow so as not to disturb her, Sean looked over at his wife. Curled up beside him on their bed, her butt tucked firmly against his hip, she slept deeply, peacefully, her breathing slow and even.

His gaze once again fixed on the dark shadows hovering near the bedroom ceiling, Sean uttered a small, mostly silent sigh of resignation—a sigh also heavily laced with full measures of annoyance and frustration.

He wasn't sure how exactly Charlotte had done it, but she'd successfully maneuvered him into allowing the limousine driver to return to New Orleans without him. In fact, recalling the flurry of activity upon their arrival at the house, he could have almost sworn that she'd planned it all along.

He had no more than unlocked the front door of the house when she'd handed Katie to him, then set about instructing the driver where to deposit their luggage. So distracted had he been trying to soothe his wailing daughter that Charlotte had been tipping the driver, then waving goodnight to the man before Sean could stop him from leaving.

His wife should have been totally exhausted by then. He'd been all but asleep on his feet himself. He had deemed it wise, however, to offer to see to his daughter's needs in the hope that he could avoid the issue of where he would spend the night.

But Charlotte had seemed to be bursting with energy all of a sudden. She had taken Katie from him, then shooed him upstairs with instructions to take a quick shower and go straight to bed. Unable to think quickly enough to pose a reasonable argument, he had done as she'd insisted as she'd whisked Katie off to the kitchen for a cup of warm milk and a small bowl of the cereal Ellen had been thoughtful enough to stock for their return.

The sluice of hot water in the shower had only served to enervate him even more. He'd no longer had the energy to make any kind of scene about their sleeping arrangements. But he'd had the presence of mind to pull on a pair of sweatpants and a T-shirt before he'd crawled into bed. He'd also planted himself as close as he could to the edge of the mattress as an added though feeble precaution.

Initially, Sean had been weary enough to fall into a deep sleep. But he'd come awake again as soon as he'd heard Charlotte in the shower, and he stayed awake long after she'd walked out of the bathroom, naked, slid into bed beside him, scooted up against him and drifted off so easily.

Sean wanted to sleep. He desperately needed to sleep so that he could think straight and act reasonably once morning arrived. He was worried about what he might do once he slipped beyond consciousness, though.

With his soft, warm, utterly desirable wife lying mere inches away from him, the temptations were not only many, but also impossible to ignore. How easy it would be to roll over on his side, to put an arm around her narrow waist, to pull her up against him so they curved together like two spoons.

He would nuzzle her neck with his lips and nip at her tender skin with his teeth. He would cup her breasts with his hands and tease her nipples into hard peaks. Then she would shift in his arms and arch her body in sensual invitation—

Sean started in his sleep, opened his eyes and realized two things almost instantaneously. Pale early morning sunlight was slipping through the wide slats of the blinds on the bedroom windows, and his wife, her clever hands shoved inside his sweatpants, was fondling him unashamedly as she trailed hot, wet, tiny kisses along the ridge of his collarbone.

Oh, hell...

He hadn't only been dreaming about making love to his wife, and now he was aching with unmistakable desire. He couldn't pretend that he wasn't interested in having sex with Charlotte. But how could he share such deeply physical and emotional intimacy with her, then gather his belongings and leave her without any promises or when, or even *if*, he planned to return?

Maybe Katie would wake up and distract them from the

perilous road they were about to travel, he thought with quiet desperation. Maybe—

"You're not playing possum on me, are you, darling?" Charlotte murmured, nipping him on the neck, likely to make sure she had his attention.

With a low groan, Sean threaded the fingers of one hand through her hair, tipped her face up and claimed her mouth in a searing kiss. There was no use trying to fight the inevitable. He couldn't have done it even if he'd wanted to. But just then all he really wanted was to sink himself into his wife's sleek, warm, welcoming depths.

Charlotte didn't seem much in the mood for foreplay, either. She made no secret of her eagerness to have him inside of her. Assuming even more control over the moment, she skillfully stripped him of his sweatpants and T-shirt. Then she straddled him with a lithe shift of her hips, opening herself to take in the full length of him without the slightest hesitation. Palms braced on his chest, she looked down at him, her eyes dreamy and her lips parted with obvious pleasure as she moved over him with a sensual rhythm all her own.

Sean allowed his wife to have her way with him only for so long. She rode him well, but he wanted more from her, needed more from her, and so he took it. Still planted firmly inside her womanly warmth, he rolled her onto her back, grinning at the way her dark eyes widened with surprise.

"Yes?" he drawled, beginning the long, slow strokes meant to send her over the edge.

"Yes." She sighed softly, then arched into his thrusts, her legs wrapped around his hips, her hand clutching his shoulders. "Yes...yes...yes..."

* * *

No matter how often Sean told himself that he should be working on an exit strategy to smooth his way out of the Mayfair house, he made absolutely no progress in that direction during his waking hours on their first day home from Almaty. Either his wife or her seemingly faithful co-conspirator, Katie, was constantly diverting his attention.

The endorphin rush that had him floating in a pleasurable haze after his lovemaking with Charlotte hadn't really started to disperse until his daughter screeched from her crib in the nursery across the hallway. Though his wife grabbed her robe and hurried away to tend to the child, she was back again in a matter of minutes with Katie perched on her hip, giving Sean only time enough to pull on his sweatpants and T-shirt.

"Here you go, Daddy. It's your turn to mind the child since I put in time with her last night." Shooting him a sexy grin, Charlotte deposited his daughter in his arms. "She's freshly diapered and ready for her breakfast. I suggest you give her a cup of milk, some cereal, and if she's still hungry, some of the vanilla yogurt in the refrigerator? Could you put on a pot of coffee, too? Please…?"

"What are *you* going to be doing?" he asked as Charlotte breezed past him.

"I'm going to be taking a shower and shampooing my hair."

She smiled again, wriggled her fingers at him and Katie, then closed the bathroom door with a firm click of the catch.

"Bah," Katie cried, pointing a delicate little finger toward the bathroom door. Then, glancing up at Sean, she batted her big brown eyes and pointed at him. "Bah, bah, *bah!*"

"Bah, all right—bah, humbug," he said to her.

He attempted to maintain a stern expression but failed completely when his daughter patted his face with her hand and giggled.

So began Sean's day, and so it continued, causing him to wonder, more often than not, what exactly had hit him. He sensed that he was being bulldozed by his wife, but in a charmingly, teasingly, good-natured, meant-to-make-him-feel-good kind of way.

She enlisted his help with Katie and with the unpacking and with the sorting of four weeks' worth of snail mail. She sent him to the dry cleaners with a huge pile of clothes, then left him home alone with his daughter while she went to the grocery store to add shrimp and salmon, fresh vegetables and fruit to the staples Ellen had already left for them.

With both Charlotte and Katie napping late in the afternoon, Sean thought that perhaps he might be able to make a run for it. He prepared a mental list of reasons why he needed to return to New Orleans, none of them believable even in his own mind. He was even ready to call the limousine service to arrange for transportation back to the city.

But then Ellen and Quinn pulled into the driveway, one after the other, apparently at Charlotte's unmentioned invitation. Ellen brought with her a pot of her gumbo and a chocolate cheesecake. Quinn carried two shopping bags full of bread and cheese and bottles of wine. Their laughing voices rang through the house, awakening his wife and daughter, much as he suspected they'd intended to do, and a party ensued.

Katie thoroughly charmed her honorary aunts. They took turns holding her and feeding her and playing with her. They insisted on perusing all of the photographs he and

Charlotte had taken of her in Almaty. They also took time to look through the books on Kazakhstan, open their gifts and produce gifts of their own for Katie.

They left eventually, and good baby that she was, Katie allowed herself to be rocked to sleep by her equally weary looking mother. Standing in the doorway of the nursery, Sean had a hard time remembering why he had been so anxious to return to New Orleans.

Surely he belonged here in Mayfair with Charlotte and Katie. But for how long? No matter how he tried, he couldn't seem to step out from under the lingering dark cloud of memories from his own childhood.

In bed that night, it was he who reached out for Charlotte in need as well as desire. It was he who took with an almost fevered desperation. But when he had spent himself in a grunting, groaning spasm of release, it was Charlotte who said, ever so gently, "I love you, Sean. I love you so much."

Sean slept soundly during the night and when he awakened at five-thirty Tuesday morning he was finally ready to do what he knew he had to do for his own peace of mind.

Quietly, he slipped from the bed, gathered some clothes and crept out of the bedroom. Closing the door behind him, he walked down the hallway to the guest bathroom.

He was showered, shaved and dressed in suit pants and a dress shirt, and sitting at the table in the sunroom alcove drinking coffee and attempting to read the paper when Charlotte appeared almost an hour later. By then, he had also called the limousine service to request that a car and driver be at the Mayfair house at eight o'clock sharp.

His wife paused in the middle of the kitchen and gazed at him with bleary eyes, her hands tucked in the pockets of her long white terry-cloth robe. She didn't say anything for several long moments. But Sean could see that the gears were starting to mesh in her mind, and he braced himself defensively in preparation for whatever she might have to say to him.

"Do you want something to eat?" she asked at last, surprising him with her offhand manner, and also taking a little of the starch out of his sails. "I'm craving waffles myself."

She busied herself getting out a bowl, the necessary ingredients and, of course, her waffle iron.

"I'm not very hungry—"

"No problem." She looked over at him and smiled in a way that all but broke his heart. "How about if I make extras, though, just in case you change your mind?"

"Sure."

Sean didn't dare say anything more to her just then, so he hid behind the sheet of newsprint he'd been trying to read while she set about preparing her waffles. She had to know that he was going back to New Orleans that morning. Yet she hadn't mentioned it. Hadn't so much as batted an eye, for that matter.

Sean wondered what she was playing at, then realized *he* was actually the one with an agenda.

What difference did it make to him how Charlotte might feel about his decision to return to New Orleans? He wasn't going to change his mind just because—

His daughter's demanding screech interrupted his reverie, but Charlotte was already on her way out of the kitchen.

"Watch my waffle, will you?" she called over her shoulder. "I'll be right back with Katie."

"Sure."

Good as her word, his wife came back again with Katie,

but not as quickly as Sean had expected. The little girl seemed to be really fussy. She rubbed her sleepy eyes with her fists and whined and kicked her little legs as she clung to her mother. She also took one look at him and hid her face against Charlotte's shoulder.

"I'd offer to take her from you, but I don't seem to be on her A list this morning."

Sean tried to inject a light note into his voice, but realized at once that he'd failed miserably.

"I don't think anybody is going to be on her A list anytime at all today. I think she had just a little too much excitement last night, thanks to Ellen and Quinn," Charlotte admitted with the slightest hint of a smile. "But don't worry. I can manage her okay. I don't want you to get your nice shirt all messed up." Then to Katie she added, "Want to sit in your high chair, big girl?"

The answer was a resounding *absolutely not* delivered in the form of a heartbroken wail as Charlotte tried to shift her daughter off her hip.

"Okay, then. Why don't you just let Mommy hold you while she eats her waffle?"

"I can take her, Charlotte—"

"No, really, you're all dressed and ready to go, aren't you?"

She didn't look at him as she asked her question. Instead, she attacked her waffle with her fork, lifted a small piece to her lips, frowned at it and set it on the plate again rather quickly.

"I have to get back to New Orleans. I've been out of the office for over four weeks now. I have a business to run, you know," he replied in a rush, definitely on the defensive now. "I've called for a car to take me into the city. There's going to be a lot for me to do, so I'm not sure when—"

"You'll be home again?" Charlotte cut in as she looked over at him, her dark eyes shadowed with obvious hurt. "That's not true, Sean, not true at all. You set up your company to run without you years ago so you could spend as much time as you wanted here with me in Mayfair. If there were any emergencies that needed your immediate attention, Elizabeth would have called you. So just be honest with yourself, Sean, and be honest with me—you're leaving us because you *want* to leave."

For another long moment, she eyed him reproachfully. Then holding Katie close she turned away from him and busied herself dumping her uneaten waffle into the trash bin.

From one moment to the next, Sean found himself transported back in time on a rush of memories that shaded the present in hues of déjà vu. In his mind's eye he could see, again, his own mother standing in the same kitchen thirty years ago, and he could hear, again, the conversation between his father and her, repeated more than once with the same sad effect.

Be honest with yourself...you're leaving because you want to leave...

Sean remembered how his mother had asked his father to stay and how his father had always made excuses about why he'd had to leave. Seeing Charlotte turn away from him, he could see again his mother turning away from his father, not in anger as he'd always thought, but in hurt—a hurt she had tried to hide just as Charlotte was doing now.

Maybe his mother hadn't started out intending to cut his father out of their lives. Maybe his father really had to leave her to earn a decent living. Maybe his mother had learned to get along without his father, not by choice but by necessity. Maybe she had eventually stopped needing him, and then, sadly, stopped *wanting* him there at all.

Now it seemed he was about to allow history to repeat itself in his own life, Sean realized.

But their circumstances weren't the same; in fact, they were quite different. Charlotte had been right. He didn't have to go back to New Orleans to take care of his business. He had made sure he could run it from Mayfair on a day-to-day basis a long time ago. Yes, he would have to go into the city two maybe three times a month, for a day or two at the most to meet with clients or his accountants. He didn't have to today, though.

"Actually, I was leaving because I thought I had to," he admitted quietly, closing the distance between him and his wife and daughter.

Katie shot him a disapproving look that made him smile as he touched Charlotte on the arm to draw her attention.

"But just now I realized that wasn't really true," he added. "This is my home and you and Katie are my family. More than anything, I want to be here with the two of you…for as long as I'm welcome."

"Oh, Sean, don't you know by now that you will always have a special place in our hearts and in our lives?" Charlotte asked, her dark eyes filled with tender longing. "I've always wanted to be a mother, but never to the exclusion of being your wife. In fact, I'm on my way to becoming a good mother not because I was meant to be, but because you've shown me how to do it. You're such a good father, Sean, and such a good husband. Don't let me down—don't let *us* down. We love you, both of us, and we will always want you to be here with us. Won't we, Katie?"

To which his daughter answered with a forceful *"Bah!"*

"I guess I'd better call the limousine service and cancel the car then, hadn't I?" he asked, his voice suddenly gruff with emotion.

"I think that's an excellent idea," Charlotte agreed. "But could you just…" Hurriedly, she shifted Katie in her arms and held the little girl out to him, a panicked look on her face. "Could you just hold her for me for a minute or two?"

"Charlotte, are you okay?" Sean took his daughter from her, then followed after her as she ran to the powder room.

"Um…no…"

Standing helplessly outside the closed door as his wife retched into the toilet bowl, holding his little girl in his arms, Sean experienced several moments of panic himself.

And when Charlotte finally appeared again, looking weak and pale and watery-eyed, he insisted in a brook-no-argument tone, "You're going to the doctor today."

"Yes, I think that would be a good idea."

Chapter Fifteen

By mid-afternoon, Charlotte was sure that she'd acted too hastily making an appointment to see her general practitioner. She had felt fine after her single bout of retching—a little tired maybe, but otherwise okay. She had even managed to eat the egg Sean had scrambled for her and a small bowl of chicken-noodle soup at lunchtime.

Sean had been adamant that she keep her appointment with Dr. Halsey, though. His concern was that she had picked up an intestinal bug of some sort while they'd been in Almaty. On the off chance that he was right, she had agreed that it was probably best to have the possible cause of her intermittent nausea checked out immediately.

Sean had intended to take her to the doctor's office himself. But then they had both realized that they'd have to take Katie with them, too, and that was impossible in Charlotte's little two-seater sports car.

She had made the drive to the doctor's office in Mayfair on her own, leaving Sean sitting in front of his laptop computer in his office. With a still-fussy Katie on his lap, he had been surfing the Internet in search of a good deal on a safe, reliable minivan to add to their small fleet of vehicles.

The wait to see the doctor was long, but he took his time asking questions about her trip to Kazakhstan and little Katie, the foods she'd eaten while out of the country, and finally the symptoms she had been suffering for the past several days. He eyed her rather enigmatically for a minute or two, made some notes on her chart, then sent her to the in-office lab for what he assured her were simple blood and urine tests.

She was then escorted back to the examination room, and after an agonizing twenty minutes, Dr. Halsey joined her again, a big grin on his face.

"Not to worry, Mrs. Fagan. You're not suffering for a dread disease of any kind."

Now driving back to the house, Charlotte stared at the road ahead of her, feeling, quite literally, stunned. She thought of Sean's vow to her just that morning. He would never leave her willingly. He loved her and Katie. He wanted to be a husband and a father.

But Sean hadn't known the full extent of what he was getting himself into then. In the time it had taken Dr. Halsey to explain the results of the tests he'd run, their world had shifted and the parameters of their relationship had changed yet again.

How would her husband respond to the news she was about to give him? Charlotte knew she was very close to finding out as she turned into her driveway at last.

The house was blessedly quiet when she let herself in

through the front door. Apparently Sean had managed to get their daughter to take a nap, for which Charlotte was grateful.

She moved quietly down the first-floor hallway to the kitchen so as not to disturb Katie and found her husband sitting at the table in the sunroom alcove, paperwork he'd obviously had faxed to him from his office spread out in front of him.

"Hey," he said, smiling as he looked up at her approach across the kitchen.

"Hey, yourself."

"I just got the little one down for a nap. She fought it all the way, but she was no match for Dad and the rocking chair." Sean paused and studied her closely for several moments, then asked quietly, "So what did Doc Halsey have to say?"

"I definitely didn't pick up a dangerous bug in Almaty," she answered him.

"That's good to know. Did he have any idea what's causing your nausea?"

"Oh, yes, he had a very good idea." Charlotte couldn't help but grin at her husband. "Tell me, did you find a minivan that you like?"

"Well, yes, but what about—"

"Good, because we're definitely going to need something roomy for hauling our family, especially eight months from now."

"Eight months—?"

Sean paused and met her gaze, then stood slowly and took a step toward her, the look in his eyes one of surprise and wonder and, best of all, jubilation.

"Yes," she said, closing the distance between them and putting a tender hand to his cheek. "I'm…I'm pregnant, Sean. I'm *pregnant*…."

"Charlotte, sweetheart…" He caught her in his arms and hugged her close. "I…I can't believe it…."

"Believe it, Sean. It's true. You're going to be a daddy again before Christmas."

"There's nothing else I'd rather be, Charlotte, than the father of your children, and of course, your loving husband…for always and forever."

"For always and forever, Sean…always and forever."

* * * * *

Every Life Has More
Than One Chapter

Award-winning author Stevi Mittman delivers
another hysterical mystery, featuring Teddi Bayer,
an irrepressible heroine, and her to-die-for hero,
Detective Drew Scoones. After all, life on Long
Island can be murder!

*Turn the page for a sneak peek at the warm and funny
fourth book,
WHOSE NUMBER IS UP, ANYWAY?,
in the Teddi Bayer series,
by STEVI MITTMAN.
On sale August 7*

"Before redecorating a room, I always advise my clients to empty it of everything but one chair. Then I suggest they move that chair from place to place, sitting in it, until the placement feels right. Trust your instincts when deciding on furniture placement. Your room should "feel right.""

—TipsFromTeddi.com

Gut feelings. You know, that gnawing in the pit of your stomach that warns you that you are about to do the absolute stupidest thing you could do? Something that will ruin life as you know it?

I've got one now, standing at the butcher counter in

King Kullen, the grocery store in the same strip mall as L.I. Lanes, the bowling alley cum billiard parlor I'm in the process of redecorating for its "Grand Opening."

I realize being in the wrong supermarket probably doesn't sound exactly dire to you, but you aren't the one buying your father a brisket at a store your mother will somehow know isn't Waldbaum's.

And then, June Bayer isn't your mother.

The woman behind the counter has agreed to go into the freezer to find a brisket for me, since there aren't any in the case. There are packages of pork tenderloin, piles of spare ribs and rolls of sausage, but no briskets.

Warning Number Two, right? I should be so out of here.

But no, I'm still in the same spot when she comes back out, brisketless, her face ashen. She opens her mouth as if she is going to scream, but only a gurgle comes out.

And then she pinballs out from behind the counter, knocking bottles of Peter Luger Steak Sauce to the floor on her way, now hitting the tower of cans at the end of the prepared foods aisle and sending them sprawling, now making her way down the aisle, careening from side to side as she goes.

Finally, from a distance, I hear her shout, "He's deeeeeeaaaad! Joey's deeeeeaaaad."

My first thought is *You should always trust your gut.*

My second thought is that now, somehow, my mother will know I was in King Kullen. For weeks I will have to hear "What did you expect?" as though whenever you go to King Kullen someone turns up dead. And if the detective investigating the case turns out to be Detective Drew Scoones…well, I'll never hear the end of that from her, either.

She still suspects I murdered the guy who was found

dead on my doorstep last Halloween just to get Drew back into my life.

Several people head for the butcher's freezer and I position myself to block them. If there's one thing I've learned from finding people dead—and the guy on my doorstep wasn't the first one—it's that the police get very testy when you mess with their murder scenes.

"You can't go in there until the police get here," I say, stationing myself at the end of the butcher's counter and in front of the Employees Only door, acting as if I'm some sort of authority. "You'll contaminate the evidence if it turns out to be murder."

Shouts and chaos. You'd think I'd know better than to throw the word *murder* around. Cell phones are flipping open and tongues are wagging.

I amend my statement quickly. "Which, of course, it probably isn't. Murder, I mean. People die all the time, and it's not always in hospitals or their own beds, or…" I babble when I'm nervous, and the idea of someone dead on the other side of the freezer door makes me very nervous.

So does the idea of seeing Drew Scoones again. Drew and I have this on-again, off-again sort of thing…that I kind of turned off.

Who knew he'd take it so personally when he tried to get serious and I responded by saying we could talk about *us* tomorrow—and then caught a plane to my parents' condo in Boca the next day? In July. In the middle of a job.

For some crazy reason, he took that to mean that I was avoiding him and the subject of *us*.

That was three months ago. I haven't seen him since.

The manager, who identifies himself and points to his

nameplate in case I don't believe him, says he has to go into *his cooler*. "Maybe Joey's not dead," he says. "Maybe he can be saved, and you're letting him die in there. Did you ever think of that?"

In fact, I hadn't. But I had thought that the murderer might try to go back in to make sure his tracks were covered, so I say that I will go in and check.

Which means that the manager and I couple up and go in together while everyone pushes against the doorway to peer in, erasing any chance of finding clean prints on that Employee Only door.

I expect to find carcasses of dead animals hanging from hooks, and maybe Joey hanging from one, too. I think it's going to be very creepy and I steel myself, only to find a rather benign series of shelves with large slabs of meat laid out carefully on them, along with boxes and boxes marked simply Chicken.

Nothing scary here, unless you count the body of a middle-aged man with graying hair sprawled faceup on the floor. His eyes are wide open and unblinking. His shirt is stiff. His pants are stiff. His body is stiff. And his expression, you should forgive the pun—is frozen. Bill-the-manager crosses himself and stands mute while I pronounce the guy dead in a sort of *happy now?* tone.

"We should not be in here," I say, and he nods his head emphatically and helps me push people out of the doorway just in time to hear the police sirens and see the cop cars pull up outside the big store windows.

Bobbie Lyons, my partner in Teddi Bayer Interior Designs (and also my neighbor, my best friend and my private fashion police), and Mark, our carpenter (and my dogsitter, confidant, and ego booster), rush in from next door. They beat the cops by a half step and shout out my name. People point in my direction.

After all the publicity that followed the unfortunate incident during which I shot my ex-husband, Rio Gallo, and then the subsequent murder of my first client—which I solved, I might add—it seems like the whole world, or at least all of Long Island, knows who I am.

Mark asks if I'm all right. (Did I remember to mention that the man is drop-dead-gorgeous-but-a-decade-too-young-for-me-yet-too-old-for-my-daughter-thank-god?) I don't get a chance to answer him because the police are quickly closing in on the store manager and me.

"The woman—" I begin telling the police. Then I have to pause for the manager to fill in her name, which he does: *Fran.*

I continue. "Right. Fran. Fran went into the freezer to get a brisket. A moment later she came out and screamed that Joey was dead. So I'd say she was the one who discovered the body."

"And you are…?" the cop asks me. It comes out a bit like who do I *think* I am, rather than who am I really?

"An innocent bystander," Bobbie, hair perfect, makeup just right, says, carefully placing her body between the cop and me.

"And she was just leaving," Mark adds. They each take one of my arms.

Fran comes into the inner circle surrounding the cops. In case it isn't obvious from the hairnet and bloodstained white apron with Fran embroidered on it, I explain that she was the butcher who was going for the brisket. Mark and Bobbie take that as a signal that I've done my job and they can now get me out of there. They twist around, with me in the middle, as if we're a Rockettes line, until we are facing away from the butcher counter. They've managed to propel me a few steps toward the exit when disaster— in the form of a Mazda RX7 pulling up at the loading curb—strikes.

Mark's grip on my arm tightens like a vise. "Too late," he says.

Bobbie's expletive is unprintable. "Maybe there's a back door," she suggests, but Mark is right. It's too late.

I've laid my eyes on Detective Scoones. And while my gut is trying to warn me that my heart shouldn't go there, regions farther south are melting at just the sight of him.

"Walk," Bobbie orders me.

And I try to. Really.

Walk, I tell my feet. *Just put one foot in front of the other.*

I can do this because I know, in my heart of hearts, that if Drew Scoones was still interested in me, he'd have gotten in touch with me after I returned from Boca. And he didn't.

Since he's a detective, Drew doesn't have to wear one of those dark blue Nassau County Police uniforms. Instead, he's got on jeans, a tight-fitting T-shirt and a tweedy sports jacket. If you think that sounds good, you should see him. Chiseled features, cleft chin, brown hair that's naturally a little sandy in the front, a smile that…well, that doesn't matter. He isn't smiling now.

He walks up to me, tucks his sunglasses into his breast pocket and looks me over from head to toe.

"Well, if it isn't Miss Cut and Run," he says. "Aren't you supposed to be somewhere in Florida or something?" He looks at Mark accusingly, as if he was covering for me when he told Drew I was gone.

"Detective Scoones?" one of the uniforms says. "The

stiff's in the cooler and the woman who found him is over there." He jerks his head in Fran's direction.

Drew continues to stare at me.

You know how when you were young, your mother always told you to wear clean underwear in case you were in an accident? And how, a little farther on, she told you not to go out in hair rollers because you never knew who you might see—or who might see you? And how now your best friend says she wouldn't be caught dead without makeup and suggests you shouldn't either?

Okay, today, *finally,* in my overalls and Converse sneakers, I get it.

I brush my hair out of my eyes. "Well, I'm back," I say. As if he hasn't known my exact whereabouts. The man is a detective, for heaven's sake. "Been back awhile."

Bobbie has watched the exchange and apparently decided she's given Drew all the time he deserves. "And we've got work to do, so…" she says, grabbing my arm and giving Drew a little two-fingered wave goodbye.

As I back up a foot or two, the store manager sees his chance and places himself in front of Drew, trying to get his attention. Maybe what makes Drew such a good detective is his ability to focus.

Only what he's focusing on is me.

"Phone broken? Carrier pigeon died?" he asks me, taking in Fran, the manager, the meat counter and that Employees Only door, all without taking his eyes off me.

Mark tries to break the spell. "We've got work to do there, you've got work to do here, Scoones," Mark says to him, gesturing toward next door. "So it's back to the alley for us."

Drew's lip twitches. "You working the alley now?" he says.

"If you'd like to follow me," Bill-the-manager, clearly exasperated, says to Drew—who doesn't respond. It's as if waiting for my answer is all he has to do.

So, fine. "You knew I was back," I say.

The man has known my whereabouts every hour of the day for as long as I've known him. And my mother's not the only one who won't buy that he "just happened" to answer this particular call. In fact, I'm willing to bet my children's lunch money that he's taken every call within ten miles of my home since the day I got back.

And now he's gotten lucky.

"*You* could have called *me*," I say.

"You're the one who said *tomorrow* for our talk and then flew the coop, chickie," he says. "I figured the ball was in your court."

"Detective?" the uniform says. "There's something you ought to see in here."

Drew gives me a look that amounts to *in or out?*

He could be talking about the investigation, or about our relationship.

Bobbie tries to steer me away. Mark's fists are balled. Drew waits me out, knowing I won't be able to resist what might be a murder investigation.

Finally he turns and heads for the cooler.

And, like a puppy dog, I follow.

Bobbie grabs the back of my shirt and pulls me to a halt.

"I'm just going to show him something," I say, yanking away.

"Yeah," Bobbie says, pointedly looking at the buttons on my blouse. The two at breast level have popped. "That's what I'm afraid of."

SPECIAL EDITION™

Look for

THE BILLIONAIRE NEXT DOOR

by *Jessica Bird*

For Wall Street hotshot Sean O'Banyon, going home to south Boston brought back bad memories. But Lizzie Bond, his father's sweet, girl-next-door caretaker, was there to ease the pain. It was instant attraction—until Sean found out she was named sole heir, and wondered what her motives really were....

THE O'BANYON BROTHERS

On sale August 2007.

REQUEST YOUR FREE BOOKS!
2 FREE NOVELS PLUS 2 FREE GIFTS!

SPECIAL EDITION®

Life, Love and Family!

YES! Please send me 2 FREE Silhouette Special Edition® novels and my 2 FREE gifts. After receiving them, if I don't wish to receive any more books, I can return the shipping statement marked "cancel." If I don't cancel, I will receive 6 brand-new novels every month and be billed just $4.24 per book in the U.S., or $4.99 per book in Canada, plus 25¢ shipping and handling per book and applicable taxes, if any*. That's a savings of at least 15% off the cover price! I understand that accepting the 2 free books and gifts places me under no obligation to buy anything. I can always return a shipment and cancel at any time. Even if I never buy another book from Silhouette, the two free books and gifts are mine to keep forever.

235 SDN EEYU 335 SDN EEY6

Name	(PLEASE PRINT)	
Address		Apt.
City	State/Prov.	Zip/Postal Code

Signature (if under 18, a parent or guardian must sign)

Mail to the Silhouette Reader Service™:
IN U.S.A.: P.O. Box 1867, Buffalo, NY 14240-1867
IN CANADA: P.O. Box 609, Fort Erie, Ontario L2A 5X3

Not valid to current Silhouette Special Edition subscribers.

Want to try two free books from another line?
Call 1-800-873-8635 or visit www.morefreebooks.com.

* Terms and prices subject to change without notice. NY residents add applicable sales tax. Canadian residents will be charged applicable provincial taxes and GST. This offer is limited to one order per household. All orders subject to approval. Credit or debit balances in a customer's account(s) may be offset by any other outstanding balance owed by or to the customer. Please allow 4 to 6 weeks for delivery.

Your Privacy: Silhouette is committed to protecting your privacy. Our Privacy Policy is available online at www.eHarlequin.com or upon request from the Reader Service. From time to time we make our lists of customers available to reputable firms who may have a product or service of interest to you. If you would prefer we not share your name and address, please check here. ☐

SSE07

HARLEQUIN®

Super Romance®

*Looking for a romantic, emotional
and unforgettable escape?*

*You'll find it this month and every month
with a Harlequin Superromance!*

Rory Gorenzi has a sense of humor and a sense of
honor. She also happens to be good with children.

Seamus Lee, widower and father of four, needs
someone with exactly those traits.

They meet at the Colorado mountain school owned
by Rory's father, where she teaches skiing and
avalanche safety. But Seamus—and his children—
learn more from her than that....

Look for

GOOD WITH CHILDREN

by Margot Early,

*available August 2007, and these other
fantastic titles from Harlequin Superromance.*

SPECIAL EDITION

#1843 PAGING DR. RIGHT—Stella Bagwell
Montana Mavericks: Striking It Rich
Mia Smith came to Thunder Canyon Resort for some peace and quiet, but with her recent inheritance, other guests took her for a wealthy socialite and wouldn't leave her be. At least she found comfort with the resort's handsome staff doctor Marshall Cates, but would her painful past and humble beginnings nip their budding romance?

#1844 THE BILLIONAIRE NEXT DOOR—Jessica Bird
The O'Banyon Brothers
For Wall Street hot shot Sean O'Banyon, going home to South Boston after his abusive father's death brought back miserable memories. But Lizzie Bond, his father's sweet, girl-next-door caretaker, was there to ease the pain. It was instant attraction—and then Sean found out she was named sole heir, and he began to wonder what her motives really were....

#1845 REMODELING THE BACHELOR—Marie Ferrarella
The Sons of Lily Moreau
Son of a famous, though flighty artist, Philippe Zabelle had grown up to be a set-in-his-ways bachelor. Yet when the successful software developer hired J. D. Wyatt to do some home repairs, something clicked. J.D. was a single mother with a flair for fixing anything... even Philippe's long-broken heart.

#1846 THE COWBOY AND THE CEO—Christine Wenger
She was city. He was country. But on a trip to a Wyoming ranch that made disabled children's dreams come true, driven business owner Susan Collins fell hard for caring cowboy Clint Skully. Having been left at the altar once before, would Clint risk the farm on love this time around?

#1847 ACCIDENTALLY EXPECTING—Michelle Celmer
In one corner, attorney Miranda Reed, who wrote the definitive guide to divorce and the modern woman. In the other, Zackery Jameson, staunch supporter of traditional family values. When these polar opposites sparred on a radio talk show, neither yielded any ground. So how did it come to pass that Miranda was now expecting Zack's baby?

#1848 A FAMILY PRACTICE—Gayle Kasper
After personal tragedy struck, Dr. Luke Phillips took off on a road trip. But when he crashed his motorcycle in the Arizona desert, it was local holistic healer Mariah Cade who got him to stop running. Whether it was in her tender touch or her gentle way with her daughter, Mariah was the miracle cure for all that ailed the good doctor.

SSECNM0707